Sophie's
Drama

Also by Nancy Rue

You! A Christian Girl's Guide to Growing Up
Girl Politics
Everyone Tells Me to Be Myself ... but I Don't Know Who I Am

Sophie's World Series
Meet Sophie (Book One)
Sophie Steps Up (Book Two)
Sophie and Friends (Book Three)
Sophie's Friendship Fiasco (Book Four)
Sophie Flakes Out (Book Five)
Sophie's Drama (Book Six)

The Lucy Series
Lucy Doesn't Wear Pink (Book One)
Lucy Out of Bounds (Book Two)
Lucy's Perfect Summer (Book Three)
Lucy Finds Her Way (Book Four)

Other books in the growing Faithgirlz!™ library

Bibles
The Faithgirlz! Bible
NIV Faithgirlz! Backpack Bible

Faithgirlz! Bible Studies
Secret Power of Love
Secret Power of Joy
Secret Power of Goodness
Secret Power of Grace

faiThGirLz!™
the beauty of believing

Sophie's
Drama

2 BOOKS IN 1

Includes *Sophie's Drama*
and *Sophie Gets Real*

Nancy Rue

ZONDERkidz

ZONDERVAN.com/
AUTHORTRACKER
follow your favorite authors

ZONDERKIDZ

www.zonderkidz.com

Sophie's Drama
Copyright © 2009, 2013 by Nancy Rue

Sophie Gets Real
Copyright © 2009 by Nancy Rue

This title is also available as a Zondervan ebook.
Visit www.zondervan.com/ebooks

Requests for information should be addressed to:
Zonderkidz, 5300 Patterson Ave. SE, Grand Rapids, Michigan 49530

ISBN 978-0310-73855-8

Published in association with the literary agency of Alive Communications, Inc., 7680 Goddard Street, Suite 200, Colorado Springs, CO 80920. www.alivecommunucations.com

Zonderkidz is a trademark of Zondervan.

Interior art direction and design: Sarah Molegraaf
Cover illustrator: Steve James

Printed in the United States

13 14 15 16 17 18 19 20 21 22 23 24 25 26 27 28 /DCI/ 22 21 20 19 18 17 16 15 14 13 12 11 10 9 8 7 6 5 4 3 2 1

So we fix our eyes not on what is seen,
but on what is unseen.
For what is seen is temporary,
but what is unseen is eternal.

—2 CORINTHIANS 4:18

Sophie's Drama

One

𝒯hat is gross," Sophie LaCroix said. She turned quickly and put her hands over her friend Willoughby Wiley's eyes. If Willoughby saw the painting, she'd probably squeal like a poodle, the way she'd been doing all morning through the entire Chrysler Museum of Art.

"I think it's *cool*," Vincent said.

Sophie cocked her head at the painting, spilling her honey-colored hair against her cheek and squinting through her glasses. "No, it isn't," she said to Vincent. "It's bloody and hideous."

"Is it totally disgusting?" Willoughby whispered.

"If you think somebody that just got their head cut off is disgusting, then, yeah," Vincent said. His voice cracked, just like it did on every other sentence he spoke.

Sophie dragged Willoughby toward the next room. Vincent shrugged his skinny shoulders and loped along beside them.

"Where's everybody else?" Willoughby said.

"They got ahead of us." Sophie looked up at Vincent as they passed through the doorway. "*They* didn't stop to look at some heinous picture of a headless person."

Fiona Bunting, Sophie's best friend, looked up from her notebook as Sophie and Willoughby headed toward her. "Oh—so you saw *John the Baptist*." She tucked back the wayward strand of golden-brown hair that was always falling over one gray eye and made a checkmark on the page. "That one's definitely repulsive."

"Does that mean it makes you want to throw up?" Willoughby narrowed her big eyes at Vincent. "You're not gonna say we should use *that* for our project, are you?"

Sophie shook her head. "No movies about people without heads. Who would play that part, anyway?"

Willoughby grabbed her throat.

"Actually," Vincent said, Adam's apple bobbing up and down, "there are some pretty cool ways we could make it *look* on film like somebody got his head cut off—"

"No!" all three girls said together. Sophie's voice squeaked, like it did when she was really making a point.

"Okay. Chill," Vincent said.

Sophie led the way to the next painting. She was the smallest of the Corn Flakes, as she and her five friends called themselves, but they mostly followed her. It had just been that way for the sixteen months since sixth grade when they'd gotten together and decided to be the group that was always themselves and never put anybody down.

"What's this one, Fiona?" Sophie said as they stopped at the next painting.

Above them was a portrait of a sober-faced lady in a gown that looked to Sophie like it weighed three hundred pounds.

"That dress is *fabulous*!" Willoughby said with a poodle-shriek. Her hazel eyes were again the size of Frisbees.

"Aw, man," Vincent said.

"What?" Jimmy Wythe came through a door from a room Sophie hadn't gone into yet. Nathan Coffey was behind him and plowed into Jimmy's back when he stopped in front of the painting. Jimmy looked at Sophie, his swimming-pool-blue eyes begging her. "It's gonna be kinda hard to do a movie about this painting."

"She's just sitting there," Nathan said. And then his face went the color of the inside of a watermelon. Sophie expected that. Nathan always got all red when he talked, which wasn't often.

"I'm gonna go find Kitty," Willoughby said. "She is going to *love* this."

"That's what I'm afraid of," Vincent said. "I guess we could pretend she's a corpse and make the movie a murder mystery."

Fiona rolled her eyes. "She is so not dead, Vincent."

Sophie looped her arm through Fiona's. "Let's go see if Kitty and them have found anything."

"Did they?" Sophie heard Vincent ask Jimmy as she and Fiona moved into the next room.

"It's all pretty much chick stuff," Jimmy said. "I mean, not that that's all bad."

"Not if you're a chick," Vincent said.

"They are so—*boys*," Fiona said when they reached the room.

"Yeah, but at least they're not as bad as *some* boys."

That was why the Corn Flakes called Jimmy, Vincent, and Nathan the Lucky Charms—because they were way nicer than a couple of guys they referred to as the Fruit Loops. The Loops were famous for making disgusting noises with their armpits and trying to get away with launching spit missiles at people, stuff like that. Now that they'd been caught doing some really bad things, they didn't get by with as much, but they were still, to use Fiona's favorite word, heinous.

13

At the other end of the room, Willoughby was jabbering at light speed to the other three Corn Flakes.

"Is it a really pretty painting?" Kitty Munford said as Sophie and Fiona joined them. Her little china-doll face looked wistful. Kitty was back in school after being homeschooled while having chemotherapy for leukemia. It was as if everything were magic to Kitty in spite of her still-bald head and puffed-out cheeks.

"It's gorgeous," Willoughby said. "That dress was, like, to die for."

Darbie O'Grady hooked her reddish hair behind her ears and folded her lanky arms across her chest. "I bet the boys put the kibosh on that."

Sophie grinned. She loved it that even though Darbie had been in the United States for a year, she still used her Irish expressions. Between her fun way of saying things and Fiona's being a walking dictionary, the Corn Flakes practically had a language all their own. It was all about being their unique selves.

"Yeah, they hated it," Fiona said. "But we put the kibosh on John the Baptist with his head chopped off."

Kitty edged closer to Sophie until the brim on her tweed newsboy's cap brushed Sophie's cheek. "I don't want my first movie in forever to be about something gross."

"No way," Maggie LaQuita said. She shook her head until her Cuban-dark hair splashed into itself in the middle. "Kitty doesn't need that." In her stocky, no-nonsense way, she was protective of all the Corn Flakes, but especially Kitty.

"I like it that you're back with us," Sophie said to Kitty.

"This is like your first field trip in forever, huh?" Fiona said.

Willoughby raised her arms like she was going to burst into a cheer, but Maggie cut her off. Sophie was glad Maggie was the one who always enforced the rules. She would hate that job. She would have to keep her imagination totally under control to do that.

Right now, in fact, Sophie was searching for her next dream character. With a new film project to do for Art Appreciation class, she hoped one of the paintings would inspire her into a daydream that would lead to a new lead character that would shape a whole movie for Film Club to do . . .

"Okay—now *that's* what *I'm* talkin' about!"

Sophie looked over at Vincent, who was three paintings inside the door, bobbing his head and pointing like he'd just discovered a new vaccine. Like a flock of hens, the Corn Flakes followed Sophie to see what he'd found. Darbie and Kitty stared, mouths gaping. Willoughby out-shrieked herself.

"We can't do a movie about this," Maggie said. Her words, as always, dropped out in thuds. "Those people are naked."

Nathan turned purple.

"Painters back then were all about the human body," Fiona said. "Don't get all appalled. It's just art."

"I don't even know what *appalled* means but I think I am that." Darbie shook her head at Vincent. "You're gone in the head if you think we're going to *touch* that idea."

Sophie suddenly felt squirmy. While the three boys wandered into the next exhibit room, Sophie put her arms out to gather her Corn Flakes around her. "You guys," she said, "we're acting like the Pops and Loops, all freaking out over naked people and talking about gross things being cool."

"*We're* not doing it," Maggie said. "The *boys* are."

"They can't help it," Sophie said. "They're just boys."

Willoughby gave a mini-shriek.

"I know what you're gonna say, Soph," Fiona said. "Even if they're being a little bit heinous, that doesn't mean we have to be."

"The Corn Pops *wish* they had Jimmy and those guys in their group," Willoughby said. She looked a little startled, curls springing out from under her headband. "Sorry—Corn Flake Code—I know we're not supposed to try to make people jealous and stuff."

Fiona sniffed. "We're so beyond that."

"Don't say anything else," Darbie said out of a small hole she formed at the corner of her mouth. "Here they come."

A group of four girls made such an entrance around the corner, Sophie was sure the paintings were going to start falling off the walls. Julia Cummings sailed in the lead with her thick dark auburn hair swinging from side to side and her glossy lips set in her usual I-smell-something-funny-and-I-think-it's-you curl. Fiona always said she looked disdainful.

She swept past the Corn Flakes with her three followers trailing after her, all dressed in variations of the skin-tight theme and curling their own lips as if they'd been studying Julia by the hour. There was a time when they would have stopped and made a remark about how lame and uncool each of the Corn Flakes was, but Sophie knew they didn't dare. The Corn Pops had been back in school for only a week since their last serious detention.

It was a sure thing they weren't going to take a chance with Mr. DiLoretto on their heels. He strode in right behind them, wearing his glasses with no rims and his curly grayish hair pulled back in a ponytail.

Sophie's high school sister, Lacie, had warned her about Mr. DiLoretto when the seventh graders switched from Life Skills to Art Appreciation for the new semester.

"He's a little weird," Lacie had said, "and he gets mad when people don't take art seriously."

So far, Sophie liked him fine because he let them choose their own groups for their assignment to do a creative project on any painting or sculpture they saw at this museum in Norfolk. And because he'd said their group could do a film. And because he was really nice to Kitty.

Even now he dodged the last of the Corn Pops and went straight to her.

"Have you done any sketches?" he asked. His voice was always edgy, it seemed to Sophie. Like he just knew that either excitement or disaster was around the next corner.

"I did a couple," Kitty said. She giggled and opened the red sketchbook she'd been carrying around. Sophie sidled closer and felt her brown eyes bulging.

Kitty's drawings looked just like some of the paintings they'd seen on the gallery tour. The lion in one looked like it was going to leap right off the page.

"Whoa," Maggie said. "I didn't know you could draw *that* well, Kitty."

"Kathryn is an exceptional young artist," Mr. DiLoretto said.

"Who's Kathryn?" Willoughby whispered to Sophie.

Kitty giggled again. Mr. DiLoretto swept the rest of them, including the nearby Corn Pops, with a bristly look. "Expect to see incredible work from her," he said.

With another proud gaze at Kitty, he hurried on, calling over his shoulder, "You have fifteen minutes left to choose your piece, and then we gather for lunch. Cuisine and Company is on your map."

"Hey," Vincent said from a doorway. "Get a load of *this* exhibit."

As the Corn Flakes headed for him, Sophie linked her arm through Kitty's. "You're gonna be a famous artist someday," she said. "There'll be, like, an entire museum of your paintings."

"I drew a lot when I was home, you know, 'cause there wasn't that much to do." Kitty hugged the sketchbook. "Now that I'm in remission, I can do a lot more."

"Mr. DiLoretto thinks you're, like, Leonardo da Vinci or somebody," Sophie said. She could hear her voice squeaking up into mouse-range. It did that when she was delighted too.

Another voice, not delighted at all, hissed from the direction of the naked-people painting, where the Corn Pops were standing in a knot.

"Pssst!" Anne-Stuart Riggins said.

Sophie was glad they weren't closer. Anne-Stuart had a continuous sinus problem, and sometimes her sounds came out wet.

"What do they want?" Kitty muttered.

"I remember when *I* was teacher's pet," Julia said.

"We *all* were," B.J. Schneider put in.

Julia gave her a green-eyed glare and went on. "It doesn't last, though. Teachers are fickle."

"Ignore them," Sophie whispered to Kitty. She nudged her by the elbow toward the door where the rest of the group had disappeared.

"I don't know, Julia," Anne-Stuart said. She gave a juicy sniff. "If Kitty kisses up to him enough, maybe he'll keep telling her she's . . ."

She waved her hand at Cassie, who squinted her close-together eyes at the artist's name next to the nude painting and read, "Bo-ti-cel—"

"Whatever," Julia said.

"Yeah, whatever, Cassie," B.J. chimed in.

They *all* glared at B.J. this time, which gave Sophie a chance to give Kitty the final push through the doorway.

"They're always so jealous of each other," Kitty whispered. "I'm so glad I'm not a Pop anymore."

"I'm glad you're not too," Sophie said. "You never have to worry about us being all jealous and stuff."

"Sophie—look at this!"

Sophie hurried over to where the Film Club was standing, staring up at a painting of a can of Campbell's soup.

"Who would paint a stupid soup can?" Maggie said.

Fiona tapped her pen on her notebook. "Some guy named Andy Warhol."

"All his stuff is weird," Vincent said. "This one's, like, a stack of boxes."

Sophie gazed at it. "Look how real that looks."

"You thought that lady in the beautiful *dress* was boring," Willoughby said. "This would put you to sleep."

"Not movie material," Vincent said.

"If somebody was, like, *under* the boxes getting crushed," Nathan said, "that would be cool."

"That would be repulsive," Fiona said.

Sophie pulled a strand of her hair under her nose. She was glad it was long enough to do that again, because it always helped her think. Personally, she liked the funny paintings of boxes and soup cans.

"What do you think of Andy Warhol's work?"

Sophie looked up at Mr. DiLoretto.

"It's—I like it," Sophie said.

"Why?" he asked.

Lacie had been right, Sophie thought. He *was* a little bit weird. She adjusted her glasses and looked back at the soup can. "Well," she said, "it's all just ordinary stuff, but up there on the wall, all shiny and perfect, it seems like it's special too."

"Well, well."

Uh-oh, Sophie thought. Did she say the wrong thing? What was it Lacie had said about him getting mad when people didn't get art?

"You have the beginnings of a good critical mind," Mr. DiLoretto said.

Sophie let go of the hair she was still pulling under her nose like a mustache. "I do?" she said.

"You don't have an ounce of talent for drawing or painting, but you show some promise as an art critic." He glanced at his watch. "Nine minutes 'til lunch."

Sophie didn't hear the rest of what he said. She was gazing again at the giant soup can—*and pawing through her large canvas artsy-looking bag for her notebook and pen. Ah, there they were, beneath the camera and the portable tape recorder and her calendar full of appointments with people who wanted her expert opinion on modern art.*

So many demands on my time, Artista Picassa thought. But I must make some notes on this piece because it fascinates me.

Very few people had her appreciation for the more bizarre artists like Andy Warhol. It was her duty to educate people, which was why she was an art critic. And possibly the most famous one in all of Virginia, if not beyond—

That was it, of course. Maggie could write it all down in the Treasure Book later.

They would do their project on one of Andy Warhol's pieces.

She could play Artista Picassa, the famous art critic . . .

And maybe artists who were jealous because she didn't praise their paintings would do something heinous . . .

Too bad they couldn't use Pops and Loops in their film. They'd be perfect as envious painters.

Sophie looked around for her group, but there was nobody left in the exhibit room.

"Rats!" Sophie said to the soup can.

She dashed into the hall, but she didn't have a clue which way to go, and the map of the museum was shoved into the bottom of her backpack.

Where's Maggie when you need her? she thought. *Maggie probably has the whole museum layout memorized by now.*

But that was why Maggie was the club's recorder and Sophie was the director. Creative people needed organized people to keep them from getting lost, Sophie decided.

The smell of food and the clattering of forks finally led her in the right direction. Mr. DiLoretto was standing in the doorway of Cuisine and Company, glaring at her from under his tangled eyebrows.

"I got caught up appreciating art," Sophie said.

He just pointed her inside. Fiona waved to her from a table across the room.

"Mr. DiLoretto wouldn't let us look for you," she said as Sophie slid into a chair.

"Tell her what we decided," Vincent said to Fiona.

"You're gonna love this, Soph," Jimmy said. His usually shy smile was wide.

Sophie looked at Fiona. "Decided about what?"

"The film," Fiona said. "Jimmy found the perfect painting for our project."

Something about the way Fiona didn't quite look back at Sophie made Sophie feel squirmy. Slipping off her shoes, Sophie pushed her toes between the close-together bars under the chair.

Maggie pushed a bowl of green soup toward her and said, "Eat."

"It looks re—what was that word?" Willoughby said.

"Repulsive," Darbie said. "It tastes better than it looks."

"It's called *The Surgeon*," Vincent said.

"The soup?" Sophie said.

"No, the painting."

"What painting?"

"The one we're going to do our project on," Fiona said.

Sophie twitched, pushing her toes farther between the tight bars, shoving them past the balls of her feet. The group had already decided? Without her?

"It's not boring at all," Willoughby said.

"And there's no blood and guts," Maggie said.

Kitty giggled. "Or naked people."

"But it's still way cool," Nathan said.

If he turned red, Sophie didn't notice. She was sure she herself was losing all color. She felt her body go rigid, and she pushed down hard again with her feet.

"I haven't even seen it," she said.

"After this, we get to go to the gift shop," Jimmy said, "and I'm gonna get a poster of it."

"All right, folks," Mr. DiLoretto said as he wove among the tables, "it's time to move on to the museum shop."

"Sophie hasn't even eaten yet," Maggie said.

"Well, now, that's her problem, isn't it?" Mr. DiLoretto said. "Kitty, you'll come with me. I want you to meet one of the artists who teaches classes here."

"Don't worry, Sophie," Darbie said, pronouncing it "Soophie" like she always did. "I've got some snacks in my bag you can eat on the bus."

Sophie didn't feel like eating. All she wanted to do was grab Fiona in the hall and find out just exactly what was going on.

But when she tried to get out of her chair, she couldn't. Her feet were stuck in the bars, and they weren't coming out.

Two

Come on, Soph," Fiona said. "Mr. DiLoretto's already mad because you were late for lunch—"

"I can't!" Sophie whispered. She tried again to pull her feet out, but they just stayed there and throbbed.

"What's going on?" Maggie said, voice thudding for all to hear.

Sophie clamped her teeth together. "My feet are stuck. Could you get me out so he doesn't see this?"

But before Darbie and Fiona could even hit the floor to inspect, Mr. DiLoretto was on the scene. One look at Sophie's feet, and his voice went straight to its edge. Sophie cringed. He had obviously seen the disaster he'd always known was coming.

"I bet if we put some butter on her foot we could slide it right out," Fiona said. She was already reaching for the pat on Sophie's bread plate.

"*We* aren't going to do anything," Mr. DiLoretto said. "*You* are going to the museum shop, and *I* am going to find a maintenance man."

"Yeah," Vincent said, nodding at Sophie's feet. "Somebody's going to have to cut those bars. I'd say you're going to have to use at least a—"

"Out!" Mr. DiLoretto shouted.

Yeah, Sophie decided. This had definitely taken him over the edge.

Everybody broke for the door, the Corn Flakes looking back at Sophie like she was about to have a leg amputated. The Corn Pops were much less sympathetic. B.J. snorted right out loud.

"I'm really sorry," Sophie said to Mr. DiLoretto.

"You're the one who's going to miss out on shopping," he said.

"But you wanted to take Kitty to meet that artist—"

The sharp cut of Mr. DiLoretto's eyes made her wish she hadn't reminded him. She chewed on the ends of her hair—until she saw a mountain-sized man in a denim shirt approaching carrying a toolbox. Sophie tossed her hair aside before she could chomp off a hunk and swallow it in fear.

The man scowled, and Mr. DiLoretto glared, and they exchanged remarks about kids not being able to just sit in chairs like normal people, as if Sophie weren't even there. Once she was sure the guy wasn't going to take her foot off at the ankle, all she could think about was what Daddy was going to say. She hadn't been in trouble for a really long time, but that didn't mean he wouldn't still take her video camera away, and all that neat film-editing stuff he'd bought her for Christmas, especially if—

"Will I have to pay for the chair?" Sophie said. Her voice sounded tiny even to her.

"Nah," the man said. "With all the kids we get coming through here, stuff like this happens."

"Not with *my* people," Mr. DiLoretto said.

Sophie was sure she wasn't one of *his* people. All she wanted to do was get to *her* people.

By the time the mountain man got the bars cut and Mr. DiLoretto did a two-second check to make sure Sophie's ankles weren't hurt, everybody was finished in the museum shop and had boarded the bus. Sophie made her way down the aisle amid posters being unrolled and kids passing bracelets and key chains to each other. The Flakes and Charms *would* have to sit all the way in the back. By the time she got to them, she felt like one of the weirder paintings in the gallery with everyone gaping at her.

"Sophie, are you *okay*?" Willoughby said when she finally made it to the last seat.

"Let me see your feet," Darbie said. She smacked her own thighs for Sophie to prop up her feet.

"How big was the saw they used?" Vincent said.

Sophie expected him to lick his chops any minute.

"This'll cheer you up." Jimmy was grinning so big it looked to Sophie like there was an extra set of his perfect teeth. Even his very-blond hair looked excited.

"He's jazzed," Fiona said to Sophie.

"Show her, Jim," Willoughby said.

Jimmy unrolled the poster like it was a royal banner, and Fiona helped him hold it in place.

"Isn't it the *best*?" she said.

It wasn't a Campbell's soup can, that was for sure.

There was a lot going on in the piece, including two men looking into another man's ear, another man having his arm bandaged by a very large woman, and a dog passing through. There were pots and pitchers and bowls all over the place, all bathed in light streaming through a window.

"You haven't heard the coolest part yet," Vincent said.

He nudged Maggie, who gave him a black look. Maggie would hardly let one of the Corn Flakes touch her, much less an actual boy.

But Sophie forgot that the minute Maggie opened the special Treasure Book the Flakes wrote important things in. The page she turned to already had her neat handwriting on it.

Sophie stared. "You started planning the film?"

"We're just getting ideas," Darbie said.

Kitty made a little circle on Sophie's jacket sleeve with her fingertip. "We wouldn't *decide* anything without you."

"Yeah, but these are great ideas." Vincent poked Maggie again. "Tell her."

This time Maggie scooted away from him, which was hard since they were sitting three to a seat on either side of the aisle. Fiona and Jimmy were on their knees on the second to last seat, facing backward so they could hold up the poster. Sophie wriggled uneasily, and not just because she was crammed between Kitty and Willoughby. It felt as if someone were sitting in *her* place. As the bus lurched, so did everything in Sophie's head. Nothing was the way it was supposed to be.

"Here's what we have so far," Maggie said. " 'The painting is called *The Surgeon*, and it's by David Ten-ee-ears the Younger.' "

"He was a painter in the baroque period," Fiona said.

Willoughby yelped. "Whatever that is."

"Get to the good part," Vincent said.

He was starting to remind Sophie of the cafeteria monitor, the way he was snapping out orders.

" 'In our movie,' " Maggie read from the Treasure Book, " 'the painter will be played by Kitty since she's the most artistic.' "

"I don't mind playing a boy," Kitty said. She pointed to her head. "I have the hair for it."

"You don't have *any* hair," Nathan said. He turned crimson even before anybody could glare at him.

Maggie read on. " 'The painter gets kidnapped by another painter who's jealous of her talent.' "

"That's Jimmy," Fiona said. She jabbed him with her elbow, and he jabbed her back.

It's like they have a secret together, Sophie thought. She gnawed at a hunk of her hair.

"'Nathan will play his evil assistant,'" Maggie read.

"He won't have that many lines," Vincent said. "That way he can do a lot of the editing since he's good at it."

"You didn't say that before." Maggie's dark eyebrows drew together. "Do you want me to write that down?"

"Not now," Fiona said. "Get to the really good part."

Jimmy grinned at her. "You mean *your* part."

Huh, Sophie thought. It sure *sounded* like they'd been deciding.

"'An expert comes in,'" Maggie read on.

Ah. Artista Picassa. Maybe this wouldn't be so bad—

"That's me," Fiona said.

"We picked her because she can say the big words without making a bags of it," Darbie said.

So can I! Sophie wanted to say. And Mr. DiLoretto had said *she* could actually be an art critic, for real.

But Sophie just chewed on her hair. They were sure to get to her part any second now, even if it wasn't Artista Picassa. She wasn't *that* attached to her yet.

Maggie went back to the Treasure Book. "'Fiona the art expert will find the clues to where Kitty the painter is—in the painting itself.'"

"This is where it really gets cool," Jimmy said.

Maggie ran her finger down the page. "'We'll set it in the ba-rock period.'"

"Ba-roke," Fiona said. "Like it rhymes with choke."

Willoughby bounced on the seat beside Sophie. "Maggie's gonna come up with fabulous costumes for her mom to make, and I get to do hair and makeup." She poodle-yipped in Jimmy's direction. "Jimmy even said he'd wear tights."

Nathan turned red.

"Vincent and I are going to do the filming," Darbie said.

Vincent nodded. "Now that we have two cameras—Sophie's and the school's—plus all our editing equipment."

"*Our* editing equipment?" Sophie said.

"Well, yours, plus the stuff Mr. Stires has." Vincent looked at Willoughby. "Go ahead and say it."

Willoughby shrieked. "It's going to be *fabulous!*"

Every face around Sophie was shining as if a painter had cast them all in some golden light. Sophie stopped squirming and let her hair drop from her mouth.

"Okay," she said. "I can direct that. You guys did good."

Suddenly nobody was looking at her—except Vincent, who said, "Actually, I'm going to direct it."

"Since it was mostly his idea," Fiona said. She glanced at Sophie, and then studied the painting as if she'd never seen it before.

Sophie swallowed a lumpy thing in her throat. "Okay—well—since it was his idea." She straightened her tiny shoulders. "So, Fiona, when do we start writing?"

Fiona looked at Jimmy—who glanced at Darbie—who bulged her eyes at Maggie.

"*What?*" Sophie said.

"We kind of already started writing it while we were waiting for you," Fiona said.

"We?" Sophie said.

"Me and Jimmy."

"They couldn't just sit here," Darbie said. "You know how they are, Sophie."

Sophie *thought* she knew how they were. But right now, sitting in what felt like the wrong spot, watching her friends fill in all the spaces that belonged to her, she wasn't so sure.

She looked at Maggie. Wasn't there a rule about this that Maggie ought to be pointing out about now?

Maggie frowned at the page. Sophie watched her hopefully, until Maggie looked at Vincent and said, "What's Sophie's part?"

"We didn't get that far yet." Fiona's voice sounded too high. "But I'm thinking she should be my servant boy."

Maggie put her purple gel pen to the page and mouthed as she wrote S-E-R—

"What does your servant boy do?" Sophie knew her voice was squeaking into only-dogs-can-hear range, but she couldn't help it. Squeaking and disbelief went together.

Fiona cleared her throat. "Back then—"

"'In the ba-roke period,'" Maggie read from the book.

"The servant helped the mistress get dressed, brought her tea, turned down her bed—"

"Then why would your servant be a boy?" Darbie said.

For the first time since she'd gotten on the bus, Sophie was grateful to one of them. It wasn't that she hadn't played boy roles before. She could play anything. And Kitty was being a good sport about her part as the male painter. But if there was no reason to be a boy—

"I'll be a servant *girl*," Sophie said. "And my name will be Johanna Van Raggs."

Fiona tucked a wayward hair strand behind her ear. "We haven't started picking names yet."

"Except David Ten-Ears the Younger," Maggie said.

Kitty giggled.

"Not 'Ten-Ears,'" Fiona said.

"Oh, let's call him that," Darbie said. "It'll be a gas!"

"We're gonna have to get serious about this," Vincent said, "if we want this film to be—" He looked at Willoughby.

"Fabulous!" she said.

"I *am* serious," Sophie said. She aimed her gaze at Fiona. "I want my name to be Johanna Van Raggs."

"It's kind of fancy for a servant girl," Fiona said.

"It's not that big of a deal," Vincent said. "It's not like anybody's actually going to say her whole name in the movie anyway."

"I like it," Kitty said. She looped her arms around Sophie's and leaned her head on her shoulder. "I wish you were gonna be *my* servant."

"Hey, wait," Jimmy said. "She could be Kitty's—David's servant—and when David gets kidnapped, Fiona could make—what's her name?—Joanne? Fiona could make her help her."

"My character would so have her own servant," Fiona said.

"But she'd use David Ten-Ears' servant because Joanne would know more about him—where he might go, stuff like that," Jimmy said.

Vincent's eyes took on a gleam. "Besides, then you could really order her around, Fiona. Y'know, treat her like your slave. Put that down, Maggie."

"Hello!" Sophie said.

Fiona leaned across the aisle toward Sophie, shaking her head. "It's not like I'm gonna bop you over the head or something, Soph."

"That'd be cool, though!" Nathan said.

"No!" Kitty and Willoughby said in unison.

Before Sophie could even say anything over the stereo squeals in her ears, Vincent said, "No violence—but let's go with Jimmy's idea."

"That'll be a bigger part for you, Sophie," Darbie said. She looked to Sophie like she'd just burped some of that repulsive green soup, and it tasted worse this time.

"It's not about who has the biggest part anyway," Fiona said.

"Can I see that book you bought, Fiona?" Willoughby said quickly. "I want to look at the hairstyles."

It seemed to Sophie that all the girls—except Maggie—were talking in way-high voices. Like maybe if they sounded "up," Sophie wouldn't be so down.

But as Sophie stared out the bus window and watched the signs on I—64 herald their approach to the Poquoson turn-off, she sank low enough to crawl under the seat. What had just happened?

She always came up with the ideas for their films.

She always dreamed up the main character and played her in the movie.

She and Fiona—or sometimes *she* and Darbie, and once *she* and Jimmy—had always written the scripts.

And there had never been any question that *she* would direct.

After all, wasn't she the one who had gotten her own camera and started making films of her daydreams with just Fiona and then Maggie, and later Kitty and then Willoughby?

If it wasn't for her, would there even be a Film Club? Would the Lucky Charms even have people to make amazing videos with?

"You okay, Soph?" Willoughby said.

"Hey, Sophie," Jimmy said, "don't forget, we have Round Table at lunch tomorrow."

"I got you something at the gift shop," Fiona said. "I hate that you didn't get to go."

"Want some crackers, Soph?" Darbie said.

Sophie tried to smile, but she had a hard time making it happen. They loved her—she knew that—but why didn't they remember who she was?

31

There was only one thing to do, she decided as the bus pulled up in front of the school. That was to show her fellow Flakes and the Charms that they needed her to be in charge.

Because if she wasn't Sophie LaCroix, the great film director—who was she?

Three

❋ ⌂ ✺

Sophie's six-year-old brother, Zeke, met her at the kitchen door when she got home. His face was smeared with jelly, and so was the doorknob, the front of the refrigerator, and the whole snack bar.

"Are you finger-painting with jam?" Sophie said.

Zeke scowled at her. Sophie grabbed his hand just before he dragged it across his sticking-up-all-over-the-place dark hair. He looked just like their father, minus the strawberry preserves.

"No," he said. "I was makin' me a sandwich."

"Where's Lacie?" Sophie said. "It's her day to play with you."

"She's not home yet," he said. "But I'm old enough to make my own snack."

"Yeah," Sophie said, "but you're not old enough to paint the kitchen when you're done. Does Mama know you're doing this?"

"No." Zeke climbed onto a stool at the snack bar where two pieces of bread were drowning in jelly. "I'm makin' her one too. It's a surprise."

"That's for sure," Sophie said.

She was headed for the sponge when Zeke said, "Mama said she wants you to come up as soon as you get here." He narrowed his blue-like-Daddy's eyes suspiciously. "You're not gonna tell her about the surprise, are you?"

"No," Sophie said. Her mind was going in another direction as she climbed the stairs. Had Mr. DiLoretto already called Mama about the chair incident?

She paused before she opened the door to Mama and Daddy's bedroom. Mama was pregnant, and things weren't going so well. If they didn't want Baby Girl LaCroix to arrive before her time in March, six weeks from now, Mama had to stay in bed. Daddy had told the three kids a bajillion times that Mama wasn't supposed to get upset.

Maybe I should have told Mr. DiLoretto that, Sophie thought.

"Is that you, Soph?" Mama called.

She didn't sound like she was going to throw a lamp or anything. Not that Mama ever had, but Sophie had figured out that being pregnant definitely made a person cranky, even soft Mama.

Sophie opened the door a crack and peeked in. Mama's usually wispy face, which people said was just like Sophie's, was puffy and white like the inside of one of Mama's home-made biscuits. Not that she'd baked any in a while. Her brown-like-Sophie's eyes were saggy and tired-looking, even though it seemed to Sophie that she took a lot of naps. Her hair, curly and highlighted, was now mostly Sophie-brown with some gray and was pulled up into a messy bun on top of her head.

Still, she smiled and held out her hand. It used to remind Sophie of an elf's hand, but now the fingers were swollen like little sausages. "Come in, Dream Girl. I've been missing you."

Sophie felt like Jell-O inside as she crossed to Mama's bed. There wasn't a sign that she'd talked to Mr. DiLoretto. And she'd called her Dream Girl, which meant at least *somebody* remembered who Sophie was.

"How was the field trip?" Mama asked.

"Horrible!" Sophie said.

Before she could stop herself, she'd knelt down and laid her head beside Mama on the bed, and Mama was stroking her hair. Sophie poured out the awfulness of everything, from the evil chair to the way her Corn Flakes had let the Film Club give her nothing but the lamest role in life.

Mama made sounds, little "oh's" and small "ah's" and tiny "ouches." By the time Sophie was through, she was all the way up on the bed, snuggled next to the baby sister inside. Even she seemed to be listening.

"I don't know what to do," Sophie said.

"Want some help?" Mama said.

But before Sophie could even sit up, the door opened and Lacie burst in. She was holding a telltale jelly-stained towel, which she thrust behind her back. Sophie knew the everything's-fine smile she pasted on was fake.

"Sorry I'm late, Mama," Lacie said.

"Did Zeke tear the house apart?" Mama said.

"Of course not. But Soph, I do need some help with— dinner."

Sophie saw the set of Lacie's jaw, which made her look like Daddy too. That, and the way she was flipping her dark pony-tail, was a clear signal for Sophie to get downstairs and help her sandblast the kitchen.

Sophie scrambled from the bed and headed for the door.

"Sophie," Mama said, "we'll talk some more later. Be sure to tell God about it, okay?"

Lacie led Sophie down the stairs, speaking low and tight. "Did you not see the mess he made down there?"

"Mama wanted to talk to me."

"Yeah, well, while you were having your little chat, Zeke dropped that whole jar, and it broke. There's jam all the way into the dining room."

"Aw, man!" Sophie said. "I'll help you clean it up."

"No — you keep Zeke away from me so I don't do him some kind of bodily harm. I'll clean it up before Daddy sees it."

Lacie wasn't kidding about the mess. There were even drippy strawberries on the kitchen ceiling. Sophie ducked out with Zeke in tow before one could drop on her. The day had been bad enough without having something gunky fall into her hair.

"I didn't get to take Mama the snack I made her," Zeke wailed as Sophie dragged him into the family room.

"Nobody can eat that much jelly, Z-Boy," Sophie said. "What video do you want to watch?"

Zeke picked a Spider-Man cartoon, and while he watched it for what Sophie was sure was the two-hundredth time, she tried to do what Mama said. She closed her eyes and looked for the kind eyes of Jesus.

It was a way of praying that she'd learned from Dr. Peter. He was the cooler-than-any-other-grown-up-on-the-planet therapist Sophie used to see every week, back when she didn't get her work done in school and daydreamed herself into trouble all the time. After she mostly got her act together, he became the Bible study teacher at church for the preteen girls.

Since Sophie was so good at imagining, Dr. Peter had taught her to get very quiet and imagine Jesus was right there with her, which, he told her, Jesus actually was, and just talk to him. Sophie didn't ever imagine Jesus answering her. Dr. Peter said that would be like writing a script for the Lord. But somehow, in ways that Sophie never would have thought up, he did answer, usually later, when Sophie least expected it.

As soon as she curled up into the corner of the sofa, eyes closed, Sophie could feel Jesus close to her. His kind eyes came right into view in her mind, soft and gentle, and understanding everything she told him.

About how unfair things were all of a sudden, and how she wasn't as important as she had been that morning when she woke up.

The thing is, she told him without words, *being the director is what you made me for. Right?*

Sophie sat with that for a moment. Of course that was right. Why else were all their films so cool? What other reason could there be for the way the Flakes got closer and closer every time they made one?

Sophie kept her eyes shut as she smiled. She'd just have to show the Flakes *and* the Charms that they'd made a mistake by taking her job away from her. The question was how to do that without breaking the Corn Flake Code about not hurting people's feelings.

She wished that for once Jesus' answer would just pop up on a billboard right away. Sophie scrunched deeper into the pillows and tried to shut out the Spider-Man theme song.

Her Corn Flakes were pretty smart, especially Fiona and Darbie. They would probably figure it out as soon as things started going wrong in rehearsals, wouldn't they?

She tried to see Jesus' kind eyes, but she was already pretty sure he was saying yes.

So she was in an almost normal-Sophie mood the next morning when she got to school. When Mrs. Clayton, one of her History/Language Arts teachers, reminded her first period that there was a Round Table meeting at lunchtime, she started to feel important again.

Round Table was the special council made up of two seventh graders—Sophie and Jimmy—and two eighth graders, and two teachers—Mrs. Clayton and Coach Nanini, a boys' PE teacher who looked like a big bald-headed bear and called Sophie "Little Bit." The council tried to help kids who couldn't seem to follow the rules, because there was almost always a reason why people acted out. Round Table was doing a lot to stop bullying at GMMS. Sophie and Jimmy had even set up a website about cyberbullying.

Sophie couldn't wait to get there that day, especially since all the Flakes and Charms could talk about during third-period PE was the new movie. Nobody showed signs of seeing that Sophie should be the director. Even in fourth-period math, Vincent passed her a note that said, "We need to edit at your house in two weeks. Put it on your calendar."

Sophie didn't write back. She couldn't think of a nice way to say, "Don't worry about it, Vincent. You won't be in charge that much longer."

When Sophie and Jimmy got to the Round Table conference room, Mrs. Clayton and Coach Nanini were in the corner talking to Mr. Bentley, the principal. Hannah and Oliver, the two eighth graders, were in their regular places. As Sophie slipped into her chair, Hannah leaned across Oliver, eyes batting at her contact lenses, and whispered, "Something's about to go down."

"What?" Jimmy said.

"I don't know, but check out Coach Nanini's face."

Sophie looked. Coach Nanini was a bigger man than even her father, who used to play football. That, along with his arm muscles being like two hams, was why Sophie thought of him as "Coach Virile." With his shaved head and heavy eyebrows, he could look like a television wrestler, but when he was helping some kid with a problem, which he did a lot, he was more like a cuddly stuffed animal.

But right now, his cheeks sagged, and his bright eyes drooped at the corners.

"He looks like we're at a funeral," Oliver said. "Who died?"

"Shut up!" Hannah said.

Sophie did as the three adults took their seats. She tried to catch Coach Nanini's eye so she could get him to grin at her, but he kept his gaze on his thick knuckles.

Yikes, maybe somebody *did* die.

Mr. Bentley folded his hands on the table and smiled that smile principals used when they were about to say something for a kid's own good.

What's he doing here anyway? Jimmy wrote on Sophie's notebook.

Sophie shrugged.

"I'm so proud of what you've done on this council," Mr. Bentley said. "Not only have you helped a number of students straighten out, but you've grown as young adults yourselves."

Sophie smiled, but she could hear a *however* in there somewhere.

"I'm eager to have more students experience the Round Table as you have," he went on. He stroked his salt-and-pepper-colored beard like he was petting a cat. "Which is why I've advised Mrs. Clayton and Coach Nanini to start with a new council each semester."

Sophie looked at Coach Virile, but he was still examining his fist. Mrs. Clayton's face had gone as stiff as her dyed blonde helmet of hair. Sophie was sure *advised* meant Mr. Bentley had given them an order.

"So that means we're out and four other kids are in?" Oliver said.

"It means you're going to get a much-deserved rest, and four other students will be given the same opportunities you've had."

"Starting when?" Hannah said.

Mr. Bentley smiled like there was actually something to smile about. "Starting now. Coach Nanini and Mrs. Clayton have already selected the new members."

Coach Nanini lifted his eyes and pressed his mouth into a sad line that made Sophie think of Charlie Brown.

"This is in no way a reflection of your work on the Round Table," Mrs. Clayton said. Her trumpet voice sounded more like a somber flute today. "You four have done an exceptional job."

"So—we're really off the council now?" Sophie said.

"Do you want them to write you a memo?" Oliver said.

Hannah poked him. "So who are our replacements?"

Sophie didn't want to hear the names. That would make it way too real.

But Mrs. Clayton read them anyway. Two eighth graders, and Ross Marley, who was a friend of the Charms, and Darbie O'Grady.

"Those are good people," Jimmy said.

"Yes," Sophie said. But she felt like a crumpled-up piece of paper.

One thing was clear as she worked her way through the hall crowd to her locker: it was more pressing than ever that the Film Club figure out she should be director. If one more important thing was taken away from her, she might just disappear completely.

The Flakes were all at their lockers when Sophie got there. Fiona's gray eyes went round when she saw her.

"Soph, what's wrong?" she said. "Did you have some kind of heinous case at Round Table?"

Sophie pulled her locker open and stuck her head inside. She didn't want Darbie to see her about-to-crumple face. When she did find out her good news, she'd realize it was Sophie's bad news. Sophie knew she'd probably offer to let her have her place.

That was the way Corn Flakes were—and it would be hard to say no.

"What's the deal, Soph?" Fiona said behind her.

"Just a minute," Sophie said. "I'm looking for something."

That was the truth. Right after winter break, all the Corn Flakes had decorated the insides of their lockers. Just about everybody in school was doing it, in fact. It made going there six times a day not so bad.

Sophie looked at the pictures she'd taped in hers and tried to find the old Sophie—the one who before yesterday felt pretty good about her life. She looked back at herself as characters like Goodsy, the cop in disguise; and Louisa Linkhart, Victorian lady.

When she got to the photo Coach Nanini had taken of her at a Round Table meeting, she pulled it off and stuck it in her pocket.

Four

W hat are you doing in there, taking inventory?" Fiona
said.Sophie swallowed the lumpy thing in her throat
and pulled her head out of her locker.

"You okay?" Fiona asked.

"I'll tell you later," Sophie said.

Fiona nodded. "We have a lot to tell you too. We got tons done
at the Film Club meeting." She turned her head and said over her
shoulder, "Come on, you guys, we have to fill Sophie in."

But Kitty, Maggie, and Willoughby were at the other end of
the locker row with Darbie, who was reading something from
a piece of paper.

"That rocks, Darbie!" Willoughby shrieked.

"Does Sophie still get to be on it?" Kitty said.

Fiona turned to Sophie with question marks in her eyes.
Sophie just shook her head.

Then she put on a smile and joined in the mini-celebration
with Darbie, although she couldn't quite bring herself to bounce
up and down like Kitty and Willoughby. When Willoughby
started making up a cheer to Darbie, Fiona pulled Sophie away.

Sophie wanted to hug her for that. She could tell Fiona how
losing Round Table left a hole in her, and she'd understand
and not tell Darbie.

But before she could even start, Fiona said, "I wanted to tell you the new stuff we decided about the movie, and now there's no time."

"Oh," Sophie said.

"Okay, here's the plan." Fiona hooked her arm through Sophie's and half dragged her toward Mr. Stires' science room. "I'll get a restroom pass, and you get one, and we'll talk for, like, five minutes in the bathroom. Mr. Stires won't care. We always get our work done."

Fiona didn't wait for Sophie to agree. She just gave Sophie's arm a squeeze and hurried to her seat. Sophie fell into hers just as the bell rang. Darbie flew through the door before it stopped.

"You're lucky, Darbie," Mr. Stires said. His voice, his toothbrush mustache, even the shiny dome that his fringe of hair erupted from—everything about him was cheerful, like always. "New rule here at GMMS."

In the back of the room, Tod Ravelli and Colton Messik, the two Fruit Loops, groaned like they'd just eaten a whole pig.

"It's not my rule," Mr. Stires said, "but since it was handed down by Mr. Bentley, I'm going to enforce it."

"So it's about being tardy," Darbie said, "since I almost was."

"Excellent reasoning," Mr. Stires said.

"So what's the rule?" Anne-Stuart said with the usual sniff.

"Three tardies in a class means an automatic detention."

Sophie let out a long breath. At least she didn't have to worry about that. She was never tardy.

But we're going to get more people coming up before Round Table, she thought.

And then she sagged miserably in her seat. She didn't have to worry about that either.

Mr. Stires gave the assignment, and the class settled down to pretending to read while they complained to each other about the new rule. Fiona nudged Sophie and went up to Mr. Stires' desk. Sophie heard her whisper to him, but he didn't write out a pass.

"One more thing, class," he said.

"Another rule?" Julia arched an eyebrow at him as if he wouldn't dare.

"Another rule. Mr. Bentley has also started a bathroom log."

"A what?" the class said in unison.

"Every time you receive a pass to the restroom, your teacher will enter it into the computer."

"That's against my civil rights!" Colton rose in his seat, ears sticking out comically from his head. "Isn't it?"

"No," Vincent told him.

"Once you have used six bathroom passes," Mr. Stires said, "you're done for the semester."

"Six in each class," Anne-Stuart said, nodding her silky blonde head like she expected Mr. Stires to nod with her.

"No, ma'am," Mr. Stires said. "Six for all your classes put together."

"What if we have to throw up?" somebody said.

"What if we have diarrhea?"

While the class named off every disease that required a toilet, Fiona held out her hand to Mr. Stires and said, "That's okay. I'll take my first one now."

She gave Sophie a you-*are*-coming-aren't-you? look as she went out the door.

But Sophie just opened her science book and shoved a hunk of hair into her mouth. Maybe it wasn't a good idea to use up a bathroom pass. Besides, she didn't want to hear any more news that was going to make the lump in her throat even bigger.

It was big enough for one day.

On Monday, Sophie was glad rehearsals for the film project would start in Mr. Stires' room during lunch. She'd spent a boring weekend doing nothing but homework and Zeke-watching. Every time she called Fiona, just so she wouldn't go mad (as Darbie would put it), she got Fiona's answering machine.

Mr. Stires and Miss Imes, the math teacher, were their Film Club advisers, but mostly they let the group work on their own. And Sophie figured out right away that Fiona and Jimmy had spent the whole weekend writing the script.

She could imagine them sitting by the fire in Fiona's living room with the Treasure Book, and Fiona's grandfather Boppa letting them toast marshmallows when they took breaks, and Fiona's doctor-mother ordering Chinese food for them, and Fiona having moo goo gai pan—Sophie and Fiona's best-friends favorite.

When she got to the part in her mind where Fiona and Jimmy were high-fiving each other over a great line they'd just thought of, she had to turn off her imagination. That wasn't easy to do. Especially when, halfway through Film Club's first read-through, Sophie realized something.

"Excuse me," she said.

Vincent blinked at her over the top of his copy. "It's not your line, Sophie."

"I know," Sophie said. "So far, I don't *have* any lines."

Kitty patted Sophie's arm. "We're not done. You'll have some."

"But I'm in *this* scene, and I'm not saying a word."

"That's because we decided to make the maid mute," Fiona said.

"Like a deaf mute?" Maggie said.

"No, she can hear. She just can't talk." She turned to Sophie. "It'll be a way more interesting character, Soph, with lots to do."

Willoughby gave a nervous yip. "At least you won't have any trouble learning your lines, Soph."

"I never have trouble learning my lines!"

"That's true," Maggie said. "She doesn't."

Fiona rolled her eyes. "That's not why we did it this way."

Sophie wished Darbie would ask why they *did* practically make her invisible in the movie, since Darbie was the only one standing up for her these days.

But Darbie was at her first Round Table meeting. Sophie didn't even want to go there in her mind. She flipped through the script again.

"So if I don't ever speak," she said, "how do I help find the clues in the painting for Fiona?"

"You mean Leona," Fiona said.

"Her character's name is Leona Artalini," Maggie said.

"I *know*." Sophie didn't comment that she thought it was the stupidest name she'd ever heard of.

"It's Italian," Jimmy said. "Some of the best artists came from Italy, so we figured — "

"Could somebody just answer my question?" Sophie said.

Vincent's big loose mouth twisted up. "What *was* your question?"

"How is Johanna Van Raggs supposed to help Leona whatever-her-name-is find the clues in the painting if she can't talk?"

Fiona propped her elbow on Sophie's shoulder and gave her a patient look. "Soph," she said, "Johanna's not the art expert; she's a servant. Leona figures out the clues. Johanna just waits on her while she's doing it." She looked at Jimmy. "Feel free to jump in any time."

A red blotch had appeared at the top of each of his cheeks. "It just seemed like it would be funny if you couldn't talk. There's a place where you use all these hand motions to try to tell her something, and she keeps thinking you're saying something else."

Fiona nodded her head until the stubborn strip of hair popped out from behind her ear. "It's really hilarious, Soph. It's in, like, scene five — "

"Which we're never gonna get to if we stop and talk about every single thing." Vincent looked up at the clock. "Fiona, it's your line."

Just about every line is Fiona's line, Sophie thought. She grabbed a hunk of hair and chowed down.

They were allowed to work on the project every day during sixth period, Mr. DiLoretto's class, which gave them more in-school time than they usually had for their Film Club movies. The only problem was that they had to stay inside the classroom — where everybody else was working with their groups too. Including the Loops-Pops bunch.

For their project, they appeared to be putting together some kind of poster about a painting called *Ship of Fools*, which, Darbie murmured to Sophie one day, was perfect for them. Since all they were doing was cutting out pictures from magazines and coloring in letters, they had plenty of time to observe the Flakes-Charms at work.

During the first rehearsal of the kidnapping scene, where all Sophie did was hide behind a chair, Anne-Stuart said to her, "Is Jimmy supposed to be a gangster or something?"

"Sort of," Sophie said.

Anne-Stuart gave a particularly juicy sniff. "He doesn't even look like a bad guy. He's way too cute."

She nudged Julia, who smiled at Cassie, who turned to B.J., poised to poke her. But Julia growled low in her throat, and Cassie retracted her poking finger.

"B.J.," Anne-Stuart said, "aren't you supposed to be working on your own project?"

Julia tossed her head. "Eddie's over there waiting for you."

Sophie looked in the direction Julia's hair had moved. Eddie Wornom was slumped in a desk in the back of the room behind a big propped-up book that said *Leonardo da Vinci* on the cover. Even though Eddie wasn't a Fruit Loop anymore, Sophie still couldn't get used to him being a decent human being.

Evidently B.J. couldn't either, because every day the Pops had to chase her off to work with him. Sophie certainly had plenty of time to watch that going on, since all she did during rehearsals was duck behind furniture and bring "Leona" cups of tea that she never drank. It was hard to get into that.

And that was very strange for Sophie. This far into the making of a film, she usually spent more time being her character than being herself. But when she tried to put on Johanna Van Raggs, she just didn't fit.

That afternoon at home, Sophie slipped into character a little in the laundry room when she had folding duty... *Johanna held David Teniers's clean shirt to her face and cried into it. Would her kidnapped master ever be returned? She scowled through her tears. Not if that ridiculous Leona Artalini had anything to do with it. She didn't know as much about* The Surgeon *as Johanna herself did. Johanna clutched the shirt in her fists. If that ignorant woman demanded one more cup of tea, she was very likely to rip her in half...*

"Hey!" Zeke said. "That's my best Spider-Man shirt! You tore it! Da-ad!"

The chunk that replacing Zeke's shirt took out of Sophie's saved-up allowance wasn't the worst of it. Mama and Daddy called her up to the bedroom for a sit-down-and-talk. Daddy did most of the talking.

"Your mother says you're having some issues with your Flakes, Soph," Daddy said, motioning for her to perch on the edge of the bed. "Does that have anything to do with your tearing a hole in your brother's shirt?"

Sophie could see the corners of Daddy's lips twitching like he was pinching back a smile, and she didn't appreciate it. This so wasn't funny.

"Better one of his than one of your friends'," Daddy said. "Seeing how he has enough of them to open a Spider-Man boutique." He tilted his big squarish head at her. "How am I doing so far?"

"You're close," Sophie said. "Except I didn't want to tear one of their shirts. I wanted to tear one of them. Well, Fiona."

Daddy lost control of his lips and grinned. "We can always count on you to be honest, Soph."

Mama ran her hand down Sophie's back. "Have things gotten worse?"

Sophie nodded. Somehow their niceness was making that lumpy thing in her throat bigger.

"Worse, as in it's affecting your schoolwork?" Daddy asked.

"Not yet," Sophie said. "But it could happen."

"You starting to daydream in class again?"

"No! That's just it." Sophie could hear her voice pip-squeaking. "I can't even get into my character to feel better."

Daddy ran his hand down the back of his head. "I can't believe I'm saying this, but that is cause for concern."

He and Mama looked at each other and had one of those parent conversations where no words were spoken, but things were said with their eyes.

Daddy put his big hand on the back of Sophie's neck. "You could talk to Dr. Peter about it at Bible study maybe." Sophie twisted to look at him. Her mother and father had also worked with Dr. Peter, and Daddy especially had become like a whole other parent. For months now they'd been handling things as a family.

"You think I'm that bad?" Sophie said.

"No!" they both said as if they'd been poked with the same pin.

"You're not 'bad' at all, Dream Girl," Mama said.

"You've really been a team player," Daddy said. "But with everything that's going on around here, we just thought you might like a little special coaching, that's all."

Sophie pictured herself sitting on the window seat in Dr. Peter's office, swinging her legs, and holding on to the face pillow that matched her mood.

"Okay," Sophie said. "Maybe I'll ask him about it at Bible study."

But she wasn't sure even Dr. Peter could tell her how she was supposed to feel.

Five

Sophie said no to having sessions with her beloved Dr. Peter because it seemed like she would be going backward. But she didn't stop dumping everything on Jesus every night.

They just aren't figuring it out yet, she told him, *even though the script is lame and the main part is too much for Fiona.*

His eyes didn't look so kind to her. *Why would they?* she thought. He was probably as mad at them as she was.

About a week into rehearsals, during sixth period, the group tried to practice the scene where Fiona was supposed to discover the final clue.

Sophie—Johanna—sat on a stool that would barely have been big enough for Zeke and watched Leona turn from the poster of *The Surgeon* and say, "Eureka!"

Sophie was supposed to get up and do a little happy-dance, which she personally thought made her look like she had to go to the bathroom. Just as she stood up, Vincent barked out, "Cut!"

"Do you have to scream?" Cassie said from just a few feet away. She waved a Magic Marker at Vincent. "You made me mess up—again."

Vincent ignored her and folded his lanky arms. It occurred to Sophie that he could have folded them over one more time and still had some arm left over.

"Fiona," he said.

"It's Leona," Maggie said.

"You're supposed to act like it's a big deal."

"I said, 'Eureka,'" Fiona said. She looked at Maggie. "Isn't that my line?"

"'Eureka,'" Maggie read from the script. "'Leona throws her arms out wide. Johanna Van Raggs does a celebration dance.'"

"You didn't throw your arms out," Vincent said.

"It looks stupid." Fiona flapped her hands like a limp bird.

"That does look stupid," Maggie said.

"So do something else to look excited," Jimmy said.

Fiona put her hands on her hips.

"No, that's not it," Vincent said.

"I know!" Sophie could tell Fiona was about to spew out her longest vocabulary words any minute now. "The point is, Leona Artalini wouldn't freak out. She's a sophisticated professional. Her reaction would be more—subtle."

"Define *subtle*," Darbie said.

"It's like keeping your feelings inside and just giving little clues."

"Okay, so do that," Vincent said.

Fiona turned to the poster and raised an eyebrow. "Like that," she said.

"I didn't see anything," Willoughby said. "I mean, no offense."

Fiona rolled her eyes. "The camera will just have to come in close to catch it."

Vincent shook his head. "I don't think anybody's gonna get it. Just try it the way I told you."

"You'll be fabulous, Fiona!" Willoughby said, flapping everything including her curls.

"Yeah," Vincent said. "Do it like she just did."

It was all Sophie could do not to roll *her* eyes. No famous art expert in the baroque period would act like she was cheering at a middle school basketball game.

But nobody's asking me, she thought.

"Go for it," Vincent said. "Your line before that is —"

"I know my line." Fiona snapped him a look and took her place in front of the "painting." Sophie/Johanna hunched down on the stool again, toes pointed inward, and pretended to be blown away by Leona's intelligence.

"I have searched every inch of this painting," Fiona/Leona said. Or at least that was what Sophie thought she said. She was mumbling like she was having a conversation with herself.

"But still something eludes me." Fiona leaned about an eighth of an inch closer to the poster. "Aha. It is here, up in this corner. Eureka." She stuck both arms out, scarecrow-fashion, and turned around in a circle.

Kitty gave a nervous giggle. Behind Sophie, Julia, Cassie, and Anne-Stuart fell over each other like a trio of gibbon apes.

"I don't think that was it exactly," Jimmy said.

"It didn't even come close," Vincent said.

"Unless she was trying out for the *Wizard of Oz*," Sophie heard Julia whisper to her gasping friends.

Fiona punched her hands onto her hips so hard Sophie was afraid she'd bruised herself. "I told you it would look stupid," she said.

Her voice had an angry edge, but Sophie knew better. What they were hearing was Frustrated Fiona. Clenched teeth would have been next if the bell hadn't rung.

Fiona snatched up her backpack and made for the door. Willoughby and Kitty took off after her, but Sophie knew the best thing to do was to leave her alone for a while. Frustrated Fiona had been known to throw things.

Besides, although the snickers from the Corn Pops and the scarecrow imitations from the Fruit Loops made Sophie cringe for Fiona, she couldn't quite bring herself to feel totally sorry for her.

"She'll be better tomorrow," Jimmy said to Vincent.

"She wasn't any better today than she was yesterday," Vincent said.

"Do you want me to write that down?" Maggie said.

"No," Darbie told her. She looked at Sophie. "Maybe you should talk to her."

"I'll handle it," Vincent said, almost before Darbie got the words out. "I'm the director."

He puffed out his chest, or at least he tried to. To Sophie, it was more like an attempt to inflate a shriveled-up party balloon.

That afternoon Mama's eyebrows puckered when Sophie took celery sticks and peanut butter to her room for snack-and-chat.

"Your face tells me things aren't better," Mama said.

Sophie sagged onto the bed with the plate. "They're worse."

When she'd told Mama the latest episode, she stuffed a peanut-butter-gooed piece of celery into her mouth. Mama just toyed with one.

"There's one thing I'm not hearing, Dream Girl," she said.

"What?"

"I'm not hearing that you've tried talking to any of the girls about this, especially Fiona." She tapped at the peanut butter with the tip of her finger. "I thought it was part of your Corn Flake Code to always talk things out."

"It's like I'm not even there, though," Sophie said. The throat lump got lumpier. "They're basically ignoring me."

"It would be pretty hard to ignore you on the phone," Mama said. "Maybe after you finish your homework, you could give Fiona a call?"

"Maybe," Sophie said.

But even after she'd done her homework on the computer in the family room, she couldn't imagine what she was going to say to Fiona. At least, not as Sophie ...

Johanna Van Raggs retreated to her stool near the hearth and frowned into the pitiful little fire she'd built. She wished she could let Leona know what she really thought of her. "You think you know all there is to know about everything," she would tell her. "I know a lot of things that would help you in your search if you would just ask me. But no—you've made it so I can't even speak—and even if I could, you wouldn't listen because you think I'm just a stupid servant." Johanna jabbed at the fire with her poker and watched the sparks scatter fearfully for their lives. If only she could stir up Leona Da-Know-It-All that way ...

"Phone for you, Soph," Lacie said. She took the fireplace poker out of Sophie's hand. "You better not let Daddy catch you playing in the fire."

She handed Sophie the phone. Sophie could hear Fiona telling her little brother and sister to "exit, stage right" so she could talk in private.

"Fiona?" Sophie said.

"Soph—I am *so* glad you're there." She didn't sound like Frustrated Fiona. In fact, her voice was a little feeble, like she'd had the flu for a couple of days. Sophie felt a flicker of hope.

"Can I ask you something, Soph?" Fiona said.

Ah. She was finally coming around.

"Ask me anything," Sophie said. She cozied up to the fire.

"Don't you think Vincent is wrong about Leona Artalini? I mean, do you really think she should be acting like one of those people on TV when they win the lottery?"

"No way," Sophie said. She was starting to glow. Mama *had* been right.

"It works for *your* character because you're, like, this uneducated peasant. But I have the lead role—*I* shouldn't be acting like I have a mental disorder."

"Well, yeah," Sophie said, squirming a little, "but—"

"And the other thing is, Vincent shouldn't have let the Pops stand there and laugh at me. I mean, I know we're not supposed to care what they think, but, hel-*lo*, rude!"

"Definitely," Sophie said. "I think—"

"I'm using Corn Flake Code on this, Soph. I'm gonna go to Vincent and just tell him that. You know, like, not in a mean way, but just say it. And I'm telling him you think the same way I do."

Sophie hitched herself closer to the fire and picked her words carefully. "You want to know what else I think?" she said.

Fiona sent her husky laugh into the phone. "I already know what you think, Soph. I always know what you think." Sophie could almost see Fiona happily rolling her eyes. "We're best friends, remember? I knew I'd feel better after I talked to you."

Fiona had to go then, and Sophie sat staring at the flames that teased her like tongues. Mama had said to try talking to Fiona.

"I did," Sophie said out loud. "But Fiona didn't try listening."

Film Club met in Miss Imes' room during lunch the next day, and Kitty was giggling so much she couldn't even eat whatever her mom had put in her Tupperware container.

"Why are you flipping out?" Vincent said to her.

"Maggie has the costume drawings! I can't wait to see what I get to wear!"

Willoughby out-poodled her loudest shriek on record, even though she wasn't getting a costume. Sophie even felt a tingle. Costumes were one of the best-best-best parts of doing a movie, especially the way Maggie's mom, Senora LaQuita, made them.

It doesn't matter if I do just stand around, Sophie thought. *At least I get to wear something period and amazing.*

They all leaned forward as Maggie propped an oversized sketchbook on Miss Imes' desk and turned to the first page.

"This is Jimmy's," Maggie said.

Kitty and Willoughby went off the scale with giggles, and Vincent grinned at Jimmy. "Dude," he said, "she did put you in tights."

Jimmy grinned back. "I wear stuff like that for gymnastics all the time."

"I heard real men can wear tights — or something like that," Nathan said. And then he skipped red and went straight to magenta.

Sophie gazed at the black billowy sleeves and the flowing cape in the drawing. If a boy's costume was this elegant, she could only imagine what the girls' would be like.

She wasn't disappointed when she saw Fiona's. Leona Artalini was to be clad in blue brocade with enough tucks and loops and puffs to upholster a roomful of furniture.

"You are going to look *fabulous!*" Willoughby said.

And so was Kitty. Her painter's outfit had green velvet breeches, a white silky shirt, and a beret with an ostrich feather that was almost bigger than Kitty herself. Sophie saw tears in Kitty's eyes as she reached out and touched the drawing. She hadn't been in a movie in so long. Sophie could almost feel Kitty's happy warmth in her own chest.

"This is for Johanna Van Raggs," Maggie said.

She flipped to the last drawing, and Sophie's warm place turned to ice.

Except for the clunky boots, everything else in the picture looked like it had been pulled from a bag of rags. The sleeves were smudgy and had gaping holes in them. The skirt was a collection of tattered strips. And the vest was laced up with a filthy piece of rope.

"Nice," Vincent said.

"That wouldn't be the word I would use to describe it," Fiona said. She tilted her head back and forth. "But it works."

"Yeah, it fits," Jimmy said. "Johanna Van Raggs in rags."

Willoughby half yelped, "Sophie, you'll look—"

"I will *not* look fabulous," Sophie said. "So don't even go there."

She barely recognized her own voice. It sounded squeezed-in, just the way she felt.

"It's definitely not fabulous," Fiona said, "but—"

Sophie didn't wait to hear the rest. She fled the scene.

Six

✳ ⌂ ✺

Reeling around the corner into the locker row, Sophie almost ran head-on into Darbie—whose chin was practically dragging onto her chest. For the moment, Sophie's image of herself in a moth-eaten dress dissolved.

"What's wrong, Darb?" she said.

Darbie sank against the bank of lockers and jabbed her hair behind her ears like it had better not even think about creeping back out.

"You never told me Round Table was going to be like this," she said.

"Like what?"

"Like we have to do individual peer counseling."

"We never did that," Sophie said. It immediately sounded fascinating to her. There were lots of possibilities for a dream character who didn't look like somebody's flea-bitten bag.

"Guess who Mrs. Clayton assigned me to?" Darbie said.

"Not one of the—"

"The worst. B.J. Schneider."

Sophie couldn't think of a thing to do except squeeze Darbie's hand in sympathy. This really was heinous. As much as she missed Round Table, she wouldn't want to do this.

"B.J.'s making a bags of her whole life," Darbie said. "She's already gotten two tardies in just about every class, and she's used three bathroom passes."

"Yikes."

"It gets worse. Yesterday she got caught going to the Mini-Mart during lunch."

"What was she thinking?"

"She doesn't think." Darbie tucked her hair back tighter. "And I guess I'm supposed to teach her how."

Darbie peeled herself away from the lockers and twirled the lock on her own. Sophie leaned in, facing her. "Did Mrs. Clayton and Coach Nanini tell you there's always a reason why somebody acts out?"

Darbie grunted into her locker.

"Seriously," Sophie said. "We learned that if we could figure out why a kid was acting like a moron, we could usually help them."

Darbie pulled out her science book like it was B.J.'s head and slammed the door. "I know why she's being an eejit," she said. "Because she is one."

Sophie couldn't argue with that. B.J. never had appeared to have much sense.

In fact, during sixth period that very day, while Vincent was making Fiona say "Eureka!" every way possible, Sophie watched B.J. plop herself down in the middle of the Corn Pops and Fruit Loops and be banished to Eddie Wornom's corner for the hundredth time.

You'd think she'd get it eventually, Sophie thought. It wasn't like B.J. didn't know that when Julia decided somebody was suddenly de-Popped, that was *it* until she changed her mind. The harder B.J. tried to get back into the group, the farther

Julia's lip curled, until by now it was halfway up her nose. It was a clear signal for Anne-Stuart to do her dirty work for her.

"B.J., are you, like, retarded or something?" Anne-Stuart said. She put her face close to B.J.'s and formed her words like her mouth was made of rubber. "You—are—not—in—our—project—group."

Cassie joined in. "Go—work—with—Eddie."

Tod cast a black look toward the corner where Eddie was still reading the da Vinci book. "The loser," he said.

Huh, Sophie thought. *Just because Eddie won't do the kind of heinous stuff you do anymore?*

"Oh, he's definitely a loser," Julia said. She made a huge production out of redoing her ponytail and then flipped it at B.J. "And anybody who works with him is a loser too."

"I can't help it if I ended up having to work with him!" B.J. said. "You wouldn't let me be in your group!"

Sophie had never heard B.J. that close to tears before. She almost felt sorry for her.

Anne-Stuart sniffed. Cassie snorted. Sophie was surprised Colton didn't just out and out hang a loogie. Julia parked her hand under her chin and looked at B.J.

"You know what you have to do," she said, "if you want back in the group."

"I can't," B.J. said, in a voice Sophie could barely hear.

"Then I guess you're not much of a friend." Julia raised her brows at Cassie and Anne-Stuart, who both shook their heads.

Sophie watched B.J. slink toward Eddie and da Vinci, and then she looked for Darbie. This was definitely something she needed to know if she was going to be able to help B.J. with her eejit issues for Round Table.

Fiona was on something like take 454. Fiddling with the camera, Darbie's eyes drooped as if she were about to drift off to sleep.

"We could be here for decades," Darbie murmured when Sophie perched on the desktop where Darbie was set up.

"I think we already have been," Sophie murmured back. "I have something to tell you about Round Table."

"Do you sit on the tables in your home, Sophie?"

Sophie looked up at Mr. DiLoretto. He squinted at her through his rimless glasses, sort of like a fish peering out of its bowl. Sophie slid off the desk and hoped the paper he was holding wasn't a detention slip for her.

He handed it to Darbie and softened his face into a smile.

"Something for you about Round Table," he said. "It's an honor to be on that council."

Darbie's always-white face suddenly looked sunburned. "I've only been on it for—"

"You're a girl of many talents. I like to see a student who's well rounded."

Mr. DiLoretto sliced a look at Sophie that indicated feet-tangling, desktop-sitting urchins like her didn't qualify as "well rounded."

I used to be on the Round Table! Sophie wanted to shout at him as he turned to go. *I practically started it!*

Mr. DiLoretto paused, and for a heart-stopping moment, Sophie thought she might have said it out loud.

"I suggest you start doing some work on this project," he said to her. "So far, I haven't seen you do much."

Before Sophie could decide how she was going to keep from exploding, he moved on to the Pops-Loops group.

Darbie looked up from the paper. "Did you want to tell me something, Soph?" she said.

Sophie clamped her teeth together and shook her head. "Never mind," she managed to say. "It was nothing."

Sophie decided it was a good thing they had Bible study with Dr. Peter that day after school. Without his twinkly grin to look forward to, she was sure she would blow up into confetti. Especially in the car on the way to the church.

Fiona's grandfather Boppa drove the Flakes in the Buntings' big Ford Expedition. Fiona was in the front seat, turned around and up on her knees so she could address the girls in the next two seats, her seat belt fastened over her rump.

"Okay," she said, "so I got really tired of Vincent telling me how to act. I even talked to him about it, but it didn't do any good."

"He's the director," Maggie said in her thud-voice. "He's supposed to tell you how to act."

Fiona twisted her little bow of a mouth into a knot. Sophie knew that look. That was Fiona trying way hard not to say something she was going to have to apologize for later. Sophie couldn't help rescuing her. Fiona was still her best friend, even if she *was* clueless.

"It's not exactly working out for you, is it?" Sophie said.

The whole car seemed to breathe a giant sigh of relief, even bald-headed Boppa.

"No," Fiona said. She beamed at Sophie. "But I think I've found the solution."

Sophie closed her eyes and tried not to grin too big. Finally, Fiona had figured it out. At this point, it wouldn't be hard for Fiona to play Johanna Van Raggs, since there were no lines. And Sophie knew all of Leona Artalini's, although the first thing she was going to do as director was change that name.

"I looked up acting on the Internet," Fiona said, "and I found this totally cool thing called 'method acting.'"

Maggie reached for her backpack. "Should I be taking notes?"

"No, it's simple. You try to become your character, not just when you're rehearsing, but, like, all the time."

Kitty blinked her china-blue eyes at Sophie. "You always do that."

"No, no," Fiona said, swatting that aside with her hand as if it were a mosquito. "You don't just pretend. You actually become it. Like, Leona's Italian, so from now until we're finished filming, I'm only going to eat pasta."

"This should be interesting," Boppa said. Sophie saw his caterpillar eyebrows wiggle in the rearview mirror. "I think we're having Chinese tonight."

Willoughby let out a little yip she'd obviously been holding back. Sophie wasn't having as much luck with her disappointment. She was sure it was smeared all over her face.

"So let me get this straight," Darbie said from the rear seat. "You and Sophie and Kitty are going to act like your characters all the time? Even in school?"

"I can't be stuffed in a closet in Miss Imes' room," Kitty said. Sophie hadn't heard her voice wind up into a whine like that in a long time. "I'll get detention!"

"I'm sure that isn't what Fiona means." Boppa glanced at his granddaughter. "It isn't, is it?"

"No—hel-*lo*!"

Fiona rolled her eyes almost up into her head. Sophie used to think it was funny when she did that. Now it crawled right up between her shoulder blades.

"You just act the way your character would act in any situation you're in," Fiona said, like she was talking to her little sister. "Wherever you are, you do what David Teniers the Younger would do."

"I don't get it," Kitty whined.

Fiona reached into the second seat and patted Kitty's hand. "Don't worry about it. Just watch Sophie and me, and you'll catch on."

When did I agree to this? Sophie thought. It was time to say something.

But as they climbed out of the car at the church, Fiona said, "Remember, you can't speak unless you absolutely have to."

Sophie stared at her.

You sure aren't going to let me forget, Sophie thought as she followed Fiona into the Bible study room. She was again ready to explode.

Each of the girls, including Harley and Gillian, their two sporty friends, the Wheaties, had a different-colored beanbag chair with a Bible in a cover to match. Sophie sank into her purple one, certain that right now her face matched it.

Fiona poked it with her toe. "Uh, Soph," she said, "you really ought to sit behind Kitty. You *are* the servant."

"I always sit here!" Sophie said.

"Shh! You're mute!"

"What gives, ladies?"

Sophie had never been so glad to see Dr. Peter. He plopped his small-for-a-man self into his own beanbag, facing them, and wrinkled his nose so that his wire-rimmed glasses scooted up. Behind them his blue eyes got their twinkly look.

"Fiona wants us to do this thing," Sophie started to say.

But once again Fiona *shhhh*ed her, this time spraying her down the arm. It felt like Anne-Stuart was in the room.

"Okay, dish," Dr. Peter said. "I need details."

He folded his hands behind his crispy gelled curls, elbows sticking out, and leaned back while Fiona told him all about their roles in the movie, and how method acting was going to make them all fabulous. When she was finished, Dr. Peter gave a familiar "Ah," and Sophie let herself breathe. If she knew Dr. Peter, Fiona was about to get straightened out.

"I think I have just the story for this situation," he said. "Grab your Bibles, ladies."

Sophie wished that for once Dr. Peter would just tell Fiona she was getting carried away instead of making them figure it out. But she did like the way he always took them through the Jesus stories, just like they were actually in them.

At least I get to pick who I want to be, Sophie thought. She sneaked a glare at Fiona.

"The Gospel of Matthew, chapter 20," Dr. Peter said. "We're going to start at verse 25, but let me give you a little background first."

He told them that Jesus had just filled his disciples in on what was going to happen to him, that he was going to be crucified, but that he would rise to life again.

"And just like a bunch of guys," Dr. Peter said, "they started arguing about who were going to be Jesus' main men in his new kingdom."

"Kind of like Anne-Stuart and B.J. fighting over Julia!" Willoughby said. Then she yelped and added, "Only Julia isn't Jesus, of course."

"You've got the idea, Will," Dr. Peter said. "Anyway, here's what Jesus said to them. Imagine that you're one of Jesus' disciples."

Sophie closed her eyes and mentally put on sandals and robe and inched along to get closer to Jesus, scuffing up dust along the way. She never wanted to miss a word the Master said.

"Sophie," Darbie whispered, "you just pushed your bean-bag onto my foot."

"Sorry," Sophie said without opening her eyes.

"Shhh!" Fiona said.

Sophie/Disciple craned her neck toward Jesus and tried to concentrate. Sometimes that was hard when *other* disciples annoyed her like pieces of sand between her toes.

"This is Jesus talking to you," Dr. Peter said. He read, "'You know that the rulers of the Gentiles lord it over them, and their high officials exercise authority over them.'"

Sophie/Disciple nodded at Jesus. Just the other day she'd seen somebody get thrown in jail for owing only a couple of dollars—

"'Not so with you. Instead, whoever wants to become great among you must be your servant, and whoever wants to be first must be your slave.'"

Sophie let the disciple fade as she clung to one word. Had he just said *servant*? Whoever wants to become great must be a *servant*?

"'Just as the Son of Man did not come to be served, but to serve.'"

Sophie was waving her hand before Dr. Peter even got his Bible closed. "So being a servant is a great thing?" she said.

Fiona started to shower her with yet another shushing, but Dr. Peter shook his head at her.

"Serving is a most *excellent* thing," he said to Sophie. And then his eyes swept over the group. "Does everybody get what he's saying?"

No! Sophie thought as everyone else bobbed their heads up and down. *I do NOT get that other people have the right to turn me into a nothing! What's so excellent about that?*

She slapped the Bible closed. Dr. Peter raised his eyebrows above his glasses; Sophie pretended to dig for something in her backpack.

If I'm supposed to be a servant, she thought as she clawed through her books, *then I will be SUPER Servant. Every one of them is gonna be so majorly impressed.*

Just wait 'til they saw Johanna Van Raggs tomorrow. They wouldn't dare ignore Sophie then.

Seven

When Sophie gave Mama a good-night hug that night, she assured her that things were definitely looking better.

"So Dr. Peter did his thing, huh?" Mama said.

"In a major way," Sophie said.

"I thank God for him every day."

Sophie did that too. Snuggled into bed, she closed her eyes and imagined Jesus and told him he was amazing about twelve times.

Thank you for showing me that I have to play the best servant I possibly can, she said to him. *That's how Fiona and Vincent and everybody are gonna see who's great.*

Jesus' eyes suddenly didn't look so kind to her. They weren't angry. They just flashed a little in her mind.

Am I being conceited? she prayed. *I don't mean to be—but don't they have to see that they're being totally unfair to me? Now Mr. DiLoretto thinks I'm a slacker, and the movie is, like, so bad right now it's embarrassing.*

Besides all that, it wasn't fun being around Fiona anymore. Fiona was—what did the Bible say?—"lording it over her."

But not so with me, she assured Jesus, just before his eyes faded from view altogether.

Johanna Van Raggs shivered into the pile of straw she'd formed into a bed before the fire. With her wonderful master, David Teniers the Younger, being held captive somewhere, there was no one to protect her from Leona Artalini the Bossy. But she had to be the greatest servant she could be—even if she couldn't talk.

In fact, she just might be able to use that to her advantage.

When the Flakes all met at their lockers the next morning, Sophie smiled until her face hurt as she motioned for Kitty to allow her to open her stubborn lock for her. Then she insisted with sign language that Fiona let her carry her backpack to first period.

"You're acting weird, Sophie," Maggie said.

"No, she isn't," Fiona said. "She's practicing method acting."

"I still don't know how!" Kitty said tearfully.

"Just—draw something," Fiona said.

Sophie pulled her colored pencils out of her backpack and handed them to Kitty.

"Sophie's into it," Willoughby said to Kitty and Maggie as the three of them went off to their class.

Fiona snapped her fingers in the air. "Come along, Johanna. I'm going to need you to wipe off my desk before I sit in it."

"You're off your nut, Fiona," Darbie said.

But Sophie just smiled. If Darbie was getting annoyed with Fiona, then this was working already.

One of the most surprising things about being a mute servant, Sophie found out that day, was how much she heard that she usually didn't.

It was incredible to discover, for instance, that most people never stopped talking, even when they were doing their class assignments. She picked up everything from the details of the Pops' last sleepover—which she decided she would have been better off not knowing—to Mrs. Clayton and Miss Hess' whispered conversation about what a pain in the neck the new restroom log was.

She also learned that maintenance people muttered to themselves when they were picking up trash, and the ladies behind the counter in the lunch line had private nicknames for some of the students—like Bottomless Pit and Stick Girl. Miss Imes hummed a lot, and Mr. Bentley had squeaky shoes.

But it was during lunch that she made her most revealing discovery.

A lot of people from Mr. DiLoretto's class were putting in extra time on their projects in his room. Film Club had finally moved on from the "eureka" scene, and Vincent was explaining how he wanted Fiona to pry open the secret door into the villain artist's dungeon where Kitty/David was being held.

"Pretend this is a crowbar," he said. He handed her a ruler. "We'll get a real one when we film this weekend."

Fiona shook her head. "Leona wouldn't use a crowbar."

"Why?" Vincent said.

"Because it doesn't feel right for my character." She turned her face so Sophie could wipe her forehead.

"Who cares how it feels? How else is she supposed to get in?"

"She'd use something clever—"

Sophie tugged at Fiona's sleeve and handed her a letter opener from the prop box.

"Maybe a letter opener," Fiona said.

"You guys," Jimmy said, pulling off his villain's mask. "Could we just practice the scene the way it is so we can get through this?"

Fiona sniffed. "I'm just exercising my creative rights."

"You're just exercising your mouth," Vincent muttered.

Sophie saw that she was the only one who'd heard him. Everyone else was debating the crowbar versus the letter opener.

71

"Use *this*!" Vincent said, and he slapped the ruler onto the table. It snapped neatly in half.

"Beautiful," Fiona said. She looked at Sophie. "Johanna, fix this."

"Rude to her," Maggie said flatly.

Darbie grunted. "It's that methodical acting thing or whatever it is."

Willoughby dug some nail glue out of her backpack, and Sophie sat in a desk in the back of the room and went to work on the broken "crowbar."

"What smells?" Anne-Stuart said, wrinkling her nose.

"Oh," Cassie said, "it's Sophie."

"Ha-ha," a male voice said. It was Eddie, slumped behind da Vinci in the row next to Sophie, sounding anything but amused.

"Yeah, they really think they're funny."

That came from B.J., who was actually sitting by him. Sophie was so surprised, she let the ruler clatter to the desktop and break apart again. She left it there and started over with the glue, but she kept her ears perked up to Eddie and B.J. Something was, as Johanna Van Raggs herself would say, amiss.

"*You* think they're funny," Eddie said to B.J.

"I used to. Not anymore."

Eddie grunted. "Not since they dumped you."

"They didn't dump me — I dumped them."

That is such a lie! Sophie thought. She furrowed her forehead over the gluing project and listened harder.

"Whatever," Eddie said. "Then why do you spend more time over there than you do helping me figure out what we're gonna do for this project? We don't even have an idea yet."

"I was spying on them," B.J. said.

Eddie paused. Sophie wanted to look to see what kind of expression he had on his face, but she just had to imagine it. She decided on being cautiously suspicious.

"Why?" Eddie said finally.

"So I could find out what they're doing, and then we can do the same thing only do it three times better and make them look stupid."

"I don't wanna do that," Eddie said.

"Do you 'wanna' get an F?"

Eddie's silence said he didn't. Sophie clutched the desk with her hands so she wouldn't jump up and yell, "Don't do it, Eddie! She's lying!"

"It's not like we'd be cheating," B.J. said. "It would be our own work."

There was another deciding pause. Sophie held on harder to the desktop.

"If I show them down," Eddie said finally, "they'll hate me worse than ever. I already got them busted last semester."

"No," B.J. said, "they can't hate you any worse than they already do."

"Thanks," Eddie said. "That really makes me feel better."

You don't want people like that liking you, Sophie wanted to say to him. She almost wished Film Club had invited him to work with them.

"Sophie, I want to talk to you."

Sophie jerked her head up toward Mr. DiLoretto, who was standing over her.

"I'm working, honest," she said. "I'm fixing a prop."

His eyes went to B.J. and Eddie, who were suddenly quiet. If they hadn't noticed her sitting there before, they definitely did now.

"Let's step out into the hall," Mr. DiLoretto said to Sophie.

She nodded and slid sideways to get out of the desk. Her hands wouldn't go with her.

She could feel her eyes bulging as she tugged first one hand and then the other. Both of them were stuck hard to the desktop, and they weren't moving.

This couldn't be happening again.

Biting her lip against the pain, Sophie gave her hands another yank, but all she got was the taste of blood on her tongue.

"What seems to be the problem?" Mr. DiLoretto said. His voice was edging toward disaster, just like last time.

"I was putting the crowbar back together," Sophie said. She swallowed the throat-lump, which was now the size of a dumpling.

"Tell me you did *not* glue yourself to that desk."

"Not on purpose!"

One look at his twisted face, and Sophie knew he wasn't buying it. Neither was anybody else who gathered around.

"She's stuck?" Cassie said.

"Ooh, Freak Show," Colton said. He and Tod high-fived each other, while the Pops rolled their eyes in unison.

"She just gets weirder by the minute, doesn't she, Julia?" B.J. said. She threw her head back and laughed too loud.

Julia squinted her face at her.

"You want me to try pulling her loose?" Eddie asked.

"No!" said all the Flakes in unison.

"All right, quiet!"

The crowd muffled its laughter. Mr. DiLoretto looked as if he were trying to control a riot.

"Whose glue was this?" he said.

"Mine," Willoughby said in a tiny voice. "I use it for my fake nails."

"Do you have any remover?"

Sophie just knew the answer was going to be no.

"What about you, Julia?" Fiona said.

"Are you kidding?" Julia tossed her hair. "My nails are real."

"Could somebody just get me unstuck?" Sophie said. Her voice squeaked; the Loops laughed, but she didn't care. A panicky feeling filled her chest. It was like being trapped in an elevator.

The bell rang, and the kids currently gaping at Sophie went reluctantly to fifth period.

"I'll stay with you, Soph," Fiona said.

"I won't write you a pass," Mr. DiLoretto said. He glared at Fiona as if she had personally glued Sophie's hands down herself.

"Call me later," Fiona said as she walked backward out of the room. "I'm leaving this period to go to the dentist. I'm sorry—"

"I'll be okay," Sophie said to her. But she wasn't sure about that, especially when one of the muttering maintenance men arrived with a large bottle of something that smelled like a beauty salon—and a real crowbar.

Mr. DiLoretto's fifth-period class was already filing in when Sophie's hands finally came loose, without the help of the crowbar.

"You've got acetone on you," Mr. Maintenance muttered. "Better go wash it off."

"May I have a pass?" Sophie said to Mr. DiLoretto.

"You're kidding, right?" he said.

He did write her one, although he seemed to take a great deal of glee in entering it into his computer.

Even though she was already late to Mr. Stires' class, Sophie hurried to the restroom. Maybe if she was only a couple of minutes after the bell, he would take pity on her.

She burst into the restroom, headed for a sink, and found B.J. leaning over one, shoulders shaking.

At first, Sophie thought she was laughing.

Come on, Sophie wanted to say to her. *It wasn't that funny. Haven't you ever seen anybody glued to a desk before?*

But as Sophie stood at the next sink and reached for the faucet, she heard B.J.'s ragged breathing. She wasn't giggling. She was sobbing.

For a second or two, Sophie considered enjoying the moment. B.J. and the Pops had driven *her* to tears more than once.

But the words *It is not so with you* rippled through her thoughts.

Sophie stepped a little closer to B.J. "Are you okay?" she asked.

"Does it look like I'm okay?" B.J. said.

"No. I guess that was kind of a lame question."

B.J. looked quickly at Sophie through a panel of her butter-blonde bob.

"Are you sick?" Sophie said.

"Yes. I just threw up, so don't go in that first stall."

"You must have eaten the hot lunch."

"No! I'm just sick of being treated like a piece of trash! They're supposed to be my friends!"

"Oh," Sophie said. "What are they mad at you for?"

"I don't know! I didn't even do anything! And now they want me to *earn* my way back in — "

B.J. stumbled over a sob. When she caught her breath again, she pushed her hair out of her face and narrowed her eyes at Sophie — which didn't take much since they were already almost swollen shut.

"I bet you're loving this, aren't you?" she said.

"Uh, no," Sophie said.

B.J. smacked at the tears on her face and stood up taller, so that she was looking down at Sophie. "If you tell anybody what I just said, I'll call you a liar."

"Who would I tell?" Sophie said.

But as she picked up her backpack and half ran to Mr. Stires' class, she knew there was one person she *should* tell.

She forgot about that, though, when she got a tardy from Mr. Stires, who looked anything but cheerful as he put it on the computer. And then the minute she walked into sixth period, Mr. DiLoretto nodded for her to join him in the hall.

I haven't been humiliated enough? she thought as she followed him. Her palms were still red and throbbing, not to mention her pride. Tod and Colton couldn't even look at her without pounding on each other like a pair of baboons.

Sophie watched Mr. DiLoretto adjust his glasses and waited for him to give her detention—or worse, tell her she had to pay to have the desk refinished. He put his hands in his pockets and jingled the contents.

"Are you ever serious at all?" he said, doubt lurking in his eyes.

"I'm serious a lot," Sophie said. "I'm serious right now."

"Can you get serious enough to give somebody in this class some acting help?"

Sophie felt her mouth drop open.

"Several people have told me you're pretty good," he said. "Including Miss Imes, Mrs. Clayton—" He shook his head, ponytail sliding back and forth. "I sure haven't seen any evidence of it. But if you want a chance to make up for the things you've pulled, you can do some individual coaching."

In spite of how little Sophie wanted to make up for anything with this person, it did feel a little bit good to be asked. It would be like directing again. As long as she didn't have to work with some Corn Pop or Fruit Loop.

"Who's the person?" Sophie said.

"Tough case," he said. "I want you to see if you can get a spark of life out of Fiona Bunting."

Eight

Sophie told Mr. DiLoretto that of course she would help Fiona, starting the next day. But late that afternoon, when she was watching Zeke, the other answers she could have given flipped through her head like radio stations. She put Zeke to work coloring in his new Spider-Man coloring book and listened to them all in her head.

Fiona took the leading role that always belonged to Sophie, and now she was supposed to help Fiona play it right?

She's not gonna let me help her! She thinks she knows everything about acting because she read something on the Internet.

And what if Sophie did help her? Vincent would say he was the director, even though that had always been Sophie's job too.

Sophie hung off the chair by the fireplace with her head upside down. Maybe she'd missed something in what Dr. Peter said. Being the best servant on the planet wasn't working out quite the way she'd expected.

Johanna Van Raggs picked up the broom and attacked the hearth with it. Dust and ashes flew, but she didn't care. Let Leona Artalini clean it up. Johanna wasn't HER servant anyway.

Johanna swung the broom hard across the stones. The Master, Jesus, said whoever wants to become great among them must be a servant. If that was true, she must be the greatest by now. What else had he said?

Johanna frowned as she swept harder and tried to remember. It used to be so easy to think when Mister David had been there, quietly painting in the corner. She could almost imagine him there, creating the smallest of details with his brush . . .

She shook her head, scolding herself. There was no time to long for him now. I must find a way to get that evil Leona—whatever her name is—to give me back my rightful place, she thought. I was never treated this way before. I don't deserve it!

She gave the hearth a resounding smack with the broom and coughed until her eyes were streaming. "I'm trying so hard to be good!" she cried. "But I feel like a slave—to everybody!"

The cottage door slammed—

Sophie jumped and dropped the broom. It fell into a layer of ashes that stretched across the hearth and onto the rug.

"What happened in *here*?" Lacie said from the family room doorway.

That wasn't the worst of it. Daddy stood next to her, only he wasn't looking at the mess on the floor. His eyes were riveted to the wall, where the *real* worst of it was happening. Zeke was putting the finishing touches on a spiderweb he'd drawn up there with a red marker.

This, Sophie decided, would be an excellent time to be the servant. Heart pounding, she started for the kitchen. "I'll clean it up," she said.

"Stop!" Lacie and Daddy said in stereo.

Sophie froze.

"You'll track it all over the house," Daddy said. "Lace, go get some—"

"I'm on it," Lacie said.

"And take Z-Boy with you."

"Sophie said it was okay!" Zeke wailed as Lacie hoisted him over her shoulder.

"No, I didn't!" Sophie said. "Daddy, I *didn't*!"

"You didn't say he couldn't. That's a yes in his mind."

Sophie put her hands on the sides of her face. "I'm sorry. I was daydreaming. I guess you figured that out."

"Sounded more like a nightmare to me," Daddy said.

"Was I saying stuff out loud?"

Daddy nodded. Sophie wished she could disappear into the ashes at her feet.

"Am I in trouble?" she asked.

Daddy's big square face got soft at the corners. "Not the kind you mean."

"What kind?"

He wiped his hand across his mouth, like he was trying to get rid of a smile. "It's a little hard to have a serious conversation when you have soot all over your face. Let's get you cleaned up, and then you and Mama and I will talk."

"About my trouble," Sophie said.

"Yeah, Baby Girl. About your trouble."

Daddy scooped her up, carried her upstairs, and deposited her in the bathroom. She would have laughed at the sight of herself in the mirror, looking like the chimney sweep in *Mary Poppins*, if she hadn't felt so confused. One thing was for sure — she wasn't going to mention this to Vincent, or he'd want her to smear ashes all over herself for the film.

Ugh. The film.

"It's the first time I ever didn't want to do a movie," she told Mama and Daddy when she was soot-free enough to sit on the edge of Mama's bed. "And it's not because I want to be the

81

star." She bumped her legs against the mattress. "Well, that's not the only reason."

"Sounds to me like it's the way it's being handled that's got you all fired up," Daddy said. He put one hand up on the bedpost and ran the other one down the back of his head. "You know, Soph, you can't control the way other people behave." He grinned. "I mean, look at Zeke."

"That's the problem," Sophie said. "I *wasn't* looking at him."

Mama laughed her little soft laugh and rubbed Sophie's back with her toe. "It happens to the best of us. Remember the time I turned my back for two minutes, and he flushed one of his action figures down the toilet?"

"The thing is, though, Soph," Daddy said, "we're afraid you might drift off into Dreamland in school again, just when you're doing so well." He slid his arm down and sat halfway on the bed next to Mama. Sophie could look right into his eyes. "And it sounds like you're pretty ticked off at Fiona. I've never seen you—uh—vent like that before."

"Venting's healthy," Mama said. "But only if you do it with the right person."

Sophie nodded slowly. "You want me to talk to Dr. Peter, don't you?"

"Daddy and I *are* getting better at helping you sort things out," Mama said.

Daddy nodded. "But if you need something a little speedier, Dr. Peter might be your go-to guy right now."

Later, after Sophie vented again—this time to Jesus—she figured maybe they were right. She did need to talk to Dr. Peter, because even when she was imagining herself as Johanna Van Raggs, she hadn't been able to remember what else he'd told them that Jesus said. Maybe that missing piece was the reason the whole servant thing wasn't making her feel so great.

What it *was* making her was the punch line for every joke in the seventh grade. Sophie caught on to that first thing the next morning when she found glue on the handle of her locker. Fortunately she smelled it before she grabbed it.

"If I got stuck again," she told Darbie, "I'd have to change schools."

"Those eejits," Darbie said.

After that she was afraid to put her hands on anything, including the bottle she found on her desk first period that had "Glue Remover" printed on it in Sharpie. One whiff told her it wasn't glue *remover* but glue itself.

All during third-period PE, Colton and Tod pretended their hands were stuck to the basketballs, and in fourth period Miss Imes was absent so they had a sub, which was the perfect opportunity for an everybody-cough at 10:45. Only they didn't cough. The whole class put their hands on their desktops and yelled "Ouch!" at the same time. Except for Darbie and Fiona and the Wheaties, who all assured Sophie on the way to lunch that half the people didn't even know why they were doing it.

"It's not about you, Soph," Fiona said. "It's about them being just—repugnant."

"I don't know what that means," Darbie said, "but I like it."

"It's like repulsive," Fiona said.

Darbie made a sour face. "Then it's perfect for what I have to do now."

"What?" Sophie said.

"Go to Round Table and try to work with you-know-who."

"Excellent timing."

They all stopped in front of the cafeteria and looked at Mr. DiLoretto, who was coming out with a *Phantom of the Opera* lunch box. "If Darbie can't work on your project during lunch,"

83

he said, "this is a good time for you" — he waved the lunchbox toward Sophie — "to work with Fiona."

"On what?" Fiona said.

Sophie wanted to open Mr. DiLoretto's lunch pail and crawl in.

"You haven't told her?" he said to Sophie.

"I didn't know I was supposed to."

"Oh, this is going very well so far." He turned to Fiona. "You're having a hard time with your part. I put Sophie on it."

Sophie felt Fiona stiffen beside her. "You gave her my part?" she said.

Mr. DiLoretto shook his head. "There is nothing more overly sensitive than a middle school girl. No, I asked her to coach you. You need help."

"It wasn't my idea," Sophie told Fiona as they hurried away from him toward the courtyard.

Fiona shrugged, but Sophie could tell by the way her mouth was knotting up that she was tucking her real feelings safely away. When the hurt disappeared from her eyes, she said, "Vincent's the one who needs help, not me."

"He didn't ask me to help Vincent," Sophie said. "I'm *your* servant, remember?"

Fiona hit her forehead with the heel of her hand. The sound made Sophie's own forehead hurt.

"Why did you hit yourself?" she said.

"Boppa told me people in Italy do that all the time. It means they just figured something out. And since Leona's Italian — "

"What did you just figure out?" Sophie said with a sigh. She'd given up hoping Fiona would figure out what Sophie wanted her to figure out.

"I don't know why I didn't think of it sooner," Fiona said. "Mr. DiLoretto doesn't get method acting either. That's why he thinks I need help." She stopped in front of one of the concrete benches and dropped her backpack onto it. "Did you try to explain it to him?"

Sophie felt bristly between the shoulder blades. "No. The thing is, if he doesn't think you're playing the part that well, maybe the whole method thing *isn't* working."

"Huh," Fiona said. "It's working for you. Ever since I taught it to you, Johanna Van Raggs has gotten way better."

"Yeah, but it isn't working for *you*, because Leona Artalinguini *hasn't*."

Fiona looked so stunned, Sophie thought for a second she'd hit herself in the forehead again. Then she realized she had just smacked Fiona herself, with a sentence.

"In the first place, it's Artalini," Fiona said. "And in the second place — I'm that bad, huh?"

"You really want to know?" Sophie asked.

"Hel-*lo*! Yes! I don't want to make an idiot out of myself!"

"Okay." Sophie sat on the bench and pointed the toes of her shoes toward each other. "You're playing Leona all stuck-up, and I don't think she'd be that way."

"Then how's she supposed to be?" Fiona said. "I mean, when I open my mouth, that's what comes out."

"You're the one who made her Italian," Sophie said. "So act Italian — and not, like, bring a plate of spaghetti to rehearsal."

"Duh!"

"More like — thump." Sophie thumped her own forehead with her palm. "Eureka!"

Fiona copied her. Even though it was only a halfway try, it was the best thing Sophie had seen Leona do yet.

"Do it again," Sophie said, "only bigger." It was better this time. Sophie felt herself smiling a little. "What if you said everything with an Italian accent?" she said. "You know, like we do when we're making pizza crust with Boppa."

"Really?" Fiona said one of her lines, bouncing the words up and down mama-mia style. Sophie giggled.

"It sounds stupid," Fiona said.

"No, it doesn't! Do some more. Do that scene where you're telling me to get you a cup of tea, only act it out. What else did Boppa tell you about Italians?"

"They always talk with their hands."

"So do that."

By the time the bell rang, Fiona was standing up on the bench, doing her eureka scene like an opera singer. Sophie was holding her sides so they wouldn't split from laughing.

"Was I good?" Fiona said.

"You were fabulous," Sophie said. She handed Fiona her backpack and steered her in the direction of the lockers.

"Let's do it for everybody in Film Club sixth period," Fiona said. "I think—"

They both stopped as they rounded the corner. B.J. was standing in front of her open locker, blocking their path.

"Excuse us," Fiona said.

When B.J. didn't move, Fiona said, "Hel-*lo*," but Sophie put a hand on her arm to stop her. The way B.J. was staring at her bare locker, it was obvious she didn't even know they were there.

"Where's my stuff?" B.J. said. Her voice was so shrill, Sophie winced as if someone had run a fingernail down a chalkboard. "It's all gone—all my pictures—all my *stuff*!"

B.J. grabbed the sides of her head and pulled at her hair. More things came out of her mouth, but she was screaming so far up into the atmosphere, Sophie couldn't tell what she was saying.

"It looks like somebody tore down all her decorations," Fiona whispered to Sophie, though there was no need. Sophie could barely hear her own thoughts over B.J.'s hysteria. Two girls entered the locker row from the other end, did an about-face, and ran. B.J. sank to the floor, her skirt puddling around her, and wailed.

"What's going on?" Maggie said behind Sophie.

"Somebody ripped off all her Corn Pop stuff," Fiona told her.

"Why?" Maggie said.

Sophie was pretty sure she knew why, and who. And, clearly, B.J. did too. She rocked back and forth on the floor, hitting her head against the bottom locker.

"This is getting scary," Sophie said. "I think we need a grown-up."

"I'll go," Fiona said.

"What should I do?" Maggie said, backing away from B.J.

"Maybe you should tell all those people to stop staring," Sophie said. She nodded to the crowd of gapers forming at the end of the row.

"Yeah," Maggie said. "They're all gonna be late."

She marched toward them, and Sophie squatted beside B.J.

"You shouldn't bang your head," Sophie said. "You might get brain damage or something."

She knew it was probably completely the wrong thing to say, but she couldn't just let B.J. keep it up until she knocked herself out.

"Maybe it was some stupid boy," Sophie said. "Or maybe it was somebody that's jealous because you're a—Julia's friend."

"NOOOOO!" B.J. cried. "She hates me! They all hate me! I don't know what to do without them. I'm nobody now."

"You're not nobody," Sophie said. "I mean—you're somebody."

"You don't understand—you've never been popular. My life is over!"

Sophie wasn't sure *what* she was supposed to say to that, but at least B.J. had stopped slamming herself into somebody's locker door.

"Maybe the way it used to be is over," Sophie said. "But—"

"I don't want it to *be* any other way! I have to have my Julia—and my Annie-Stew—"

"You call her 'Annie-Stew'?" Sophie said.

B.J. nodded. Some strands of her hair caught on the tears on her cheeks and plastered themselves to her face. "We all have cute nicknames." Her face crumpled. "Had."

"You'll find another Annie-Stew."

"I can't. There isn't one. I just want to die!"

"Whoa, whoa—there's no dying in the locker hall."

Sophie had never been so glad to hear the high-pitched-for-a-man voice of Coach Nanini. He squatted beside the two of them and tilted his shaved head at Sophie. "What's up, Little Bit?"

"B.J.'s friends broke up with her," Sophie said. "She's kind of upset."

"I have to get out of here!" B.J. said. "I can't stay here!"

She scrambled up and tore for the hallway. Two steps later she was sprawled out, and she stayed there, pounding the floor with her fists.

"Okay, Beej," Coach Nanini said. His words were soft. "Take it easy now..."

Sophie watched him talk down her sobs and her shouts and her flailing around. The B.J. he helped off the floor was limp and shaky, hunched over at the shoulders. Sophie had to look twice to make sure it was still her. As Coach led her away, Sophie swallowed down the lump in her throat.

Who knew I could feel so bad for a Corn Pop? Sophie thought. And then she grunted. *So bad that I forgot to ask Coach Virile for a pass.*

This was going to mean another tardy from Mr. Stires. But right then, it didn't seem like the worst thing that could happen to somebody.

Nine

The Corn Flakes didn't have a chance to talk again until sixth period. By then, Darbie was fuming and shoving her hair behind her ears.

"I wasted a whole lunch period waiting for B.J., and she never showed up."

Fiona rolled her eyes. "That's because she was having a major meltdown at the lockers."

Sophie looked over at the Corn Pops. The way everybody else in the entire class was whispering, surely the Pops had heard about B.J. by now. But they were acting like one of their former best friends hadn't thrown herself on the floor an hour ago because they had rejected her. Julia was drawing a heart on the back of Tod's hand with a red Sharpie, and Anne-Stuart and Cassie were looking on as if Julia were Leonardo da Vinci himself, giving them an art lesson.

Who needs friends like that, B.J.? Sophie thought.

"So-oph, hel-*lo-o*."

Sophie looked quickly at Fiona, who said, "Let's do that scene for them."

Sophie shook B.J. out of her head and made room for Johanna Van Raggs. The rest of Film Club watched as she and

Fiona acted out the eureka scene just as they'd done it in the courtyard, only better, of course, since they had an audience.

When they were finished, Willoughby did her poodle thing, Kitty clapped, and Maggie said to Darbie, "I wish you would've been filming that."

"That rocked," Jimmy said.

Nathan nodded without even turning red.

Fiona lowered her chin at Vincent. "Well?" she said.

Vincent leaned his chair onto its back legs and rubbed his chin.

Fiona slitted her eyes at him. "You irritating little man."

"Say it for me, Willoughby," Vincent said.

Willoughby squealed, "That was *fabulous!*"

Vincent parked his pencil behind his ear. "So what made you get so much better, like, overnight? Was it what I said yesterday?"

"No," Fiona said. She gave him a smug little smile.

Sophie stood up straighter and got ready to be modest. She would, of course, compliment Fiona back on taking direction so well—

"I just got the idea to do it ultra-Italian," Fiona said. "I was playing her way too conceited, you know?"

Jimmy snapped his fingers. "That's what it was. I kept thinking there was something wrong."

"I figured it out." Fiona popped her palm against her forehead, and everybody laughed.

Everybody except Sophie. All she could do was stare at Fiona.

You *got the idea?* You *decided to play her Italian?* Sophie was ready to stomp her foot through the floor. *You didn't figure it out, Fiona. I did!*

"Okay, we're on a roll," Vincent said. "Try another scene."

Darbie picked up the camera. "I'm going to film it this time. I want you to see how class you are, Fiona."

Sophie had to sit on both hands so she wouldn't reach up and snatch the camera and bonk Fiona over the head with it.

I can't believe I'm thinking that! she told herself.

But she couldn't believe Fiona was taking all the credit for her performance either. It made Sophie's neck prickle and her sight narrow down to pinpoints. Her mind darted around for a way to get back what was rightfully hers. She landed on one the minute Vincent said, "Action!"

"Maid! A cup of tea!" Fiona/Leona said.

"Cut!" Vincent said.

"What?"

"Do it with the Italian accent."

"Oh," Fiona said. "I forgot."

"Take 2."

Fiona said her line again, this time sounding like she was calling out an order at a pizza place. Sophie leaped up, curtsied several times, and bounded for the exit they'd made out of two desks. Just before she got there, she made the perfect pratfall. She heard kids all over the room laughing like they knew a good piece of slapstick when they saw it.

"Cut!" Vincent cried.

"Would you quit cutting?" Darbie said. "Just go on, would you?"

Fiona continued her lines, and Sophie waited for her entrance. Should she come in with the teacup balanced on her head, or the teaspoon tucked behind her ear the way Vincent carried his pencil?

Whatever I do, she thought, *it has to be better than what Fiona's doing.*

She decided to do both the spoon behind the ear *and* the teacup on the head, and was rewarded with appreciative guffaws from the growing number of other kids who were watching. That made it easier to come up with more things, like making faces at Fiona/Leona behind her back and imitating her every move.

When the scene was over, there was a round of applause from the rest of the class. Fiona bowed.

She thinks they're clapping for her, Sophie thought. Didn't anybody else see that she was taking all the credit for herself when she didn't even know what she was doing?

It didn't seem like it. Vincent wasn't even paying attention. He was arguing with Darbie about who was supposed to shoot from what angle. Nathan and Jimmy were laughing with the rest of the class. Maggie was bent over scowling at her script. They didn't get it.

Sophie folded her arms. Dr. Peter hadn't gotten it either. Maybe if she could make *him* see, he could help her with everybody else.

"I need to take the camera home tonight," she told Darbie.

"You can watch yourself then," Darbie said. She gave a little grunt.

"What?" Sophie said.

"Nothing," she said, although there was obviously *something*, the way she was shoving her hair. She stuck the camera in its bag and handed it to Sophie. "Wasn't Fiona just grand today?"

Thanks to me! Sophie wanted to say.

But it was okay. She could say it to Dr. Peter that very afternoon and show him the evidence.

"Sophie-Lophie-Loodle!" he said to her when she arrived at his office.

She felt her smile almost reaching her earlobes. It hadn't done that in days. When she hopped up onto the window seat where she and Dr. Peter always sat, she chose the pillow with the biggest lopsided grin and held it against herself.

"The Happy Pillow is an interesting choice, Loodle," Dr. Peter said.

"I'm just so glad to be here," Sophie said. "*You* understand, and right now it feels like everybody else on the whole planet doesn't."

He twinkled his eyes at her and inched his glasses up with a wrinkle of his nose. "I can't do anything about everybody else on the whole planet, but I can listen to *you*."

"Fabulous," Sophie said, "because I have a lot to say."

She poured out absolutely everything, from the day at the museum when Film Club had planned the whole project without her to that very afternoon when Fiona had let everybody think she had created the new Leona all by herself.

"And you know what?" Sophie said.

"No," Dr. Peter said, "but I bet I'm about to find out."

His eyes were very still, as if he'd turned off their twinkle. Sophie considered not telling him this next thing about Fiona. He was already looking disappointed enough.

"You don't think bad of Fiona because I'm telling you all this, do you?" Sophie said.

"I'm just interested in what *you* think. It's good that you're concerned for Fiona, but remember—"

"Whatever we say in here stays in here," Sophie said with him. She took a big breath. "Okay, so here's the rest of it. When we did another scene, not the one I helped her with, she went back to being terrible as Leona. I can even show you."

"I'm all over it," Dr. Peter said.

He plugged her camera into the TV on the shelf with the collection of frogs that had feeling words on them, and Sophie curled into the corner of the window seat. It was so good to be back here. It was going to be okay. It always was with Dr. Peter.

"Ready?" Dr. Peter said.

"Action!" Sophie said.

The screen flickered to life with a close-up of Fiona demanding a cup of tea in a stiff voice. The camera stayed on her with Vincent in the background yelling, "Cut!"

"I love the creative process," Dr. Peter said.

Fiona was back, calling for her tea, when suddenly something bounded across the screen, blocking Fiona and everything else with a bug-eyed face.

"That's me!" Sophie said.

"You're a little hard to miss, Loodle," Dr. Peter said.

That was definitely the truth. Through the whole scene, every time the camera settled on Fiona, laughter erupted in the background, and the camera panned dizzily to Sophie.

At least Sophie *thought* it was herself. She remembered being in the scene, but this obnoxious person couldn't be *her*. In fact, she reminded Sophie of somebody else—she just couldn't quite remember who.

Not until Fiona/Leona began to search the "room," looking for clues and chattering away like she had a mouth full of pasta. Sophie was right there, in front of her whenever possible, rolling her eyes and mocking Fiona's walk. Sophie played to the audience so that their laughter drowned out everything Fiona's character was saying.

Then she realized who that girl grabbing all the attention reminded her of. Sophie was acting just like B.J., showing off for the Corn Pops. Trying to get back what used to be hers.

"Dr. Peter?" Sophie said. "Could you turn that off?"

Dr. Peter punched the Off button like he'd been waiting for her to say the word. The obnoxious girl on the screen blipped away.

"You didn't like what you saw?" Dr. Peter asked.

"I was heinous," Sophie said. She shoved the Happy Pillow aside. "Do you have a pillow that looks like it can't stand itself?"

Dr. Peter joined her on the seat and wrinkled his glasses up his nose again. "No. You don't really want to hold on to that feeling, do you?"

"I'd rather hold a porcupine—but it's the truth!"

"Then let's get to work."

Sophie sagged against the pile of puffy ears and noses and lips. "You want to know why I was trying to steal the attention away from Fiona."

"Right."

"And you want to know because that's not who I really am."

"Uh-huh."

"Only it must be kind of who I am because I'm acting that way."

Dr. Peter nodded. "Go ahead. You're on a roll."

"Downhill!" Sophie said.

"That's okay. It's a direction."

Sophie resituated on the seat, although she couldn't find a comfortable position. "It's not because I have to be the star all the time."

"Okay."

"That's part of it—which is repulsive—but it's not because I think I know everything about acting and directing. I mean, it's repugnant enough that I think I know more than Vincent does. Only I can't help it because it's like *in* me—and they just keep taking it, and they can't do that because it's not fair! That's why I was acting like a Corn-Poppy obnoxious little brat-child!"

She had to stop to take a breath.

"Anything else?" Dr. Peter asked.

Sophie gave her head a miserable shake. "No. Is that enough?"

"Oh, I think it'll get us started."

At least his eyes were twinkling again. Sophie knew hers weren't.

He rubbed his hands together like he always did when they were about to dig into Sophie's troubles. She wished she felt as eager about it as he looked. "Okay," he said, "first of all, we need to work on the name-calling."

"Did I call somebody a name?" Sophie said.

"Yeah—one of my favorite people." He leaned forward. "You."

"Me?"

"You said you were heinous. Repulsive. Obnoxious. What was the other one?"

"Repugnant."

"That's it. You have to be careful what labels you put on yourself, Loodle, because you'll start to believe them. And basically we act out what we believe."

"I believe I'm all tangled up!"

Dr. Peter wiggled his eyebrows. "Then you've come to the right place. Shall we get out the de-tangler?"

He reached for the Bible he always kept on the shelf under the seat.

"Uh-oh," Sophie said.

"What, uh-oh?"

"That's how I got all knotted up in the first place."

"You mean the story we read in Bible study?"

She nodded as she watched him flip to Matthew 20, her stomach turning with the pages. "Jesus said if you wanted to be great you should be a servant, and I tried to be, like, this amazing Johanna Van Raggs, and it just made me a moron."

Dr. Peter blinked. "Jesus wasn't talking about a movie, Loodle."

"I know," Sophie said. "But I thought that's why you wanted me to hear it—to tell me to show Fiona and everybody that they were making a mistake. I thought I was supposed to be Super Servant in our film."

She could tell by the way he blinked at her again that that wasn't it at all. She smacked her forehead with her palm.

"Before you start bullying yourself," Dr. Peter said, "let's look at it. I think you missed something."

"I know!" Sophie said. "I keep thinking that."

Dr. Peter grinned. "Then let's go in."

He read the passage again. Sophie remembered it all, until he got to the last line.

"'Whoever wants to be first must be your slave—just as the Son of Man did not come to be served, but to serve.'"

Dr. Peter peeked over the top of the Bible at her. "How are we doing?"

"That last part, about just like Jesus didn't come to be served—"

"Yeah?"

"That's the part I missed."

"Aha! We're making progress."

Sophie suddenly felt all the stuffed noses and lips on the pillows poking into her back. "I don't think I'm serving the way Jesus did. But I still don't get it. I always thought I *was* helping people when I directed our movies."

"You were," Dr. Peter said. "A couple of them really got me thinking. But Loodle, there are a lot of different ways to serve. Seems like you're learning some of the other ones right now."

"What are they?" Sophie said.

"This could be hard to hear," Dr. Peter said.

"I'm ready," Sophie said.

Right now she didn't care if she had to spoon-feed Fiona her lunch, if it would get the knots out of her own stomach.

Ten

Dr. Peter did the hand-rubbing thing again. "The good news is, Jesus didn't give us tough things to do and then just expect us to figure out how to do them on our own. Remember? He's right here with us."

Sophie squirmed.

"I know that wiggle," Dr. Peter said. "What?"

"Jesus' eyes haven't been so kind lately," she said. "I thought he was disappointed in Fiona and the others, just like I was."

"Not to worry," Dr. Peter said. "He understands when we don't get it."

Sophie grabbed the cushion with the big furry eyebrows that pinched together. Anxious Pillow seemed like the only choice right now.

"Number one," Dr. Peter said. "Jesus didn't worry about being great. He just did whatever job God gave him. Sometimes it was healing somebody from some horrible disease, and everybody went, '*Wow*.' Other times it was washing people's nasty feet, and everybody went, '*Yuck*.' Most of the time when he did something great, he told people to keep quiet about it." He tilted his head at Sophie. "How you doing so far?"

"I feel like a—"

"Careful now."

"I feel like I've been doing it all wrong."

"Then you need number two. Jesus was the perfect Servant, which we can't be. But he forgives us when we aren't, and that's called grace, right?"

Sophie nodded.

"So you can stop beating yourself up and keep on growing."

"I wish I was already grown."

"And miss all this fun? Are you kidding?" Dr. Peter grinned. "Wait 'til you hear number three. Have you ever played 'Mother, May I?'"

Sophie groaned.

"I take it you didn't like it that much?"

"It wasn't fair. Even if I said, 'Mother, may I?' every time, Lacie—she was always Mother—could tell me to take two giant steps backward or something."

"So there was nothing you could do except what you were told."

Sophie felt her eyes bulging. "Are you gonna say God's, like, playing 'Mother, May I?' with me?"

"No, thank goodness. But it can feel like it when Jesus says things like, 'For he who is least among you all, he is the greatest.' What's that about?"

"I don't know."

"That's where number three comes in. What does it mean to 'be great'?"

Sophie pulled a panel of her hair under her nose, and Dr. Peter waited.

"Being the best at something?" she said. "Being the first one to do it?"

"Like being at the head of the line when you're in first grade."

Sophie rolled her eyes. "Zeke thinks he's all that when he gets to lead the line."

"Does he get to lead it every day?"

The eyes rolled again. "Uh—no. We hear about it when he doesn't. He's all, 'It's not fair!'"

"Did somebody promise him fair?"

"Nobody ever promised *me* that!" Sophie said.

"Picture where you are in line right now in your Film Club."

"I'm totally at the back." Sophie closed her eyes and saw Vincent at the head of their imaginary line, with Fiona right behind him, and Darbie following with a camera.

"What's happening now?" Dr. Peter said.

"Mr. DiLoretto's taking Kitty to the head of the line because he thinks she's an amazing artist—I mean, she is."

"So he's bringing her from the back of the line—where she was when she was having chemotherapy."

The lump in Sophie's throat expanded to its all-time biggest.

"I know that look, Loodle. Don't go guilty on me."

Sophie opened her eyes. Dr. Peter's were saying, *I'm not kidding.* "It wasn't fair that Kitty got leukemia in the first place. It isn't fair that your sweet mama has to stay in bed until the baby's born. And it really wasn't fair that your friends shoved you to the back of the line the *way* they did."

"Then I have a right to be mad at them?"

"By the world's rules, you do." Dr. Peter lowered his head to look at her over the tops of his glasses. "But whose rules are we trying to play by?"

"God's," Sophie said.

"Bingo. And part of playing by his rules is that we have to go against what the world expects us to do sometimes."

"So I shouldn't be mad at Fiona?"

"You *are* mad at Fiona. She's taken unfair advantage of you, and she doesn't even seem to know it. God understands why you're angry, but he wants you to take this chance to practice the servant life."

Sophie dug her fingers into the pillow's cheek. "And just let her take all the credit and mess up the movie?"

"Why not?"

This time Sophie's eyes nearly bulged from her head. "Are you serious?"

Dr. Peter shrugged. "What else can you do? You can't take her place in line and knock her to the back. You already tried that."

Sophie's face felt hot. He hadn't been kidding—this *was* hard to hear.

"I know," he said. "Not fair. But in God's world, it's not about fair. It's about grace. He serves us by giving us forgiving grace, and we have to do the same for each other."

"Forgive her? That's it?" Sophie couldn't swallow the lump. "But won't she keep shoving me to the back of the line if I let her?"

"Ah!" Dr. Peter's eyes lit up like birthday candle flames. "That's just it. Who says you're really at the back of the line? You aren't the star this time, or the director, but didn't you help Fiona be a better star? Didn't you show Vincent something about directing without him even knowing it?"

Sophie squinted her eyes behind her glasses, so maybe she could see it clearer. "So, like, I helped them get ahead in the line?"

"You did. You're still using some of your best gifts, Loodle. The ones nobody sees. That might not put you ahead in the world's line—"

"But it pushes me up in God's line?"

Dr. Peter leaned forward, so his eyes looked right into hers. "Number four is the best part, Sophie. With God, there *is* no line. You're right where he wants you to be, even if you can't figure out why."

It was so much to think about, Sophie could hardly concentrate on her homework that night. When Lacie brought her the phone, she realized she'd been staring at a page of math problems for ten minutes without even writing any of them down.

"It's some guy," she whispered.

She gave Sophie a sly look as she left the room, which made Sophie want to roll her eyes right out onto the floor. It was worse when she heard Vincent's voice on the other end.

"We need to talk," he said.

Only Dr. Peter's words in her head kept Sophie from grunting at him.

"What about?" she said instead.

"I want you to start studying Fiona's part."

"I already know Fiona's part," Sophie said, trying not to grit her teeth too hard.

"Excellent," Vincent said, "because I think you might have to take over for her."

Sophie clenched the phone. "Why? Is she sick?"

"You haven't noticed how—uh—challenged she is?" Vincent's voice chipped off into some high place on the *challenged*. "The only scene she's ever done halfway good as Leona was the one today that you guys had already practiced."

Sophie chomped down on her lip. It would be so easy to slide straight to the head of the line right now.

"We have to film this weekend, starting Friday after school," Vincent went on, "and Fiona's not even close. Just be ready to do her part, okay?"

Sophie did grunt this time. Two answers shoved each other back and forth in her head. She couldn't say either one.

"Jesus?" she whispered later when she'd turned out her light. "I'm gonna try to do what Dr. Peter said, but this is way hard. I hope you have a double scoop of grace waiting for me."

Sophie woke up the next morning feeling like a rubber doll whose arms were being pulled in two different directions.

There is no line in God's world, she kept reminding herself.

But if that were the case, she wondered as she climbed off the bus in front of the school, how come it was so hard to *be* in God's world right now?

Johanna Van Raggs hurried up the steps in search of Leona Artalini. As much as she detested it, she had to fetch the imperious art expert's chamber pot and help her dress. Another day of grueling service. It was her God-given job, and she must do it well — even though she was certain she could have found her master herself by now, as smart as she was. Should she break her vow of silence and speak up — or stand by and let Leona Artalini make a bags of the whole thing? Yanking up her wool stockings and cinching tight the strings on her overdress, she hurried on. She wasn't sure, but perhaps it would come to her when she saw her.

But the chamber pot was empty, and Leona was not at her closet as usual. There was someone else in the room, grumbling into a wardrobe. "Excuse me, Madam," Johanna said, "but may I be of some assistance?"

"No!" said the young woman, and she slammed the wardrobe door and stomped away.

Sophie blinked and watched Darbie disappear around the corner, shoulders hunched up like she was beyond annoyed.

For a few seconds, Sophie thought she should go after her. After all, Corn Flakes talked about their problems to each other.

The lump swelled in Sophie's throat again, and this time she knew what it was.

It's a big ol' wad of guilt, she told herself. *Because I haven't talked about my problem to Fiona or any of the other Flakes.*

Jesus didn't tell them to do hard things without being there for them, Dr. Peter had said.

I hope you're right next to me, Sophie prayed, *because it doesn't get any harder than this.*

She was already composing the note in her head that she would write to Fiona when she got to class, but Fiona was absent first and second periods. She wasn't there when the girls were dressing for PE either, and none of the other Flakes knew where she was. Sophie threw on her track pants and T-shirt and double-timed it to the gym to find Vincent. He was watching Jimmy shoot layups.

"I have to ask you something," Sophie said.

"Wait a sec. I'm calculating Jimmy's average."

Sophie grabbed him by his sweatshirt sleeve and dragged him off the court. Hands on hips, she said, "Did you already tell Fiona you were replacing her with me?"

"I haven't even seen Fiona," Vincent said. "But I'm gonna tell her when I do. I mean, that is, if you can do her part. We could do one big rehearsal in class today and then just shoot Friday afternoon and all weekend." His voice cracked up into the stratosphere. "You can do it—you're, like, the best actress in our whole group. I wish I'd picked you for the part in the first place."

Suddenly the balls that bounced around them seemed to be bouncing inside Sophie's head. How long had she waited for Vincent to get a clue and figure this out? She'd imagined herself nodding somberly and assuring Vincent she only wanted what was best for the project.

Instead, she grabbed a hunk of hair and gnawed at the ends. Somehow this didn't feel at all like she'd imagined it.

Coach Virile gave his whistle a blast, and everybody scurried to their lines for roll check. Sophie saw Fiona skitter into her place, and she grabbed Vincent's shirt again.

"Don't say anything to Fiona yet, okay?" she said.

"I have to tell her. I'm the director." Sophie followed his gaze in Fiona's direction. She looked like she was practicing her Leona stance in line. "On second thought," Vincent said, "you tell her. She'll take it better coming from you."

"Thanks," Sophie said. She wanted to curl her lip at him, Corn Pop-style. But at least this gave her a little bit more time to decide what to do.

Coach Yates, the girls' coach, came down the row and counted everyone off. After she moved past, Sophie whispered to Fiona, "Where have you been?"

"I had to go back to the dentist," she whispered back. "But Boppa helped me with my Italian accent on the way there and back, so it was cool."

Sophie was for once glad that Fiona was a three and she was a four, so they were in different groups for the passing drills. It was almost worth it to be in a group with Julia, Tod, B.J., and Eddie, just so she didn't have to talk to Fiona yet.

Eddie passed the ball to Sophie first, soft enough so she could actually catch it. She did the required three dribbles and handed it off to Tod. She expected him to make some you're-so-lame face, but he turned his focus at once on B.J. and thrust it at her. It landed squarely in the middle of her face and bounced back.

B.J. plastered both hands over her nose, but blood was already gushing out.

"Dude!" Eddie said. "You didn't have to throw it so hard."

"I can't help it if she can't catch," Tod said.

Julia casually tightened her ponytail. "He didn't even throw it that hard. B.J. cries if she breaks a nail."

To Sophie it sounded like B.J. had broken her whole face. She was crying so hard, blood was spattering through her fingers.

"I'll take you to Coach Yates," Sophie said to her.

But Coach Yates was already there, yelling, "Nothing to see here. Everybody get back to practice."

"You did that on purpose," Eddie said to Tod when B.J.'s wails had faded into the locker room.

"You can't prove it," Tod said as if making somebody bleed was all in a day's work.

"So if it was an accident," Eddie said, "how come you didn't say you were sorry?"

Tod smiled with only half his mouth and tossed the ball to Julia. "Because I'm not," he said.

Eddie shook his head at him, and without a word he turned on a squeaky heel and headed toward Coach Nanini.

Julia dug her gaze into the back of Eddie's head as he went. "He's so gonna go tell Coach you said that."

"He'll be sorry then, won't he?"

Julia flashed a smile at him, and Sophie wondered if she was using those whitening-strip things on her teeth. She also wondered if they'd forgotten she was there. Just in case they hadn't, she picked up the ball and pretended to practice her dribbling. She could still hear them talking. She decided it must be all that practice being mute.

"He's not the one I want sorry," Julia said.

"So — why can't it be a two-for-one deal?"

"Whatever," Julia said.

"Hey, where's the ball?" Tod said.

It was all Sophie could do not to pass it right at his nose.

Eleven

When Coach tooted his whistle for the end of class, Sophie rushed toward the locker room ahead of the other Flakes. She still wasn't ready to talk to Fiona, and that whole bloody-nose thing had distracted her from making a decision. But before she could even get out of the gym, Coach Virile called out, "Hey, Little Bit. I need to talk to you."

Okay, so maybe Fiona would already be gone when she got there. She met Coach Virile on the bottom seat of the bleachers. His eyebrows were hooding his eyes, which didn't look happy.

"How's your friend Darbie?" he said.

Sophie felt a little pang of guilt. "Um—she seemed kinda funky this morning, but I haven't found out what's wrong."

He nodded his shiny bald head, as if he'd expected that very answer.

"Do you think she likes being on the Round Table?" he asked.

Ew. How was she supposed to answer that?

"I'll take that as a no," Coach said. "I'm not trying to put you on the spot, Little Bit. I just want her to have as good an experience as you did on the council."

Sophie didn't even try to swallow the guilt wad in her throat. She'd never thought about whether Darbie was having a good experience. It had been too hard to think about Round Table at all.

"I think she's struggling with a project we gave her," Coach Virile went on, "and I wonder if you could help her with it. I know your friends all look up to you—as well they should." He grinned down at her. "You're very wise for such a Little Bit."

Only Dr. Peter's warning kept her from saying, *No, I'm the most selfish person in life!*

The locker room felt empty when Sophie got there. The only voices she heard before she could get to her row belonged to the Corn Pops. She stopped and let the words filter out to her.

"Are you serious?" B.J. was saying. Her voice was shrill.

"Totally," Julia said. "Aren't I?"

"Absolutely," Anne-Stuart said, with Cassie chiming in.

Sophie didn't even have to know what they were supposed to be serious about to tell they were lying their heads off.

"Tod only threw the ball so hard because Eddie made him," Julia said. "Everybody thinks Eddie's all changed and he's all like Mr. Sunday School now, but that's so fake." Her voice dropped so that Sophie had to inch forward to hear the rest. "He has something on Tod, only Tod won't tell me what it is—but it's so bad that Tod will do just about anything Eddie tells him."

"Including hit you in the face," Anne-Stuart said. Even from where she was, Sophie could hear her sniff. "Are you okay, B.J.?"

"I am now," B.J. said. "Now that y'all are my friends again."

Your friends? Sophie wanted to scream. *Are you* kidding *me*?

"I love that," Julia said. "And you know what? You're the only one who can save Tod for me."

"Whatever it takes," B.J. said.

"Go to the gate during lunch. We'll tell Eddie to meet you there. Tod will take care of the rest."

"We'll tell Eddie you want to work on your project for art class," Anne-Stuart said.

"Why would I want to meet him out there for that?" B.J. said.

"We'll *handle* it." Julia's voice went tight.

"I don't have to go *outside* the gate, though, right?" B.J. said. She sounded like an egg about to crack. "I got in trouble that time I went to the store to get you candy."

"No," Julia said. "You won't be the one going outside. Just leave it to Tod."

"Oh, I get it," B.J. said.

So did Sophie. She also got that she had about two minutes to change clothes and get to fourth period. As soon as the Corn Pops clattered out, she scrambled.

The same math problems she hadn't been able to focus on the night before still stared her in the face during Miss Imes' class. All she could think about was whether to warn B.J., who might not listen, or alert Darbie, who might not listen either, come to think of it. There was no way to write Darbie a note, not under Miss Imes' pointy see-all gaze. And before Sophie could get to her when the bell rang, Darbie bolted from the room.

"We're having our Film Club meeting in here today," Miss Imes said as Sophie wove among the desks to go after her. "Mr. Stires and I want to get caught up on how this movie is coming together for Mr. DiLoretto's class."

Even as she spoke, Vincent stopped in the doorway, turned to look at Sophie, and said, "Perfect."

"Why perfect?" Fiona said.

"Come on," Sophie said, hauling Fiona toward the door by the arm. "Let's go get our lunches. We'll be right back."

With any luck, Sophie thought, they'd be abducted by aliens before they could return to Vincent and his grand scheme for fixing the movie and probably ruining everything else.

111

"We have to rehearse the last two scenes," Fiona said as she trotted after Sophie toward their lockers. "We don't have time to sit around yacking our jaws—and besides—I want to show everybody what Boppa taught me."

Sophie stopped short at the end of the locker row, and Fiona plowed into her from behind. Darbie was leaning against her locker, swiping at the tears that had the nerve to slide down her face.

"You're crying?" Fiona said. "You hardly ever cry."

Sophie gulped down her guilt and hurried to Darbie's side. "It's about Round Table, isn't it?"

"Yes!" Darbie cried. "I'm making a bags of the whole thing. I'll never be as good at it as you were, Sophie. I'm rotten compared to you!"

"What's going on?" Maggie said. She marched up to them and studied Darbie's face. "Did some Corn Pop do something?"

"Yes!" Darbie said. "I don't know! It's B.J.—who can keep up with whether she's in or out from hour to hour?"

"Darbie—" Sophie said.

"She blew me off the other day, so I scheduled a meeting for right now—and she isn't showing up again."

"Darbie, I know—" Sophie said.

"And now I won't have my Action Plan for tomorrow, and Coach Nanini and Mrs. Clayton will think I'm an eejit, especially since Sophie was so perfect when she was on it."

"Darbie, I can help—" Sophie said.

"You think you're just the best at everything, Sophie, and sometimes it gets a little sickening!"

Somewhere in the circle of Flakes that had formed around Darbie, there was a frightened poodle-yelp and a nervous giggle. A familiar voice thudded, "I don't think we're supposed to say stuff like that to each other."

"I know I've been acting all jealous and silly," Sophie said. She planted her hands on the sides of Darbie's face. "But you have to listen to me. I know where B.J. is, and she's about to get into big trouble."

Darbie's face went so white that her freckles seemed to stick out from her face. "Where? Should I go there? I don't know what to do, Sophie!"

"If you'd hush for a minute, she'll probably tell you," Maggie said.

"She's at the gate," Sophie said. "She's setting Eddie up for Tod to push him off the school grounds so he'll get in trouble—"

"Why?" Fiona said.

"Because Julia told her to, and B.J. thinks she's back in the Corn Pops."

Willoughby shook her head, curls flying. "I know them—they're just tricking her—"

"Go, Darbie," Sophie said. "Get to her and help her. That's what Round Table does."

Darbie nodded, but she didn't move. "Come with me, Sophie. I don't know what to say to her."

"We'll tell Miss Imes you had an emergency," Fiona said to Sophie.

Sophie didn't realize until she and Darbie were almost to the gate that the lump in her throat was gone. But once they got closer, B.J. looked like she had a supersized one in hers. She was leaning against the fence that separated the school's back field from the parking lot at the Mini-Mart. Although B.J. was bundled up from toboggan hat to suede boots, Sophie could see her shivering, and she was pretty sure it wasn't from the cold. Sophie linked her arm through Darbie's, since neither of them had stopped to put on a coat, and headed toward her.

"You do the talking, Sophie," Darbie whispered. "I don't know what to say to her."

But there was no chance for anybody to say anything. As Darbie and Sophie approached from the school side of the fence, somebody wearing a down jacket the size of a comforter and a black ski mask emerged from the bushes on the other side and crept toward B.J. from behind.

Sophie broke into a run, still dragging Darbie with her. Darbie got herself loose and dived for one of B.J.'s arms while Sophie grabbed the other one.

"Get off me!" B.J. cried.

"We had to get you before he did!" Darbie shouted back at her, jerking her head.

B.J. glanced back just as the down jacket disappeared into the foliage. It rustled as whoever it was tried to get untangled for a getaway. Sophie, B.J., and Darbie made theirs in the other direction, and they didn't stop until they reached the empty baseball field. The two Corn Flakes pulled B.J. down onto the bleachers with them.

"That was Eddie Wornom!" B.J. said as she wrenched her arm away from Sophie.

"Eddie Wornom's way taller than that," Sophie said.

B.J. got her other arm untangled from Darbie's. "Who else would act like he was going to pull me through the gate and get me in trouble?"

"I don't know exactly who *that* was," Sophie said, "but I know what the plan was."

Talking as best she could with her teeth chattering, Sophie told B.J. what she'd heard Julia and Tod say in the gym. B.J.'s face seemed to freeze harder with every word. She could barely move her mouth when Sophie was finished, and she

114

said, "How do I know you're not making that up just to make me feel horrible?"

"For the love of Mike, B.J.," Darbie said. "If we wanted you to feel horrible, we would have let that blaggard drag you off school grounds and get you suspended for the rest of your life."

B.J. gave Darbie a long look, as if she'd never really seen her before. "Oh," she said. "I guess that's right."

"Of course it's right."

"So Julia and them really didn't try to make it so I could finish the project with Eddie and not flunk and also help them get Eddie in trouble ..."

Her voice faded out as Darbie shook her head. And then she started to cry, with a stiff face, without tears. It looked like every sob hurt.

"What am I supposed to do without friends?" she said.

Darbie looked at Sophie, eyes expectant.

Sophie opened her mouth, and then she closed it. She knew what to say to B.J. But Darbie probably did too. She was doing fine so far, and besides, she needed to do it. For lots of reasons.

"Darbie can help you with that," Sophie said. "I have to get to class, but Coach Nanini will give you guys passes since you're doing Round Table business."

She wrapped her arms around her freezing self and started for the building. She heard Darbie's footsteps behind her.

"Psst! Sophie!" she hissed. "You're leaving me? What am I supposed to say to her?"

Sophie stopped and grabbed Darbie's hands. They were like cold little claws.

"Just tell her what you know about real friends."

"You mean, like our Corn Flake Code?"

115

"Great idea."

"But you're the one who's good at this, Soph."

Sophie turned Darbie around to face B.J., who was huddled on the bleachers like an abandoned puppy. "You can do this," she whispered. "I know you can."

As Darbie started toward B.J., Sophie broke into a run. There still might be time to make it to fifth period before the bell rang. Just before she got to the double doors, they opened, and Mr. Bentley emerged importantly into the sunlight. Julia was on one side of him, and Tod was on the other. Sophie slipped behind the trash can, thankful that they were engrossed in conversation and hadn't spotted her.

"Now, you're sure she said she and Eddie Wornom were going to sneak out the back gate."

"Oh, she was all proud of it," Julia said.

Tod stepped out in front of them and walked backward. "We should hurry. Eddie said they were gonna go right about now."

Sophie couldn't see Mr. Bentley's face when they went past, but from the way his back straightened into a pole, she knew he believed them.

That's okay, she decided as she tore down the hall toward the stairs. *They're not gonna find anybody at the gate when they get there. Except maybe Colton Messik in a ski mask.*

But Colton was just flying into Mr. Stires' room when Sophie got to the end of the hall. Just as the door shut behind him, the bell rang.

Sophie was late again. For the third time.

Twelve

Mr. Stires looked like he would rather swallow a test tube than give Sophie detention, but a rule was a rule.

"We'll see you tomorrow after school," he said.

"Okay," Sophie said. It really didn't matter what day life as she knew it ended and Daddy grounded her and took away the camera.

Sophie gasped, right out loud. Film Club was supposed to film this weekend. They had it all planned for two cameras. And if she was under house arrest, she couldn't be in the film. At all.

Mr. Stires gave the assignment, and Sophie hid behind her science book to try to figure something out—and to get warmed up. She was shivering from the inside out. Two notes fell onto her desktop, and she opened them with stiff, raw hands.

You didn't talk to Fiona yet, Vincent had written. *What's the deal?*

What happened out there? Fiona's said. *The meeting was weird. Vincent is all freaked out about something.*

Sophie didn't answer. She stayed hidden, tucked into a ball at her desk. Then Darbie came in, gave her pass to Mr. Stires, and scribbled a note, which she dropped on Sophie's desk on her way to the pencil sharpener.

Thank you SOOOOO much. I think I helped B.J., but I couldn't have done it without you.

Sophie peeked over the top of her book. Darbie's eyes were sparkling like sun on snow, and it was the first time Sophie had seen her smile in days. Things started to melt in Sophie's chest.

And that was when she decided what to do.

Give me twenty-four hours with Fiona, she wrote to Vincent. If she's amazing by rehearsal tomorrow, I think she should keep the part.

She didn't write down what would happen if Fiona wasn't amazing. She *would* be amazing, just like Darbie obviously was. And nothing could feel better to Sophie herself than that.

"Why didn't you write me back?" Fiona said after class when they were on their way to Mr. DiLoretto's room.

"Because we should talk instead," Sophie said.

She got Mr. DiLoretto's permission to take Fiona out into the hall. "Whatever it takes to get her up to speed," he said.

Sitting on the floor beside her best friend, Sophie told her the truth about everything. Fiona's eyes displayed every emotion known to the human heart, Sophie was sure. They filled up with tears, sent out anger sparks, and rolled right up into her head in disgust. But in the end, they looked deep into Sophie's and said, "Will you help me? I really want to do this."

"Will I breathe?" Sophie said.

Mama was thrilled when Sophie called her after school, and she said of course Sophie could go to Fiona's and work until eight o'clock, as long as she got her homework done. Math was all she had, and Fiona coached her through it. After that, it was nothing but Leona Artalini 'til Daddy picked Sophie up.

"You look like somebody took a hundred-pound sack off your shoulders, Baby Girl," Daddy said.

"Yeah," Sophie said. "But there's still some left."

On the way home she told him about the detention. When they pulled into the driveway, she watched him run his hand down the back of his head. That only meant he was thinking. Beyond that, she couldn't tell, and she couldn't stand it.

"So am I grounded for the weekend? Are you going to take the camera away?"

"It's hard to punish you when you were trying to help somebody," Daddy said. "This is a tough call. Let me review it with your mother."

Sophie bit back further questions. At least he hadn't just said, "Yes. Your life is over."

"I will say this, though." He swallowed Sophie's shoulder with his big hand. "Whatever your consequences have to be, I'm sure proud of you. You made a big sacrifice."

He wasn't the only one who was proud, Sophie decided when she finished her talk with Jesus that night. His eyes looked very, very kind again.

The next morning, Sophie met Fiona an hour before school started so they could work some more. They each got a restroom pass in every class so they could take five minutes at a time to work out Leona's trouble spots. That used up all their passes for the rest of the school year, but they agreed it was worth it. Fiona was showing definite improvement. They slaved during lunch, except for the time it took to try on the costumes Maggie brought in.

Sophie put on her ragged petticoat, laced up her patched-over dress, and tied on the cap that fit right around her face. When she looked in the mirror in Mr. DiLoretto's room, an impish Johanna Van Raggs—ready to skip around and duck behind things—looked back. Not like Fiona and Kitty, who could barely move in the brocade outfits Senora LaQuita had made for them.

"What's with the hips?" Vincent said as Sophie helped Fiona move sideways between the desks.

"Those are farthingales," Maggie said. "They're like big pillows tied underneath. It was the style."

"Ouch! Willoughby, what are you doing to me?" Fiona said.

Willoughby leaned down from the desk she was standing on and showed Fiona what looked like a metal-net cap spray-painted gold.

"I'm putting your hair up in this," she said.

"*Torture* was the style?" Jimmy said.

"I love my costume, Maggie," Sophie said. "Thank you."

She swayed back and forth and watched the strips of skirt make fun patterns over the petticoat. Then she stopped.

Who was going to play Johanna Van Raggs when the Film Club started filming after school? She wasn't going to be there. She had detention.

Maybe they could start with the scenes she wasn't in. But she was in all except two. And if they didn't get more than that done this afternoon and tonight, it wouldn't be finished by Monday. Besides, Daddy might ground her—

"Don't you all look class!"

Sophie glanced up as Darbie made her way through the costumed Jimmy and Nathan and Kitty and Fiona, patting the farthingales and teasing the boys about their tights. When she got to Sophie, she pulled her to a corner.

"B.J. is doing *so* much better, thanks to you," she said.

"You're the one who's doing it," Sophie said. "Don't tell anybody I had anything to do with it. You should have the credit."

Darbie shook her head. "There's one thing I don't have any idea how to help her with, and I'm desperate. Who knew I would ever want to help this girl, eh?"

"What's up?" Sophie said.

Darbie lowered her voice to a murmur. "She doesn't have a project for this class. She hasn't been cooperating with Eddie, so he's just done his own thing with da Vinci. She's going to get an F, which is wretched enough, but heinous when you don't even have any friends to cheer you up."

"No doubt," Sophie said.

Darbie brought her face in closer. "You have an idea, don't you?"

"Maybe," Sophie said. "I'll let you know."

There really was only one way for Sophie to help B.J. *and* keep her own group from getting a lower grade just because she'd gotten herself in trouble at a crucial point.

Still, she talked to Jesus about it during the lab in fifth period. It was a good thing Fiona, her lab partner, knew what she was doing, because Sophie wrote every figure in the wrong place and turned over a caddy of test tubes before Fiona took over. At least she thought she saw approval in Jesus' eyes.

As soon as she got to sixth period, Sophie went to Mr. DiLoretto's desk. For maybe the first time ever, he smiled at her.

"Looks like your hard work is doing wonders for our Fiona," he said. "Why didn't your group make you the director? Somebody made some bad decisions—"

"I want to give my servant part to B.J.," Sophie said.

Mr. DiLoretto looked as if he'd just been quick-frozen. Only his eyes moved to squint at her.

"You want to what?"

"If you would give me credit for helping Fiona, B.J. could have my part. It didn't work out with her partner, and I don't want her to get an F."

He thawed out enough to fold his arms and cock an eyebrow. "It looked to me like the reason it 'didn't work out' was because she was too busy hanging out with another group."

"She's changed now, though," Sophie said. "And it would help Darbie too—that's a whole other thing."

"Well, aren't you just the little fixer?" Mr. DiLoretto said.

"No," Sophie said. "It's just what I'm supposed to do right now."

For a minute he looked at her, and then he stood up and perched on the edge of the desk. "I think I was wrong about you," he said. "I hope people like B.J. and Fiona appreciate what you do for them."

B.J. and Fiona might, Sophie thought as she took a big breath and headed for her group. But she wasn't sure about everybody else.

When she told them what Mr. DiLoretto had agreed to, the Film Club stared at her like a group in a snapshot. Vincent was the first one to break with his cracked voice.

"The whole thing's gonna be ruined now!"

"The servant doesn't even have any lines," Sophie said. "You told me yourself it wasn't that important of a part."

"Yes, it is, Sophie!" Kitty said. "Nobody else could play it as funny as you."

"Especially not B.J.," Willoughby muttered.

"I was playing it *too* funny," Sophie said. "Fiona's the star. The attention should be on her."

Jimmy was wiggling his foot. "Can B.J. learn the part by, like, this afternoon?"

"We *have* to start filming after school," Vincent said.

"I'll help her all I can." Everyone turned to Fiona as she spoke.

"I know the Johanna Van Raggs part inside out," Fiona said. "I kept thinking Vincent was going to make me switch with Sophie, and I wanted to be ready."

Willoughby leaned in and whispered, "How's B.J. gonna fit into Sophie's costume? I don't mean to be rude, but—hel-*lo-o*!"

Nathan turned red.

Maggie grunted. "I can do stuff with safety pins. It's not that big a deal."

"I just wish you'd talked to me about it first," Vincent said, voice splitting in two. "I'm the director."

"Oh, for Pete's sake, Vincent," Darbie said. "It isn't about you, now, is it?"

While Vincent fumbled for an answer, Darbie snuck her hand into Sophie's and squeezed. Fiona was less subtle. She gave Sophie a big ol' thumbs-up.

Detention that afternoon was worse than any of the medieval tortures Vincent had found on the Internet and wanted to put in the movie. It wasn't that cleaning the science lab was so bad. It was knowing that her best friends were all in the art room, filming without her. Sophie had felt so warm and good during sixth period, even watching B.J. stumble clumsily through her new part.

But now she hurt.

Jesus is with me, she told herself. *I forgot where I was in line and just did the jobs he gave me. I'm serving the way he would have if he went to middle school.*

But she still felt like somebody had cut a piece out of her. It was going to be hard to fill in that hole.

So hard that she didn't really want to see the group when Mr. Stires let her go early. Deciding she would just watch the film with everybody else in the class next week, Sophie went straight to the front of the school to wait for the late bus. Daddy was there instead, sitting in his truck.

Sophie ran toward him with her heart coming up her throat. Was it Mama? Was the baby coming?

But he was smiling and waving to her, and Sophie slowed down. He probably came to make sure she brought the camera home. Maybe she could get it from Fiona tonight...

"So did you serve your time?" Daddy said as she stood on tiptoes to look into his window.

"Well, here anyway," Sophie said. "I can go back in and get the camera from Fiona if you want."

"How are you going to film this weekend without the camera?"

Sophie lowered her heels. "You're not taking it away?"

Daddy shook his head. "What more could you learn from that than you've already learned from everything you've been through?" He shrugged. "That's the only reason we ever punished you anyway, so you'd learn." He grinned a little. "I'm not sure it's working with your brother."

"You mean I'm not grounded either?"

"No. That's what I came to tell you. If they're still working, you can go back inside."

But Sophie just trudged to the other side of the truck and climbed in. "I think I just want to go home now," she said.

"How come?" Daddy said.

"Because I think I need to cry," she said.

And then she started right there beside Daddy, who drove her home without asking any more questions.

Sophie did watch all the filming that weekend, and Vincent let her work with the actors. He didn't have much of a choice, as far as Sophie could see. They kept asking her, especially B.J., who wasn't as hard to work with as everybody had thought she'd be. In the first place, she couldn't say a word as long as they were filming. And in the second place, she seemed to use something she'd learned from the Corn Pops: if you don't go with the group, you get thrown out.

But that isn't true for us Flakes, Sophie thought as she watched Fiona go through a scene with B.J. for the thousandth time. Willoughby patiently tucked all of B.J.'s blonde bob into a cap too small for her. Nobody teased Nathan because he turned into a radish every time B.J. even looked at him.

We could get selfish and compete as much as the Pops and Loops, though, Sophie told herself. And then she smiled. *If we didn't have grace.*

They showed their film to the class on Tuesday, and they got a standing ovation. Even Colton clapped, until Tod and Julia glared at him. Sophie could see it in every Corn Pop and Fruit Loop face: they weren't finished with B.J. yet. Or Sophie.

"Why weren't *you* in it, Soapy?" Julia said to her at the end of the period.

"Are you kidding?"

Sophie turned to look at B.J., who had appeared beside her.

"She was the best thing about it, Julia," B.J. said.

She darted off then, but not before Sophie saw her chin tremble and tears fill her eyes. It was the first time Sophie ever thought she knew how B.J. might feel.

Darbie had done good work with B.J., Sophie decided. She was going to have to tell her that.

She wriggled through the crowd at the door to try to catch up to her. But it was Coach Nanini and Mrs. Clayton she ran into in the hall.

"Got a minute, Little Bit?" Coach said.

Sophie looked wistfully at Darbie's disappearing back, but she nodded. They were having a celebration party at Fiona's. She could tell her then.

"We have a proposition for you, Sophie," Mrs. Clayton said.

"What's a proposition?" Sophie said.

Coach Virile grinned. "It's an offer you can't refuse. How would you like to serve on the Round Table as an adviser for new council members?"

Mrs. Clayton almost smiled, which didn't happen often. "We heard you were wonderful with Darbie," she said.

"She did all the work," Sophie said. "Honest. She wasn't even supposed to tell you!"

"She didn't," Coach Virile said. "But she was about the only one who didn't."

"We heard it from Mr. Stires and Mr. DiLoretto."

"And you'll never guess who else, Little Bit," Coach Virile said.

Sophie didn't even try. There were way too many surprises happening.

Coach Virile shook his head. "She sure could've knocked me over with a feather," he said. "It was B.J."

"So what's it going to be, Sophie?" Mrs. Clayton said. "Will you serve with us?"

Sophie could feel all the lumps and hurts and shivers draining from her. Everything but her smile.

"As long as you put it that way," Sophie said, "of course I will." Because she was really beginning to like this servant role.

Glossary

amiss (uh-MISS) when something seems to be incorrect, or doesn't make any sense

appalled (uh-PAWLD) being really shocked—almost disgusted—when something happens

baroque period (ba-ROHK PEER-ee-uhd) refers to a time in the 17th century when art, music, and clothes suddenly became very frilly and detailed—some people might say *too* detailed

disdainful (dis-DAYN-full) when you think you're better than someone else, and look at them with so much disgust that you show your feelings on your face

farthingales (FAR-then-gales) called "French farthingales," these were stiff, crescent-shaped pads that fashionable women in the 17th century tied around their waists so their skirts would look wider

gibbon apes (gib-en apes) small apes with very long arms, and cute, hairless faces. They are known for their very loud calls to each other, which sound like crazed laughter

heinous (HEY-nus) unbelievably mean and cruel

kibosh (KI-bosh) putting an end to something you don't like; to vote an idea down

Medieval (meh-DEE-vul) something or someone from the middle ages, which lasted from the 5th century to the 15th century. This wasn't a happy time to live in, because of the painful punishments and disease, but there were kings, knights, and cool castles.

pratfall (PRATT-fawl) when you fall or land on your rear end in a really humiliating way, causing others to laugh really hard

remission (re-MIH-shun) when a disease, like cancer, disappears with treatment. If the disease doesn't come back for many years, the person may be cured.

repugnant (re-PUG-nent) something so incredibly offensive that it can make you very angry

repulsive (re-PULL-sehv) gross, disgusting, and so icky you feel ill just thinking about it

subtle (SUH-tul) so small or quick that you have to look really hard to notice it

Sophie Gets Real

One

"Sophie. Yo—Sophie LaCroix!" Sophie looked up at her best friend Fiona and blinked behind her glasses.

Fiona pointed. "Are you putting both feet into one leg of your sweats for a reason?"

Sophie looked down at the bulging left side of her PE sweatpants. Fiona sat beside her on the locker-room bench, one magic-gray eye gleaming. The other one was hidden by the golden brown strand of hair that always fell over it.

"Are you thinking up a new character for a film?" Fiona said. "Yes! We haven't done a movie in so long that the whole Film Club's going into withdrawal."

Sophie shook her honey brown hair out of her face. "I wish that was what I was thinking about." She got untangled and pulled on her PE sweatpants. "I can't keep my mind off my mom."

"What's wrong with your mom?" Willoughby, another member of their group, bounded in and stopped in front of Sophie, brown curls springing in all directions. "Um, Soph? How come you have your sweats on backward?"

Sophie groaned and wriggled out of them again.

"Her mom's been in labor since early this morning," Fiona told Willoughby. "Sophie's a little freaked."

Willoughby's hazel eyes, always big to begin with, widened to Frisbee size. "Your mom's having your baby sister today? Why are you even here? Why aren't you at the hospital?"

"It could take all day, and it's not like Sophie could help deliver the baby," Fiona said. "She can't even get her clothes on right. Soph, your shirt's on inside out."

Sophie looked down at the fuzzy backward letters GMMS—for Great Marsh Middle School—and groaned again. "I'm not even gonna be able to change her diapers. I'll probably put them on her head or something."

"You put diapers on somebody's head?" At the end of the bench, Kitty's china-blue eyes went almost as round as Willoughby's.

Kitty was the fourth member of their six-girl group. She was just back from changing clothes in a restroom stall. Although she was finally sprouting spiky hair after her chemotherapy for leukemia, she still had a tiny hole in her chest. It let the doctors put in medicine and take out blood without sticking her every time. She always changed her shirt out of sight of the girls a few lockers down—the mostly rude ones Sophie and her friends secretly referred to as the "Corn Pops." Those girls decided what was cool. A hole in the middle of somebody's chest *wasn't*.

"What about diapers on her head?" Kitty asked again.

"She hasn't put Pampers on her little cranium so far," Fiona said. "But then, the baby's not born yet."

"Any minute now," Willoughby told Kitty. And then she let out one of her shrieks that always reminded Sophie of a hyper poodle yelping.

Kitty giggled and threw her arms around Sophie, just as Sophie pulled her T-shirt off over her head. A few tangled moments passed before Sophie could get it off her face and breathe again. By then, Darbie and Maggie, the final two, were there. Maggie shook her head, splashing her Cuban-dark bob against her cheeks.

"You can't wear your shirt for a hat," she said, words thudding out in their usual matter-of-fact blocks.

Maggie was the most somber of the group, but that was just Maggie. Although the lip-curling Corn Pops called them "Flakes"—which was where their very-secret name "Corn Flakes" came from—Sophie and her friends let each other be the unique selves they figured God made them to be.

Only at the moment, Sophie wasn't feeling unique. Just weird.

Darbie hooked her straight reddish hair behind her ears. "You're all in flitters, Sophie," she said.

Darbie still used her Irish expressions, even though she had been in the U.S. for more than a year. Sophie loved that, but she barely noticed now.

"Her mom's having her baby sister right this very minute," Willoughby told Darbie, with a poodle-shriek. "Our newest little Corn Fl—"

"Shhhh!" Maggie said.

Willoughby slapped her hand over her own mouth, and Sophie glanced down the row of lockers to make sure the Corn Pops hadn't heard. It didn't look like it.

Nobody outside the group knew about the Corn Flake name. Being a Corn Flake was a special thing, with a code that was all about behaving the way God wanted them to. The Corn Flakes had agreed a long time ago that they couldn't risk Julia and her group finding out and twisting it all up.

Still, it was hard not to talk about it, especially when it came to Sophie's soon-to-be-born sister. They had plans for making her the newest Corn Flake.

"Sophie's so nervous about the baby," Kitty said to Maggie, "she's about to put a diaper on her head."

"Of course she is," Julia Cummings said as she walked by. She was the leader of the three Corn Pops, who all rolled their eyes in agreement.

But that was all they did. The Corn Pops had gotten into so much trouble for bullying the Corn Flakes in the first six months of seventh grade, they didn't dare try anything they'd get caught at. Or, as Fiona put it, there would be "dire consequences." That was Fiona language for "big trouble."

And now that her Corn Flakes were all around her, helping her get her shoes on the right feet, Sophie didn't feel quite so much like the pieces of her world had been mixed up and put back together wrong. A new baby was big stuff, but Fiona, Willoughby, Kitty, Darbie, and Maggie could make even that easier.

As the Flakes hurried into the gym, a whistle blew and Sophie jumped.

"Does Coach Yates have to toot that thing so hard?" Willoughby said. "Doesn't she know Sophie's mom is having a baby?"

"I don't think so," Maggie said.

Coach Yates, their PE teacher with a graying ponytail so tight it stretched her eyes at the corners, gave the whistle another blast.

The Flakes skittered into line for roll call. In the next row, a way-skinny boy with a big, loose grin that filled up most of his face turned to Sophie. "So when's Film Club gonna do another film?" His voice cracked, as usual, bringing titters from Corn Pop Cassie in front of him.

"Not now, Vincent," Kitty said. "Her mom's having a baby."

"What's that got to do with it?" Vincent said.

"Boys," Willoughby whispered to Sophie. "They're so clueless."

Sophie nodded, but she really did wish she was deep in daydreams about a new and fabulous character for a Film Club movie the Corn Flakes could make with the Lucky Charms. That was the name the Flakes had secretly given to Vincent and his two friends, partly because they weren't absurd little creeps like *some* boys they knew.

"Is your mom okay?" Jimmy Wythe said. His eyes, as blue as a swimming pool, were soft.

But before Sophie could answer him, Coach Yates gave an extra-obnoxious blast on the whistle that brought even the Corn Pops out of their huddle.

"Singletary!" Coach Yates yelled. Nobody could holler like Coach Yates. "Are you looking for a detention your first day? Get yourself down from there."

Sophie looked in the direction Coach Yates was yelling. Her mouth dropped open.

"Somebody's making a holy show of herself," Darbie said.

A girl with bright red hair was shimmying up one of the volleyball poles. Even with Coach Yates still shouting, the girl reached the top and looked down triumphantly at the entire seventh-grade PE class.

"Who is *that*?" Julia said.

Beside her, Corn Pop Anne-Stuart gave the usual sniff. Sophie wondered where all the stuff in Anne-Stuart's nose could possibly come from.

"She'd better get down," Maggie said. "She's gonna get in so much trouble."

"Is she mental?" Darbie said.

Sophie was sure of it when Red-Haired Girl suddenly let go of the pole and leaped to the gym floor. Her flight landed in a roll that brought her right to Coach Yates' feet. Vincent clapped—until Coach Yates shot him the Coach *Hates* look.

She ordered them all to get into their teams for warm-up and pulled Red-Haired Girl to her feet. Coach Nanini joined them — the big man Sophie thought of as Coach Virile. He had muscles as big as hams and one large eyebrow that ridged his eyes. He was the boys' coach, but Sophie secretly called him hers.

Sophie tried to hear what he was saying to Red-Haired Girl in his high-pitched-for-a-man voice, but Coach Yates blasted the whistle yet again and sent them all scurrying. The Charms went to get a ball while the Corn Flakes gathered on their court.

"What was *that* about?" Fiona said.

"She'll get double detention for it," Maggie said.

Fiona rolled her eyes. "That's, like, something my little brother would do."

"So's that," Darbie said, nodding toward Coach Nanini and Red-Haired Girl. The girl was rolling the front of her T-shirt onto her arms so that her bare belly showed. Somebody on another team yelled, "Woo-hoo!" Probably one of the Fruit Loops, Sophie thought. They were the boys famous for such talents as burping the alphabet, booby-trapping toilets, and far worse.

"She acts like she's in about fourth grade," Willoughby said.

With an eyebrow raised, Sophie looked around the circle.

"Oops," Darbie said. "We're breaking the Code, aren't we?"

Maggie gave a solemn nod, and Sophie knew she was about to list the entire Corn Flake Code for them.

"Never put anybody down even though they do it to you," she said as if she were reading it. "Don't fight back or give in to bullies; just take back the power to be yourself. Talk to Jesus about everything, because he gives you the power to be who he made you to be. Corn Flakes are always loyal to each other."

"I always make a bags of that 'don't put anybody down' part," Darbie said.

Kitty nudged her. "Shh. Here come the boys."

The Corn Flakes spread into a circle so the Charms could join them for warm-up. Nathan, the third Lucky Charm, soft-served the ball to Fiona, his face going strawberry-red for no reason at all except that he was Nathan.

"So what was with the girl on the pole?" Jimmy said.

"I think we're about to find out." Willoughby jerked her curls toward Coach Yates, who marched in their direction with Red-Haired Girl right behind her.

"Do you think she heard us?" Kitty whispered to Sophie.

"Not with that whistle going off all the time," Sophie whispered back.

Coach Yates stopped, and Red-Haired Girl plowed into the back of her.

"Team One," Coach Yates said to them, "meet Brooke Singletary."

Brooke rolled her forearms up in her shirt front again. Nathan turned scarlet.

"Hey," Brooke said. "I'm on your team now."

Sophie was sure Brooke must have a hundred freckles per square inch on her face. They seemed to jump around when she talked, just like the rest of her. Sophie wondered if she might have to go to the bathroom.

Fiona waved. "I'm Fiona," she said.

The rest of the group said their names, except Nathan, who just bobbed his head and went radish colored. Before they even got to Sophie, Brooke said, "I'm serving first," and snatched the ball from Fiona. Then she tore toward the serving corner of their court, untied shoelaces flapping.

"Yeah," Fiona said, staring after her, "why don't you just do that little thing?"

This, Sophie decided, was going to be a real test of their ability to uphold the Code.

Before all the Flakes and Charms could get into position, Brooke smacked the ball and sent it sailing just over the net. Colton Messik, a Fruit Loop, turned in time to smack it back over. Maggie jumped toward the ball, hands in perfect position to set it up, but a blaze of red was suddenly there. Brooke's head collided dead-on with Maggie's, and Maggie staggered backward. Jimmy stepped in and caught her.

The court burst into a chaos of shouts.

"You should have let her set it up—"

"You're supposed to play your position—"

"Are you gone in the head, girl?"

"You can let go of me now!"

That last shout came from Maggie, who squirmed away from Jimmy and glowered at Brooke. "That's not the right way to play," she said.

"I don't know," Tod Ravelli called from the other side of the net. "I thought it was slammin'!"

Colton and Tod did an instant replay of Brooke ramming into Maggie, and Julia exchanged lip-curled smiles with Anne-Stuart and Cassie.

"You okay, Mags?" Willoughby said.

While she and Kitty examined Maggie's forehead, Sophie watched Brooke. She tossed the ball in the air and stumbled after it, this time falling into Nathan, who went past red and into the purple color family.

"I think this might be beyond the Corn Flake Code," Fiona muttered to Sophie.

Sophie turned to Darbie, who was shoving her hair behind her ears, over and over.

"I think she needs some Round Table help," Sophie said to her.

Darbie directed her bird-bright dark eyes down at Sophie. "That's easy for you to say, since you're not on it, and I am."

"I'm a consultant," Sophie said, lifting her chin. "And I think I should *consult* with Coach Nanini."

Darbie sighed. "You're always so good, Sophie. I'd rather toss her out by her drawers and be done with it."

But Darbie followed Sophie to Coach Nanini, who was one of the Round Table advisers. Round Table was a council of faculty members and students who tried to help kids that couldn't seem to follow the school rules. Coach and the other teachers thought most kids acted out because something was bothering them, and instead of just being punished, they should be helped. Sophie had been on Round Table for the first half of the year until a new council came on, but Coach and Mrs. Clayton, the other adviser, had asked Sophie to be a consultant.

"It's Little Bit and the Lass," Coach Nanini said when they reached him. "Those are some serious faces."

"That's because we have a serious problem," Darbie said.

Coach Nanini folded his big arms and said, "Okay, let's hear it."

Sophie filled him in, while Darbie punctuated with little grunts. When she was finished, Coach Nanini peered beneath his hooded brows in the direction of Team One's court. The ball was just sailing from Tod Ravelli straight to Brooke—who had her back to him as she gawked at Kitty on the sideline waiting to rotate in.

"Heads up, Brooke!" Fiona shouted.

But the ball hit Brooke in the back of the head and bounced away. "Hey!" she said. "What jerk threw that at me?"

Coach Yates blasted the whistle, and Coach Nanini nodded his shaved head. "She looks like Round Table material to me. I'll talk to her after class."

Sophie felt a wisp of guilt as she and Darbie joined the team again. *I feel like I just passed Brooke off so we wouldn't have to deal with her,* she thought.

But by the time Coach Yates sent the class to the locker room, all traces of regret had disappeared. Within thirty minutes, Brooke had fallen into the net, told Vincent he had big lips, and wrestled Fiona for the ball until Coach Yates nearly popped a blood vessel blowing her whistle.

"I know this isn't Corn Flake Code," Fiona said to Sophie as they headed for the locker room, "but that girl is harder to be around than the Corn Pops."

"Maybe she has issues," Sophie said.

"Yeah, well, if she ever tackles me on the volleyball court again, she'll definitely have an issue." Fiona sighed and rolled her eyes. "Okay. I'll pray for her. Besides ..."

But Sophie didn't hear the rest. She pulled Fiona to a stop by the sleeve and pointed.

"My sister's here," Sophie said, her voice cracking. "This can't be good."

Lacie was standing in the doorway to Coach Yates' office, looking way too serious for a fourteen-year-old. Even the scattered freckles across her nose looked pinched in.

"Lacie?" Sophie called.

Her sister turned toward her with tears in her eyes. Lacie never cried. "We have to go to the hospital," she said.

"Is the baby born yet?" Sophie said.

"Yeah, and Soph—I think there's something wrong with her."

Two

Boppa, Fiona's grandfather, was waiting in front of the school to take the LaCroix girls to the hospital. Sophie was full of questions for Lacie as they hurried to his car.

"How do you know something's wrong with the baby?"

"I just—"

"Did you talk to Mama?"

"No, but—"

"Did Boppa tell you?"

Lacie shook her head, swishing her dark ponytail from side to side. "He just said Daddy needed to stay there with Mama. That alone tells you something."

"What does it tell me?" Sophie said.

"That something's not right."

"Not really," Sophie said. "Maybe the baby's just so adorable Mama couldn't wait till after school for us to see her."

Lacie gave her a big-sister look before she opened the car door. "Right. Daddy's going to take us out of school for that. Frogs might sprout wings and fly too."

Sophie slid into the second seat of Fiona's family's SUV. Boppa, who was usually ready with a grin and a wiggle of his caterpillar eyebrows, looked at her as if his soft face were about to crumple. Hard fingers of fear wrapped themselves around Sophie's heart and stayed there.

"Okay, Mr. Bunting," Lacie said as she buckled herself into the front passenger seat. "I wish you'd tell us what's going on."

Boppa shook his partly bald head. "Your dad just wants everybody together for your baby sister."

Lacie gave Sophie a what-did-I-tell-you look over the front seat.

Poquoson, Virginia, and then Hampton seemed to pass in slow motion as they rode through the February bleakness, but Sophie's mind was on fast-reverse.

Mama had had to stay in bed for the last several months because Baby Girl LaCroix wanted to be born too soon.

Nobody was supposed to upset her—and Sophie was sure she had at least a dozen times—not to mention the trouble her six-year-old brother, Zeke, had gotten into pretending to be Spider-Man. Had they caused the baby some kind of problem?

Mama had gotten paler and puffier, and early that morning when Daddy took her to the hospital she'd looked even worse to Sophie—like a bloated marshmallow.

Did all that mean the baby was born sick?

Or that Mama herself had something wrong?

Sophie groped in her mind for a daydream character to escape into. Ever since the Corn Flakes had started making movies early in sixth grade, Sophie's dream people had become as real to her as actual people. They almost always became the main characters in their films, even after the Lucky Charms joined them in Film Club. Dr. Peter, once her therapist and now her Bible study teacher, had told Mama and Daddy that Sophie should always use her imagination. He believed that doing productions would help her channel it instead of letting it get her in trouble for daydreaming.

If the Flakes and Charms were working on a film right now, she could dive into her role as a superhero or something and imagine her way through this baby thing somehow.

But when Boppa took Lacie and Sophie to Daddy inside the hospital lobby, it was all too real. Their tall, big-shouldered father was white-faced, and his mouth was pressed into a line that quivered at the corners. His short dark hair looked as if he'd been raking his fingers through it.

Daddy held out both arms and folded the girls into them. Sophie thought he smelled nervous, like sweat and coffee.

"What's going on, Dad?" Lacie said.

He didn't answer for a minute, and when he did, his voice was thin. Very un-Daddy-like.

"We have a new LaCroix," he said. "Hope Celeste. Six pounds, one ounce." His arms squeezed tighter. "She's beautiful, just like her big sisters."

"Is she okay?" Lacie said.

There was a pause so long that the fingers of fear had another chance to grip Sophie's heart.

"She *will* be okay." Daddy loosened his hold so they could look up at him as they walked down the hall. "They're doing some tests."

"Tests for what?" Lacie said.

Sophie couldn't grab hold of any of her darting thoughts. Only one came out of her mouth. "She isn't going to die, is she?"

"Hel-*lo*—no!" Lacie said.

Daddy stopped them just outside a door and smothered Sophie's shoulder with his hand. "That's a fair question, Soph," he said, "and we think the answer is no. But she has to be checked because—"

His voice broke, as if something had chopped the words off in his throat. Sophie clutched at his big hand.

"Because," he said, "Hope was born with something called Down syndrome."

Lacie gasped right out loud.

"What is Down syn-whatever?" Sophie said.

"It means she'll be re—um, mentally challenged, right?" Lacie said.

Sophie stared, first at her, and then at her father.

"I'm not sure of everything it means," Daddy said. "She'll learn slower than other kids, and she'll look a little different."

"Like the kids in the Special Olympics," Lacie said.

Sophie had no idea what that was, but she could tell from the way Daddy nodded with his eyes closed that the "Special" was like the special in "Special Ed." Like the kids whose classrooms were near the Corn Flakes' lockers—the kids the Pops and Loops referred to as "'tards" and imitated behind their backs.

Then what Lacie had started to say was true. Baby Hope was retarded.

"Do you want to see her?" Daddy said. "Mama's asleep, but she said to let you meet Hope as soon as you got here. She knew you'd be excited."

Excited wasn't exactly the word Sophie would have used. She pulled a strand of hair under her nose, a thing she always did when she was confused. Her heart beat double-time as she followed Daddy through the door into a small hallway lined on one side by a window.

The room on the other side of the glass was softly lit. It took Sophie a moment to realize there was a clear, small, bathtub-style container just beyond the window. In it was a tiny, pink, kicking baby, waving her fists.

"That's your little sister," Daddy whispered.

Sophie was afraid to even peek at her. What if she had a giant head or two noses or something?

"Oh—she's adorable," Lacie said. "She looks like you, Sophie."

"Yup. Spitting image of you when you were born," Daddy said.

Sophie shuddered. *How can she look like me?* Sophie knew what "special" kids looked like. She stood on tiptoe to peer into the baby's bed, and she could feel her eyes bulging.

"Did I have all those tubes in me?"

"You had more," Daddy said. "You were really sick."

"Did I have Down syndrome too?"

Daddy pulled Sophie almost roughly to his chest and held on. "No, Baby Girl," he said. His voice sounded broken again. "You didn't have it."

"I'm talking about her hair and her little cheeks," Lacie said. "Check it out, Soph."

Sophie tried to look past the tiny mask over baby Hope's nose and mouth and the tube that fed into a vein in her little head. She did have a fuzz of golden hair, almost like a miniature halo. Her skin was pale with a whisper of pink, just like Sophie's and Mama's. And she was tiny—the tiniest person Sophie had ever seen.

"She's going to be the shortest one in the class, just like me, isn't she?" Sophie said.

"If she ever goes to schoo—"

"Lacie," Daddy said.

Sophie glanced back to see Lacie biting her lip.

"Let's go see if Mama's awake," Daddy said.

Sophie took another long look at her baby sister, who had drifted off to sleep. She didn't have as many things going in and out of her as Kitty had had when Sophie visited her in the hospital. That had to be a good sign. And although Sophie hadn't seen all that many newborn babies, Hope looked perfectly normal to her. All the fingers and toes were there. She had two eyes. Her ears were sort of rolled up, but maybe that was because they weren't all the way open yet. When Darbie's dog had puppies, it took two weeks for their ears to pop into shape.

"Come on, Soph," Daddy said. He smiled a tired smile. "You'll be able to look at her for the rest of your life."

Mama was sitting up in bed when they got to her room, and her face was pinker and less puffy than Sophie had seen it in a long time. She almost looked like regular Mama again, except that Sophie could tell she'd been crying. That was *not* a good sign.

"Is she getting more beautiful by the minute?" Mama said as she hugged Lacie.

"Yes—even though she does look like Sophie." Lacie grinned back at Sophie and wrinkled her nose.

Sophie edged carefully up to the bed to give Mama a kiss. Mama pulled her right into her arms.

"I won't break, Dream Girl," Mama said. "I'm going to be back on my feet any minute now. Then we can get back to normal, huh?"

Lacie looked at Daddy, who cleared his throat.

"You told them," Mama said to him.

Daddy nodded.

"It's not ever going to be normal again, is it?" Lacie said.

Sophie thought her heart would squeeze to a stop.

"It's going to be a new normal," Daddy said. "Our little rookie will have special needs, and we'll learn how to meet them. We'll work together as a team. New game plan, that's all."

Daddy always talked about the family like they were headed for the Super Bowl. But the tears sparkling in his eyes weren't part of his usual game face.

"The first thing we're going to have to do," Mama said, "is make sure Zeke doesn't use Hope for a football."

"Or try to climb up the wall with her like Spider-Man," Lacie said.

"She might be the first Spider-*Baby*." Daddy laughed. It sounded like a laugh he had to make up, because he couldn't find a real one.

"It's going to be okay, my loves," Mama said. "God will show us everything we need to know."

She put out her hands for the girls to take hold. Mama's was icy cold in Sophie's. Daddy's was clammy. It made Sophie wonder if they really believed it would be okay at all.

Sophie tried that night to imagine Jesus before she went to sleep. That was what Dr. Peter had taught her to do. With Jesus' kind eyes in her mind, she could tell him and ask him anything she wanted. She didn't imagine his answers, though, because Dr. Peter said that would be speaking for him, instead of waiting for the truth to appear in the days to come.

Sophie couldn't have thought up answers for Jesus that night anyway. She couldn't even think up questions. It was so confusing, and all she could do was fall into a restless sleep. When she woke up the next morning, she was holding her hair under her nose again.

Zeke flew into Sophie's room and threw back the filmy curtains that hung around her bed.

"Daddy's taking us out for breakfast!" he announced. His volume was always on LOUD.

Sophie tried to pull one of her purple-and-pink pillows over her head, but Zeke yanked if off and sailed it across the room. He was dressed in full Spider-Man garb, including a red mask that covered everything except his eyes, and unfortunately, his mouth.

"Daddy's not gonna let you wear that into a restaurant," Sophie said.

"We're goin' to Pop's Drive-In!" he shouted. "You can wear anything you want. I'm even wearin' it to the hospital." He threw himself onto Sophie's bed and kneeled over her on all fours. "Hopey doesn't know about Spider-Man yet."

"But she's about to find out," Lacie said from the doorway. "Hurry up, Soph."

Lacie coaxed Zeke out with promises of cartoons. Sophie put another pillow over her head—because uninvited thoughts were barging in.

Would this be the last time they got to go to Pop's for breakfast? Would they be able to take Hope out in public if she was—different?

Sophie tried again to imagine Jesus with his kind eyes, and there he was. Only his eyes were sad, as if he didn't think everything was going to be okay, either.

That made it hard to climb out of bed.

When they got to the hospital, Daddy dropped Zeke off in Mama's room. He and Sophie and Lacie headed for the nursery to say good morning to Hope.

Sophie held a hunk of hair under her nose all the way down the hall. The closer they got to the nursery, the slower she walked. By the time she reached the window, Daddy and Lacie were already there, waving excitedly to someone on the other side of the glass.

"Look who's up!" Lacie said.

Sophie slid reluctantly between her and Daddy, to see a nurse in a mask holding Hope in her arms. The tubes that had been taped to the baby's face were now gone.

"She's breathing on her own," Daddy said. "Look at that—she's doing it."

"She's amazing," Lacie said.

Sophie couldn't take her eyes off the tiny person's face. Without half of it covered, Sophie could see a nose so small it almost didn't exist. Unlike Sophie's eyes, the baby's murky-blue eyes tilted up a little at the outer corners. From her baby-pink mouth, a matching tongue poked out. And stayed there.

"She's so precious," Lacie said.

"Her eyes will probably turn brown like yours did, Soph," Daddy said.

But Sophie could barely keep from crying out, *It's just like you said, Daddy. Our baby is different.*

The nurse let Daddy in so he could hold little Hope, and Lacie pressed her hands and nose against the glass. Sophie backed silently away and walked, stiff-legged and fast, until she found a cubicle that said FAMILY WAITING ROOM on the door.

She plopped down on one of the sofas and closed her eyes. But she couldn't erase the picture of her baby sister with a tongue that lay on her lips like a wilted rosebud. It reminded her of kids she'd seen at school who couldn't control their own faces and bodies.

Is she always going to look like that? Sophie thought.

How was she supposed to eat?

How was she going to talk?

Sophie squeezed her eyes shut tighter. Would she ever even learn to talk? What about all the dreams the Corn Flakes had had of teaching her to use Fiona-vocabulary—like "dire" and "fabulous" and the Corn Flakes' favorite, "heinous"?

Sophie watched those dreams swirl away down an imaginary drain, but she shook her head. It would be at least two years before even a normal little kid could say those words. Maybe there would be a cure for Down syndrome by then. Maybe Sophie would be the first one to read about it and tell Hope's doctor. Maybe she would even—

The doctor straightened up from the microscope and worked hard at not smiling—at not running around the laboratory, shouting, "I've found it! I've discovered the cure!" After all, she couldn't be completely sure yet. There were more tests to do. And if she revealed how close she was now, it would be in all the news reports, because everyone had complete faith in her work. She could already see the headlines: DR. DEVON DOWNING FINDS CURE FOR DOWN SYNDROME.

But fame was not the reason the good Christian doctor was so devoted to this work. If she could just see one Down syndrome child's eyes and ears and tongue become normal, if she could hear one say "heinous" and know that one was enjoying breakfast at Pop's Drive-In on a Saturday morning, it would all be worthwhile.

Dr. Devon Downing picked up her notebook of findings. She must make sure that she was as close as she thought she must be to—

"What are you doing down here reading a magazine?" Lacie said.

Sophie looked up with a jerk.

"The nurse said we could come in and hold Hope," Lacie said.

"Only one of us can hold her at a time." Sophie hugged the magazine to her chest. "You go first since you're the oldest."

Lacie put her hands on her hips, just like Daddy did when he was suspicious. "We can only hold her five minutes each, so don't take too long." She stepped back toward the door. "And since when do you read *Sports Illustrated* ?"

Sophie pulled the magazine out just enough to see the title.

"This isn't the best time in the world to be daydreaming," Lacie said. "Daddy said we all have to pull together as a family."

"I'm pulling," Sophie said.

Lacie disappeared, and Sophie tossed the magazine aside. It had been a long time since she'd gotten in trouble for lapsing into one of her imaginings and forgetting what she was supposed to be doing. It had hardly happened at all since Daddy had given her the video camera a year and a half ago. She knew if it became a problem again, he'd take it away.

Sophie sighed back into the sofa cushions. Would she even be able to make movies anymore? Was she going to be so busy pulling together with the family that she wouldn't have time to write scripts and act and direct?

Dr. Devon Downing straightened her white lab coat. There were always sacrifices to be made when a doctor was on such a quest as she was, but it was all right. "I will find a cure for Down syndrome," she said. "And that is all that matters."

"Wouldn't that be great?"

Once again Sophie jolted up, only this time Daddy stared down at her. He didn't put his hands on his hips, though. He sat beside her on the couch. Sophie had never seen dark smudges in the skin under his eyes before.

"I wish you or anybody else *could* find a cure, Baby Girl," he said.

"Somebody will," Sophie said. "They find cures for things all the time."

"Not for this." Daddy pinched the top of his nose with his fingers. "Whether a baby is going to have Down syndrome is decided way before she's born, when the chromosomes get handed out. They carry the genes that tell whether she's going to have brown eyes like you or blue ones like Lacie and Zeke. If she gets an extra chromosome, that decides she'll be—like Hope."

"Can't they just change the chromosomes or take one back out?" Sophie said.

Daddy shook his head like it hurt to move. "Once a baby is born with Down syndrome, that's it. She'll always have it. And no matter how hard you dream, Soph—there's nothing you can do about it."

Three

✳ 🏠 ✺

Sophie let everybody else in the family take turns holding baby Hope. Sunday morning she begged Daddy to let her go to church instead of the hospital, but he said they were having a special thanksgiving service for Hope in the hospital chapel, and she needed to be there. The only thing that made that bearable was that Dr. Peter was there too.

She spotted him right away, standing outside the chapel door. There was no mistaking his short gelled curls, his smile full of mischief, and the wire-rimmed glasses he always pushed up with a wrinkle of his nose. The eyes behind them twinkled when Sophie ran up to him, and the inner fingers that kept squeezing her heart let go a little. Any hard thing was easier with Dr. Peter on the scene.

"Sophie-Lophie-Loodle," he said in a hospital-low voice. "How's the big sister?"

Sophie's throat went tight. Dr. Peter nodded.

"What do you say we talk after this, huh?" he said.

That got her through the service. Lacie said it was pretty, with the candles and the tiny pink tea roses and the prayers Daddy and Mama and Dr. Peter said. All Sophie saw were the tears behind Mama's and Daddy's smiles. She was ready to cry a few of her own when it was over.

Dr. Peter said, "Want to go downstairs and have a soda?"

The table and plastic chairs in the corner of the cafeteria weren't Dr. Peter's colorful office with its window seat and pillows with faces on them, but it didn't have to be. Once Sophie was seated across from him, a cherry Coke in front of her, she finally felt like she could tell someone everything. Still, she started slow.

"You know my little sister has Down syndrome," she said.

Dr. Peter pressed his lips together and nodded.

"I guess you know what that is."

"I do. Do you?"

"My dad told me. It can't be cured, you know."

"I know," Dr. Peter said.

The last piece of Sophie's dream was chipped away. She'd dared to hope that Dr. Peter, being a psychologist, would know something Daddy didn't. Right now, he looked as sad as everybody else.

"Are you scared, Loodle?" Dr. Peter said.

"Yes. Only don't tell my dad. We're supposed to be pulling together as a family."

"That doesn't mean you can't be afraid. Do you want to talk about why you're making a mustache out of your hair again? I haven't seen you do that in a while."

Sophie let her hair drop and took a sip of her cherry Coke. It didn't taste as good as it usually did.

"There's this new girl in my PE class."

Dr. Peter didn't ask her what in the world that had to do with her new sister, like most grown-ups would.

"She's out of control," Sophie said. "It's like she forgets there's anybody else around, so she runs all over, like, plowing into people and hitting them in the head with the ball. She can't pay attention, so she gets bonked with it too. And, seriously, she can't be still. I keep thinking she has to go to the bathroom."

Dr. Peter nodded.

"There's something way different about her—not, like, unique, but like something's wrong with her." Sophie discovered she had to swallow hard. "The other kids, you know, like the Corn Pops—"

"And the Fruit Loops?"

"Yeah—they all make fun of her. It's even hard for *us* not to say bad stuff about her. I bet she doesn't have any friends and—Dr. Peter?"

"What, Soph?"

The lump in Sophie's throat broke, and she felt her face wad up into tears. "I'm scared that when Hope goes to school, the kids are gonna be even meaner to her because she's—because she's—retarded!"

She pushed her Coke aside and folded her arms on the table so she could cry into them. Dr. Peter let her.

"Y'know, Loodle," he said, "I'd be worried about you if you *didn't* admit that you were afraid. Maybe mad too."

"Mad? At who?" Sophie said.

"Whoever's responsible for Hope being born with Down syndrome."

Sophie sat up straighter. "Who? What do you mean?"

"Remember when we first found out Kitty had leukemia?"

"Uh-huh."

"I told you when something happens that seems so unfair like that, instead of asking God *why*, it's better to ask, *what now?* I think that's what your dad means by pulling together as a family."

Sophie suddenly felt cold, as if she'd stepped right into her icy drink. "Are you saying you think *God* did this?" she said. "Oh—sorry. Is that bad to ask?"

"It's not a bad question, but that puts us back at *why?* and *who?*" Dr. Peter scooted his glasses up with a nose-wrinkle. "Do *you* think God made this happen?"

"How could he? Everything he does is for good, right?"

"We can trust there's a good purpose behind everything. And he's definitely in the *what now?* Do you think he'll help you know what to do with all this?"

Sophie couldn't answer right away. Other words—not very nice words—were in her head, shouting at her. She wasn't sure even Dr. Peter would want to hear them.

He leaned on the table, searching Sophie's face with his eyes. "Don't hold back, Loodle."

She looked away from him.

"You need to get this out—"

"I don't see why God didn't stop that one evil chromosome from getting into my sister," she blurted out. "Since he didn't stop it, maybe he's not involved at all. Not even in the *what now?* "

Sophie put the back of her hand up to her mouth. She would have given up her video camera just to have those words back.

But Dr. Peter didn't look disappointed. "You're having doubts."

"Yes, but I'm not supposed to doubt God. I mean, he's—God!"

"Which is why he can handle it. If you didn't have doubts, Loodle, you wouldn't ask questions. And if you never asked questions, you'd never get answers."

Sophie pulled her hair under her nose again.

"I know it's scary," Dr. Peter said. "But go ahead and pour out all that stuff to Jesus tonight when you imagine him. Tell him you don't know what to do next."

"He won't get mad?"

"Nah. Of course, don't expect the whole answer right away. You know how that works."

Sophie nodded glumly. Dr. Peter pushed her drink toward her.

"Now, about that wild thing in your PE class?"

Sophie blinked until she remembered Brooke.

"I doubt your little Hope is ever going to act like that. I don't know for sure without actually meeting the girl—"

"Brooke," Sophie said.

"Brooke. But it sounds to me like she *might* have ADHD— attention deficit hyperactivity disorder."

"I've heard of that," Sophie said. "Lacie says she thinks Zeke has it sometimes when he can't sit still."

"Zeke doesn't, but if Brooke does, she can't focus, can't stay on task. She gets distracted easily. She really can't help the impulse to do things without thinking about them first," Dr. Peter said. "The point is, your little sister won't act like that because her brain is very different." His eyes twinkled behind his glasses. "She'll probably be just as wonderful as you are."

Although Sophie finished her cherry Coke and the rest of the day without crying again, she felt dreary when she climbed into bed that night. She wasn't sure Dr. Peter was right about this telling-God-your-doubts thing, but he'd never steered her wrong before. She closed her eyes and tried to imagine Jesus.

She couldn't see his eyes, kind or sad or any other way. It was as if there was a fog separating her from the look she depended on.

Are you there? she asked in silence. *I mean, I know you are — it's just that I really need to know — how am I supposed to be a good big sister if I'm so confused?*

It wasn't at all what she'd intended to pray, and she still wasn't sure she should have prayed it at all. But Dr. Peter was right about one thing: there were no answers right away.

By the time third period came around on Monday, Fiona had already told Darbie about Hope. But Kitty, Willoughby, and Maggie arrived in the locker room with a banner that read CONGRATULATIONS BIG SISTER SOPHIE and enough candy pacifiers for all the Corn Flakes. Sophie took one look and burst into tears.

There was a lot of whispering as Darbie and Fiona filled them in. And then there was a lot of Corn Flake hugging and promising to help Sophie with *anything.*

"Thanks," Sophie said as they walked into the gym together. "But there isn't anything anybody can do."

Willoughby's eyes grew round. "I never heard you say that before, Sophie."

"Don't ever say it again, either," Darbie said. "You're scaring the bejeebers out of me."

A whistle blasted, which scared the bejeebers out of *Sophie.*

"Everybody up in the bleachers!" Coach Yates yelled.

"Will you be okay, Sophie?" Darbie whispered to her as they found seats.

Sophie didn't have a chance to answer.

"Do you smell something, Cassie?" Julia said.

Sophie stifled a groan, and Fiona nudged her in the side. The three Corn Pops sat in the row in front of them, all filing their fingernails.

"Yes, I do smell it." Cassie let her already-close-together eyes narrow. "Do you smell it, Stewie?"

"Definitely," Anne-Stuart said, with a juicy sniff. "I can't place it, though."

"Is it garbage?" Cassie said.

"Nuh-uh," Anne-Stuart said. "That's pooh if I ever smelled it."

"You're both wrong," Julia said. "That is the stink of some-body that lives in a ..." She curled her lip. "Mobile home."

"Eww," Cassie said.

Tossing her silky hair back, Anne-Stuart gave the longest sniff in sinus history. "Where's it coming from?"

Julia paused in her manicure and pointed a silver file with the jeweled head of a cat on one end. In spite of herself, Sophie followed it with her gaze toward the red head in front of Julia, next row down.

"That's heinous," Fiona whispered into Sophie's ear. "Brooke has to be able to hear her."

At that moment, Brooke stood up and snuffled into the air like a bloodhound. Darbie grabbed Sophie's knee. Fiona put her hand over Willoughby's mouth before she could poodle-shriek.

"I smell it too," Brooke said. She turned to Julia. "Want me to find out who it is for ya?"

Julia cocked her head of dark-auburn hair to one side. "Would you? I'd like to know so I can—uh—"

"Help them out a little," Anne-Stuart finished for her.

Cassie had already collapsed into a heap of giggles.

Brooke charged down the bleachers, stopping only to lean over and nuzzle at people with her nose. The girls the Corn Flakes called the Wheaties, because they were fun and ath-letic, reared away from her. Colton sniffed back and pretended to pass out on Tod. Nathan turned purple. Before Brooke could start in on the student aide, Coach Yates blew her whistle and froze the whole gym.

"What in the *world* are you doing, Singletary?"

Brooke thrust a finger toward the Corn Pops. "She said she smelled somebody so I was just—"

"Just what?" Coach Yates said. "Giving everybody the sniff test?" She turned to Coach Nanini. "How about it, Coach? Why don't we all just choose up sides and smell armpits, huh?"

While the class erupted into hysteria, Sophie crossed her arms over her chest to keep the hard fingers of fear from squeezing her heart to death. No matter what Dr. Peter said, that could be Hope Celeste LaCroix down there someday, with even a teacher making fun of her. Coach Nanini bent his head low to talk to Brooke, but it didn't help Sophie. What if there was no Coach Virile for her sister? What if not one single person tried to help little Hope?

Coach Yates tooted the whistle again. "We'll review the volleyball rules for your written test tomorrow," she said. "I'm going to start on this end and drill you—"

That was the last thing Sophie heard Coach Yates say that period. She was too busy coming up with a plan. The minute Coach dismissed them, Sophie bolted for Brooke—who was perched on the bottom row of the bleachers, chewing on her fingernails.

"Hi," Sophie said as she sat beside her.

Brooke leaned over and tugged at Coach Nanini's sweatshirt. "Hey—Coach What's-Your-Name. Can I talk to her?"

Coach Nanini looked at Sophie and grinned. "Yes—she's the perfect person for you to talk to. Go change, and I'll see you back here after fourth period. We'll go together."

"Come on," Sophie said to Brooke. "I'll walk in with you."

Brooke looked Sophie over with green eyes that didn't stay any more still than the rest of her.

"We're on the same team," Brooke said.

"That's for sure," Cassie hissed as she sailed past.

Sophie caught sight of her Corn Flakes in the doorway, faces full of the question: *What are you doing, Sophie?*

I'm being decent to this poor kid, Sophie knew she would tell them later. *Because somebody has to.*

But when, for no apparent reason, Brooke pulled Sophie's glasses off and stuck them on her own face, Sophie wasn't quite sure why that somebody had to be her.

Four

Sophie had barely reached her locker when Brooke careened around the end of the row with her school clothes tucked under her arm.

"I'm changing here," she said as she threw her stuff on the bench.

"Sure," Sophie said.

"Won't they give you a locker?" Julia said from the other end of the row.

"She can change wherever she wants." Sophie patted the bench. "Here's a spot for you, Brooke."

Julia made a face and turned her back.

"Oh," Fiona said to Sophie, "I get it." Fiona gave a huff as if she were talking herself into something and looked at Brooke. "So — how come you just transferred into this class?"

"Where's my sock?" Brooke said, pawing through the pile she'd just dumped. "I can't find my sock."

"Maybe you dropped it on the way from your locker." Willoughby glanced at Sophie and added, "Want me to help you look?"

"I'll just borrow one." Brooke straightened up to face them. "Anybody got an extra sock?"

Sophie pulled out her toe socks, the ones with the turtles on the bottom. "You can borrow these. I don't need socks with my boots—"

"Sweet!" Brooke said and swept them out of Sophie's hand. She was feeding her toes into them before Sophie could finish her sentence.

Brooke still wasn't ready when Sophie left for fourth-period math class. Out in the hall, the Flakes were on her like Velcro.

"It's cool that you're being nice to her, Soph," Fiona said, "but you know I don't do nice as well as you do."

"She was digging through my bag," Willoughby said. "She said she lost her own brush."

"She looked at my hair all weird," Kitty said. She gave a nervous giggle. "I'm afraid she's gonna say something about it."

"I won't let her," Maggie said, words falling out like chunks of wood. "I won't be mean about it, but—"

"It's okay," Sophie said. "You guys don't have to be all friendly to her just because I am."

They all stopped at the end of the math hallway and looked at Sophie as if she'd grown an extra eye.

"Like we're really gonna let you do this by yourself," Fiona said.

"Hel-lo!" Willoughby said. "We're all Corn Flakes."

"Just don't expect me to be as patient as you are, Sophie." Darbie hooked her hair behind her ears. "When she gets to foostering and into everybody's things, I start to go mental. But if you just tell us what to do—"

"Hey—girl!" somebody yelled behind them. "Where's your fourth-period class?"

Brooke hurried toward them, her backpack half open with papers sticking out of it. One flew out and was immediately trampled by Brooke's own tennis shoe.

"I hope that wasn't important," Fiona said.

Brooke looked behind her and shrugged. "It's just my math homework. I didn't finish it anyway."

"Won't you get in trouble?" Maggie said.

Brooke shrugged again. Sophie noticed that her short neck disappeared when she did that. *She's sort of like a Raggedy Ann doll*, Sophie thought.

"You want me to zip your backpack up for you?" Willoughby said.

"Zipper's broken." Brooke looked at Sophie. "So — what's your name?"

"I'm Soph —"

"Dude!" Brooke stared toward the math room. "Is that your teacher?"

Sophie glanced at the very pointy Miss Imes, their math instructor, who was standing in the classroom doorway raising her arrowhead eyebrows at the students hurrying in.

"Yeah," Sophie said. "That's Miss —"

"What's *your* name?"

"Sophie!" the rest of the Corn Flakes said.

Brooke pulled her head back. "Dude," she said, "you don't gotta yell."

"That's it," Darbie muttered to Sophie as they hurried toward Miss Imes. "I'm going mental."

Although it wasn't good to lose focus in Miss Imes' class, Sophie couldn't concentrate that period. If she wasn't picturing Hope growing up and driving everybody "mental," she was imagining herself trying to have a conversation with Brooke, who obviously couldn't stay on one subject for more than half a second.

And then Sophie didn't *have* to imagine her, because Brooke was standing in the hall, outside the open door. She waved to Sophie with a grin that set all her freckles dancing.

"May I help you, young lady?" Miss Imes said.

"It's that weird chick," Colton said.

Miss Imes pointed a finger at him, even as she moved to the doorway. Sophie wanted to squirm right out of her skin.

Just don't let her tell Miss Imes she was waving to me, she prayed.

"I was just saying hi to somebody," Brooke said.

"Did your teacher give you a pass to come say hi to somebody?" Miss Imes's voice grew as pointy as her nose. "Or is there some other place you're supposed to be?"

Brooke bolted from the doorway. Miss Imes took off after her.

"Busted," Tod said and high-fived Colton.

Sophie looked at Fiona. Her bow of a mouth was drawn into a knot, and she shook her head. It was clearly an *I-hope-you-know-what-you're-doing* message.

The Corn Flakes discussed it at lunch, minus Darbie, who had a Round Table meeting.

"Okay," Fiona said. "Can we review the Corn Flake Code again?"

Maggie reached into her bag and, without even looking to see where it was, pulled out the Corn Flakes Treasure Book. Sophie knew she always kept the special purple notebook in exactly the same place. She guarded it like a CIA agent with a top secret document. After all, it held every one of the scripts for the eleven movies they'd made, plus the Corn Flake Code, and almost everything they'd ever said in a meeting that Maggie could write down in her slow, careful handwriting.

"You want me to read it out loud?" Maggie said.

"Not *loud* loud." Willoughby glanced over her shoulder.

Maggie read the code in a voice only slightly softer than her usual thuds. She looked up at the group.

Fiona poked her fork into a chicken tender. "It doesn't say we have to let the people we help get *us* in trouble."

"Who's in trouble?" Sophie said.

Fiona pointed the fork at her. "*You* would have been if Miss Imes had known who Brooke was out there waving to."

"That wasn't Sophie's fault." Kitty's giggle was nervous again.

"It doesn't matter with Miss Imes," Fiona said.

Maggie nodded solemnly. "Besides, if somebody gets in trouble, Sophie always gets in it with them."

"You in trouble, Soph?" Jimmy appeared and straddled the chair next to Sophie. Vincent and Nathan stood behind him.

"Not yet," Fiona said. "But if that Brooke child stays around, it's only a matter of time."

"We're being nice to her, though," Willoughby said pointedly.

"Don't look at *me*," Nathan said. "I'm not gonna be mean to her."

Sophie figured he wouldn't even look at her if he could help it. His face was already the color of a radish, and Brooke wasn't even there.

"We think she has issues," Maggie said.

"She's probably ADD," Vincent said. "Maybe ADHD. Or OCD."

"*What* are you talking about?" Willoughby said.

But Sophie nodded. Dr. Peter had said Brooke might have ADHD. Vincent probably read about it on the Internet.

Jimmy did a drum roll on the back of the chair. "So—we came to talk about a movie. Miss Imes asked me if we had anything going. Whatcha got, Soph?"

"Can we please *not* do a movie about ABCD or whatever it is?" Willoughby said.

"That could actually be cool," Vincent said, his voice cracking on the *cool*.

"No," Fiona said, "it would be heinous. I personally don't want to play the part of somebody that climbs up a volleyball pole in the middle of roll check."

Suddenly everybody looked at Sophie.

"*What?*" she said. Her own pip-squeaky voice went up almost as far as Vincent's.

"We know you, Soph," Fiona said. "So let's agree: no movie about being hyperactive, starring Brooke Singletary."

There was much holding of breath until Sophie nodded. "Okay," she said. "We can be nice to her and not put her down, but we don't have to include her in our next movie."

"That's a relief," Kitty said.

But Sophie didn't feel relieved. She felt ... well ... *itchy*.

"At least Darbie won't go mental now," Fiona said as they walked toward fifth-period science.

"I think she already has." Sophie pointed at Darbie, who was charging toward them. "Are you okay?" Sophie said when Darbie screeched to a halt in front of them.

"Thanks to *you*, Sophie," she said, "no, I am *not!*"

She stormed into the science room.

"What did I do now?" Sophie said.

"I'm afraid to ask," Fiona said.

But Sophie did ask, as soon as she could get to her desk and write a note to Darbie, which Fiona delivered to her while the smiling—and sometimes clueless—Mr. Stires took attendance. He was their science teacher and Film Club adviser. Everything about him was cheerful, including his gray toothbrush-shaped mustache.

Darbie, on the other hand, looked about as cheerful as the day after Christmas vacation. She flashed her dark eyes across Sophie's note, snatched up her pen, and scribbled on the paper with such force that Sophie was sure she'd engrave the letters into the desktop.

"We have a special lab tomorrow," Mr. Stires said. "You're going to dissect a lizard."

"Sick," Julia said.

While Mr. Stires assured Julia that the lizard would be freeze-dried, Darbie's note made its way to Sophie's desk.

Thank you VERY much, Sophie, for telling Coach Nanini that Brooke needed to go to Round Table. GUESS who he assigned her to. ME! I will absolutely go mad—I mean it. I said I would be nice—I didn't say I could fix her!

"I won't touch something dead, Mr. Stires," Julia said.

"I won't either," Anne-Stuart said. "It's against my civil rights."

"Try again," Vincent said. "That's not covered in the Constitution."

That conversation could go on for days, Sophie knew. She wrote back to Darbie.

Who guessed they'd assign her to you? But you'll be perfect.

Sophie pulled up a picture in her mind of B. J. Schneider, a former Corn Pop her "friends" had dumped on so badly, she'd transferred to a private school. Darbie had helped her—

Remember B.J.? Sophie added to the note.

Vincent was still on the Fourth Amendment. Fiona slipped the note to Darbie, who answered at the speed of light.

B.J. was completely different. In the first place, she didn't start chumming up to us like THIS girl. And B.J. didn't act retarded. I'm telling you, Sophie, Brooke is not the full schilling.

Sophie stared at the note until her eyes blurred with tears, but she could still see the word *retarded*. And she could see baby Hope in her mind. The fear fingers squeezed Sophie until she had to write—

She's mentally challenged—not retarded. And I'll help you—I AM the consultant—and we'll be so fabulous to her that she'll be cured.

"Hurry up, Soph," Fiona whispered. "Mr. Stires is about to give the assignment."

Sophie shoved the note across the desk. It came back just as Mr. Stires turned to write on the board.

I'm sorry I said retarded, Darbie had written, *but just so you know, after the way she acted at Round Table, I don't even want to be around her anymore.*

"Okay," Mr. Stires said, happily rubbing his hands together. "Be sure to answer all the questions so you'll be ready for your lizard tomorrow."

Dr. Devon Downing closed her eyes. She was weary to her bones, but she couldn't stop working. Maybe the lizard's brain would show her what she needed in order to find the cure for—for ADHD. Surely THAT wasn't in the chromosomes, like that other poor baby's problem. Dr. Devon opened her eyes and went straight to her text. Before she even touched the specimen, she would find that out—

"Good job, Sophie," Mr. Stires said. "Class, I want everybody working like Sophie's doing."

Sophie heard Fiona clear her throat. A cough had always been the signal for Sophie to pay attention and not drift off into Sophie World. Okay—she would read the assignment now, but when she got home, she was going to email Vincent.

Vincent sent her a list of what looked like a bajillion websites for ADHD, and most of the articles were hard to understand. Sophie had to keep stopping to look up words like *hyperactivity, impulsivity,* and *inattention.* She finally figured out that kids with ADHD were just like Dr. Peter described—they had trouble paying attention, got distracted, couldn't seem to follow directions, forgot information, and lost things. Kids with ADHD were just like Brooke.

What a devastating condition, Dr. Devon Downing thought. It's a wonder the poor child can even function in school.

Putting her luscious hair up into a bun and securing it with a pencil, she burrowed further into the articles, like the amazing medical researcher she was.

There was no cure for ADHD, the Internet told Sophie, but symptoms could be controlled if the child had lots of structure and routine, was rewarded for self-control, and had a very healthy diet. There was some disagreement, it seemed, over whether too much sugar made ADHD worse, but Sophie decided it couldn't hurt for Brooke to cut back.

She will be my test case, Dr. Devon wrote in her notebook. A plan was forming in her scientific brain. Perhaps there was no cure now, but there had to be a cure for everything. Even Down syndrome. But she shook that off. One brain issue at a time. And meanwhile, there was much she could do for Raggedy Ann-D-H-D. She would begin tomorrow.

Five

"Just give it a try for one day," Sophie said to Darbie on the way into the gym for PE the next morning.

"What am I supposed to do?" Darbie said. Her eyes were narrowed so far down, they looked like hyphens.

"I'll start by telling her the rules for taking a test in Coach Yates' class. If she follows them, we'll reward her."

"With what?" Fiona said on the other side of Sophie. "I, like, forgot my American Express card."

"We're supposed to give her money?" Kitty spiraled up into a whine.

"No," Sophie said. "Praise."

"Oh," Willoughby said. "Like, 'Good job,' 'All right, Brooke.' That kinda thing?"

"Yeah, just be her cheerleader," Sophie said.

Darbie sliced Sophie with a glance. "How about, 'Thank you for not crawling under me during the test and getting marker all over my leg. Excellent.'"

"She's not going to do that—is she?" Kitty said.

"She did it yesterday during Round Table." Darbie stopped inside the gym doorway, and the Corn Flakes huddled around her. "Coach Nanini and Mrs. Clayton had a bunch of colored markers so we could write out a plan for Brooke. She snapped them together into a tower until they broke apart and rolled under the table." Darbie rolled her eyes. "She dove down to get them and crawled right under my legs—"

"Nuh-uh," Kitty said.

"Yes. And somehow she got purple all over my calf." Darbie pulled up her pant leg to reveal a faded lavender blotch on her skin. "I was in the tub for an hour last night, and I still couldn't rub it off."

Willoughby out-poodled herself. Kitty giggled so hard, she collapsed into Maggie.

"I don't see what's so funny about it," Darbie said. She looked at Sophie, eyes like a pair of darts. "I'll give it one more day, and if she doesn't improve, I'm resigning from Round Table."

Coach Yates blew her whistle, so there was no time to protest. Sophie just prayed that her plan would work and climbed up the bleachers.

The average person does not understand how long these studies take, Dr. Devon reminded herself as she took her place in the great scientific arena. I must be patient and lead the way.

Sophie positioned herself behind Brooke and whispered the test rules to her while Coach Yates checked the roll.

"No talking—like, don't say a single word. Keep your eyes on your own paper. And don't move from your seat. Got it?"

"Yeah," Brooke said. "You got a pencil I could borrow?"

She is displaying all the symptoms, Dr. Devon Downing thought. I must record everything.

In the Treasure Book, Sophie thought. Since Maggie was already in test mode, she decided to fill her in later.

Meanwhile, there was a lot for her to remember about Brooke's behavior. The minute Coach Yates passed out the test papers, Brooke dropped the pencil Sophie had just given her under the bleachers and attempted to slip below to retrieve it. Coach Yates blew her whistle, making everybody in the silent gymnasium jump, and told Brooke to move down to the front row.

Two minutes later Brooke announced mondo-loudly that her pencil lead had broken.

Five minutes after that, Coach Yates caught her nudging Gill, one of the Wheaties.

"I just wanted to borrow an eraser," Brooke said.

Just as Coach Yates yelled out that time was up, *Brooke* yelled out that she'd erased a hole in her paper, and she needed a new one.

"Good job, Brooke," Darbie muttered to Sophie as they made their way down the bleachers. "You made it through the whole test without writing on anybody."

"Thanks," Brooke said—because she was suddenly right there with them, bouncing an eraser from one palm to the other. "I'm gonna eat lunch with you guys today."

Darbie's glare went right through Sophie's skin as Brooke bolted off to the locker room.

"I've been thinking about this film thing." Vincent came up behind Sophie and Darbie. He had Jimmy with him, and Fiona joined them.

Vincent's eyes had an idea gleam. "Why *don't* we do a film about ADHD?"

"I'd rather be shot," Darbie said.

"No, seriously. Mr. Stires wants us to do another project, and we could get extra credit in his class since we're studying the brain."

"I don't need extra credit," Fiona said.

Sophie sneaked a glance at Darbie. She could almost see steam coming out of her ears. But something about the idea did seem right—

"You have a new character." Jimmy's blue eyes sparkled at Sophie. "I've seen you thinking about her."

"Dr. Devon Downing," Sophie said.

Darbie groaned.

"She's looking for a cure for ADHD."

"And she needs a subject to study." Vincent wiggled his eyebrows.

"Oh," Fiona said. "Like Project Brooke."

"Only we can't tell her she's a project," Sophie said.

"She'll just be another character in the film," Jimmy said.

Darbie jammed her hair behind her ears so hard, Sophie was sure she would rip it out. "That's a flick I won't be participating in."

"Wait, Darb," Fiona said. "This could be your solution to helping Brooke for Round Table."

"I'm your consultant," Sophie said.

Darbie's eyes narrowed down to points. "Why do I feel like I don't have any choice?"

Sophie grinned. "I'll get my camera from Mr. Stires' room right after fourth period."

Everything at home was upside down over the next several days. Sophie was glad she had the film to concentrate on. Mama and Hope were still in the hospital, which meant Daddy was gone almost every evening to be with them, and Lacie was in charge. And *that* meant they ate macaroni and cheese (unless the other Corn Flakes' parents sent over casseroles) and rescued Zeke from every place Spider-Man could get to, including the rafters in the attic. Boppa finally rescued Sophie and Lacie and kept Zeke at his house until bedtime.

So Sophie was glad to become Dr. Devon Downing. She observed Brooke and trained the Corn Flakes to work with her during lunch and sometimes after school, when Brooke didn't have "something else to do."

"Like drive somebody else mental," Darbie muttered more than once.

On those days, with Brooke not there, they shot the scenes of Dr. Devon Downing and her able assistant, Test Tube Tess, played by Fiona. Darbie and Vincent filmed, Jimmy set up the shots, and Nathan stood around turning red.

Since there wasn't much makeup involved in the movie, which Willoughby usually handled, she concentrated on the praise-Brooke department. During PE, she'd say, "Go, Brooke—you almost hit it that time!" or "Yay—good job not stepping on Maggie!" Jimmy restaged that later for filming.

Fiona showed Brooke how to line up her clothes on the bench in the locker room so she wouldn't lose them. She rolled her eyes nearly up into her head when Brooke still ended up with somebody else's bra. That part Darbie didn't catch on film.

Maggie complained that there were no special costumes to make, but she quickly got the hang of reciting all the table rules for Brooke every day when they sat down to lunch in the cafeteria. No interrupting people. No talking with your mouth full. (Kitty's mother wanted to know why she was getting so much food on her clothes all of a sudden.) No borrowing lunch money. And no jumping up from the table every other minute. Footage of Maggie talking woodenly into the camera wasn't the best they'd ever taken, but Sophie said it had to be there.

Kitty became the best at rewarding Brooke with a small handful of Cheerios when she got something right. It seemed that Brooke would eat just about anything, including items from Darbie's lunch, when she wasn't looking.

"*You* weren't eating it," Brooke said when Darbie demanded to know where her brownie had disappeared to.

"I was *going* to," Darbie said, and then she gritted her teeth at Sophie. That was some of their best footage.

They got together without Brooke Thursday morning before school in Mr. Stires' room to check their progress on the film editor.

"This is some of our best stuff," Vincent said.

"It looks so real," Kitty said.

Maggie grunted. "It *is* real."

"Too bad it isn't working." Darbie's eyes were pointy. "As long as we're blathering at her," she said, "she does what she's supposed to. But the minute we look the other way, she starts foostering about again."

Now everybody looked at Sophie, and she felt prickly — the way she did when she had to take Lacie's turn with Zeke or the dishes. Why did she have to be responsible for everything on the planet?

"What does everybody else think?" Sophie said.

"What difference does it make?" Fiona said. "When it comes to doing the right thing, you always know."

"Do you think it would be right for us to just suddenly dump her?" Sophie said.

"Do you?" Willoughby said.

"No." Sophie knew her voice sounded prickly.

Vincent rubbed his hands together. "Then let's get back to work. Project Brooke could be our best production yet."

Sophie didn't say that she wished they'd stop calling Brooke a project. Or that she wished they wouldn't be so ready to give up all the time.

Or that she needed somebody *else* to come up with some answers for a change.

She just packed her camera into its bag and returned it to the shelf in Mr. Stires' storage room. Everything felt like a wool sweater itching her. She was afraid if she opened her mouth, she would scratch somebody.

But then, on Thursday, it looked like maybe Brooke was making progress. At the lunch table, almost before Vincent could get the camera rolling, Brooke sat down, pulled a sandwich out of a brown bag, and chewed an entire bite before she started talking.

176

"Good job!" Willoughby said.

Kitty dug into the huge box of Cheerios she'd gotten at Sam's Club. "You get a reward for remembering your lunch and not talking while you're chewing."

"All right!" Willoughby said.

"A reward?" Julia said.

Sophie looked up to see Julia and the Corn Pops standing at the end of the table with their trays. Sophie shook her head at Vincent, but he just pointed the camera at them.

"What is she, a puppy in training?" Cassie said.

"No," Brooke informed her. "I'm getting rewarded for not being rude."

Now would be a good time to hush up, Brooke, Sophie thought.

"Cheerios?" Anne-Stuart snuffled, taking away Sophie's appetite for cereal or anything else. "I'd hold out for M&Ms if I were you, Brooke."

Brooke snapped her head toward Kitty. "Yeah. How come I don't get candy?"

"Because sugar makes you even more—" Darbie started to say.

"Sugar isn't good for anybody," Sophie said.

"It's fine for me," Anne-Stuart said. She looked down at her twiglike body. "I never gain an ounce."

"Okay, I'm bored with this conversation," Julia said. With a toss of her thick hair, she whisked the Corn Pops away.

"I need something to drink," Brooke said.

She pushed her chair back so hard it banged into the kid behind her.

Sophie groaned. It was Tod Ravelli.

"Hey, step off, would ya?" Tod said. His spiked hair seemed to poke up taller as he stood his otherwise short self up. "That's like the eighth time you've touched me, chick." He put his face closer to hers. "I don't like to be touched."

Brooke looked at him for no longer than a millisecond before she gave him a poke in the chest with her finger.

"Hey, Brooke!" Sophie sang out as she shoved back her own chair. "Let's go get you a drink."

"He's a punk," Brooke said for all to hear.

Sophie put her hand in front of the camera and whispered, "Turn that off," before she led Brooke toward the drink counter. Brooke looked back over her shoulder.

"What's Tod doing?" Sophie said.

"Talking to that kid with the stick-out ears. They're both punks. I don't like punks." Brooke moved closer to Sophie as they walked—and didn't seem to notice that she pulled Sophie's shoe half off with the side of her foot. "But you," she said. "You I like."

"Oh," Sophie said. "Thanks."

But as Brooke filled a cup to overflowing with milk, Sophie wondered whether it was a good thing that Brooke liked her. After all, that wasn't the point of making this film with her. Was it?

"When do I get to see myself in the movie?" Brooke turned to Sophie and slopped milk over her hand and onto the floor. Sophie stepped back just in time to keep her tennis shoes from being drenched.

"Um, maybe after school—soon," Sophie said.

"Can't be Monday or Wednesday. I think I have to go to—" Brooke stopped and shook back her hair, splashing more of the contents of her cup. "Whatever. Anyway, I like movies. Can me and you go to one—like, a real one?"

Sophie was more than grateful when the bell rang. That way she didn't have to answer Brooke's question, or her own. What was she supposed to do if this hard-to-be-around girl wanted to be her new best friend?

All the questions made her want to scratch an itch she couldn't reach. That was not the way Dr. Devon Downing would handle it, she thought as she got ready for the lizard lab in fifth-period science.

A dedicated medical researcher such as myself does not have time to concern herself with these personal matters, Dr. Devon thought as she tucked her notebook neatly and professionally under her arm and headed for the laboratory. Today, for the first time, she was going to look into the brain of a lizard, and if things went as she hoped, she would find the final clue in her search for a cure. Then she would no longer have to worry about Raggedy Ann-D-H-D.

Dr. Downing's lab assistant, the devoted Test Tube Tess, uncovered the deceased lizard. It lay with its feet pinned down, ready to be opened up for medical science.

"We're supposed to cut from the neck down," Tess said.

But Dr. Downing placed the tip of her scalpel on the lizard's head and deftly spit it open. Although Test Tube Tess coughed loudly, there was no blood, nothing at all disgusting. Freeze-drying had taken all the grossness out of the procedure. Even if it had been a nasty job, Dr. Downing would have pressed on as she did now, peering at the reptile's tiny brain. The clue was in there; she could sense it. But it was far too difficult to see. She would have to extract —

Dr. Devon Downing skillfully pinched the brain with her tweezers and tugged. It was stubborn, so she pulled again, this time with more force. The tiny organ broke free, and Dr. Downing's arm flew back. There was a shocked silence, and then a cry —

"What is that?" Julia screamed.

"Where?" Anne-Stuart said.

"In my hair! It came flying at me! What is it?"

Vincent examined the top of Julia's tresses. "Looks like lizard brains to me."

Julia balled her hands into fists and screamed until Sophie was sure the noise would shear everyone's scalps off. "Get it out, Anne-Stuart!"

"I'm not touching it!"

"Get it out!"

"I'll get it out," Vincent said.

"Don't touch me!" Julia said.

Fiona looked slyly at Sophie from behind her hanging hunk of hair. "I wish we'd gotten that on film," she whispered.

That night, as soon as Sophie closed her eyes to imagine Jesus, Brooke was there instead.

That was the way it had been for a lot of nights now. Sophie tried to see her image of Jesus' kind eyes so she could talk to him and tell him how hard things were. But it was always something else she saw—like the little tongue her baby sister couldn't control, or the shenanigans (as Darbie called them) that Brooke couldn't control. Not being able to "see" Jesus the way she had before made it harder and harder to believe he was listening when she told him how everything was changing, and how scary it was.

She tried not to think her itchiest thought: that maybe he wasn't even there right now.

Six

✽ ⌂ ✺

I't's one of God's miracles," Mama said that next Saturday morning. "She's just a little more than two weeks old. Even with all the problems they thought she had when she was born, she's home with us, healthy."

Sophie looked at the rest of the family, gathered in the family room around Lacie, who was holding Hope. She hadn't let go of the baby since Mama walked in the door with her from the hospital. Zeke was dangling a Spider-Man figure in the baby's face like he expected her to grab it and say, "Cool!"

Did no one else see that Mama didn't get it? Sophie thought. Hope wasn't healthy. She had something *huge* wrong with her.

"Okay, so here's the game plan," Daddy said. He clapped his hands together as if they were all about to take the field. "Everybody's going to want to hold the baby all the time, and that's good because we all love her." He looked straight at Lacie. "But she has to rest in her crib sometimes, where she can stretch out."

Lacie wrinkled her nose at Daddy and gazed down at Hope as if she were *her* baby. *Maybe nobody'll notice that I'm not holding her*, Sophie thought.

"When can she play?" Zeke frowned at Hope. "You sure sleep a lot."

"I tell you what," Mama said. "It's time for a bottle, so why don't we let Sophie feed her, since she hasn't had a chance yet."

"Sorry, Lace," Daddy said. "You're going to have to hand her over to your sister."

Sophie felt her face freeze. *I'm not ready for this!* she wanted to tell him and Lacie and anyone who would listen.

But everybody was scrambling around, putting pillows in place for Sophie to prop her arm on and warming a bottle in the microwave. Mama rewrapped Hope in her blanket so she looked like a little burrito with a tiny golden head. Before Sophie could escape into Dr. Devon Downing or anyplace else, she was on the couch, arms positioned like Lacie showed her.

"Be careful of her head," Lacie said. "You have to support it because she's not strong enough to hold it up by herself yet."

"Lacie," Daddy said from behind the couch, "why don't you go see what your brother is doing? We've got it handled."

The first thing Sophie noticed when Lacie placed Hope in her arms was how warm the baby was. The second thing was that she immediately wiggled and drew her face into a knot.

"What's going on?" Sophie could barely hear herself, her voice was squeaking up so high.

"She's hungry," Mama said. "Personally, I think she can smell formula from a mile away. Here you go."

She handed Sophie a warm plastic bottle. Hope made a sound like a baby bird and opened her tiny mouth so wide it seemed to fill her whole face. Her tongue pointed at Sophie.

"Just put the nipple in," Mama said, voice soft. "She'll grab onto it."

Sophie aimed the nipple for Hope's mouth, but it wasn't as easy to get in as Mama said. Her tongue was in the way.

"Just wiggle it around a little," Mama said. "Down babies sometimes have trouble with those tongues—keep trying."

Sophie tried pointing the nipple at an angle, but Hope's tongue was still right there. She scrunched up her face and gave an angry squawk.

"Hang in there, Little Rookie," Daddy said. "Sophie's working on it."

Sophie made another attempt and got the nipple in, but Hope spit it back out.

"Maybe she wants you to feed her," Sophie said to Mama, holding out the bottle.

"You'll be fine," Mama said. "I had trouble the first time too. Just press down a little on her tongue—there you go!"

The bottle slid in, and Hope sucked at it.

"Look at her eat," Daddy said as he leaned over the back of the couch. "That's my rookie."

"Now you can both just relax and enjoy," Mama said.

A shout erupted from the kitchen, followed by Lacie shouting back, "Spider-Man does *not* eat bugs, so get that nasty thing out of your cereal!"

"I'm on it," Daddy said and headed for the kitchen.

"You're doing great, Soph." Mama put her arm across the back of the couch. "She's very content right now."

Sophie looked down at her little sister, who was staring straight ahead as she drank. Her eyes were still a murky color, and Sophie couldn't tell if she was really seeing anything. Could a baby with Down syndrome see like everybody else? What if the whole world looked different to her? Was that one reason she'd be—mentally challenged?

Without meaning to, Sophie's arms tightened. Baby Hope stopped sucking on her bottle and thrust out her tongue. With it came a stream of white stuff that splattered all over the blanket.

"She's throwing up!" Sophie said.

"That's just a little dribble," Mama said. "Just tilt her up a little bit—"

"No, you take her, okay? I'm doing it wrong."

"Sophie, honey—"

"Here!" Sophie pushed the upchucked-on bundle of a baby into her mother's arms.

"I'll go get a washcloth," Sophie said.

"You don't need to. I have a wipe right here—"

Sophie ignored her mom and bolted for her room.

Sophie decided it was the longest weekend she'd ever lived. She spent a lot of it in her room, pretending to do homework, but mostly imagining Dr. Devon Downing so she wouldn't have to think about her baby sister.

But even that didn't work entirely. There was a constant hubbub of Hope wailing and Mama showing Lacie how to change diapers and Daddy telling Zeke what toys he could and could not put in the crib with the baby.

"She needs stuff to play with," Zeke said at least a hundred times.

And every time, Sophie thought, *Will she ever really hold things and play?*

She and the Corn Flakes had dreamed of teaching her little sister the joys of imagination, of becoming whatever she wanted to be. Thinking it might never happen made the fingers of fear curl around Sophie's heart tighter than ever.

By Monday, Sophie could think of only one thing to do to keep the fear away, and that was to concentrate on something else: Project Brooke. First, Sophie had to figure out what to do about Brooke wanting to be attached at the hip. Sophie just wasn't ready for that. Besides, even though they were almost finished filming, Brooke still hadn't shown as much improvement as Sophie needed to see. They needed more time.

"Maybe we should get some footage of her in some of her classes," Sophie said to the Corn Flakes on the way to third period.

"I never even see her in the halls," Willoughby said.

They all agreed that was strange, since Willoughby could hardly walk two steps without somebody saying hi to her.

Dr. Devon Downing made a mental note to get into the database and find Raggedy Ann-D-H-D's schedule. She felt a bit uneasy, but she chased that away. A medical researcher had to do whatever it took to gather information. It was for the good of all children with mental defects.

"There she is, right over there," Maggie said, pointing to the locker room door where Brooke was swinging, hands gripping the doorknobs and knees clamped.

"We should get some film of that." Kitty giggled.

"We have enough pictures of her shenanigans," Darbie said. "We need some of her improving."

Sophie sighed and headed for the door. When Brooke looked up, every freckle on her face seemed to darken.

"Hi," Sophie said.

Brooke watched as if she expected Sophie to pick her pocket. "What?" she said finally. "You're looking at me weird."

Actually, Sophie thought, *you're the one who's looking at me weird.* The suspicion in Brooke's eyes made her uneasy. "Um," she said, "want to do some more work on our movie with us?"

"You already took like twenty hours of me eating lunch."

Sophie blinked. *Okay,* she thought, *what happened to Brooke sticking on me like a shadow?*

"What if we filmed you in one of your classes?" Sophie said. "Do you have a teacher that's cool? We could ask her if we could do some shots of you at your desk—"

"No!" Brooke let go of the door handles and staggered backward. "I hate my teachers!"

She stumbled into the locker room and let the door close in Sophie's face.

"That went well," Fiona said in a dry voice.

But Sophie nodded. "That's like what I read about ADHD. Kids who have it don't do well in school because they can't pay attention, so they hate it."

"Don't even think about us helping her with her homework, Sophie," Darbie said. "Or I know I'll eat the head off her for sure."

"Okay, forget that," Sophie said. "We'll think of something else."

"*You* will," Willoughby said.

But Sophie didn't. When they got to the gym, Brooke was sitting on the floor, surrounded by Corn Pops.

"*That* can't be good," Fiona muttered to Sophie.

"I bet they're making fun of her," Kitty said.

Maggie shook her head. "Doesn't look like it to me."

It didn't to Sophie, either. Brooke was chattering nonstop, as usual, while Julia appeared to be giving her a manicure and Anne-Stuart coaxed her strings of red hair into a French braid.

"I *know* the Corn Pops." Willoughby twisted one of her own curls around her finger. "They wouldn't be nice to Brooke if they didn't want something from her."

Fiona raised an eyebrow. "No offense, but what does Brooke have that they would possibly want?"

"I don't know," Sophie said, "but we should find out. She *is* our project."

Darbie groaned. "I was afraid you'd say that."

Coach Yates blasted away on the whistle, and the Corn Flakes hurried to their line. Brooke passed them on the way to her place, but she didn't look at Sophie or any of them.

"She has something stuffed under her shirt," Maggie said. She demonstrated, pulling her own shirt out at the waist.

Sophie glanced back at Brooke, and her gaze snagged on Julia. Her eyes were gleaming with that hard kind of mirth Sophie knew was trouble. Whenever a Corn Pop thought something was funny, it was usually at somebody else's expense.

As soon as roll was taken, the Corn Flakes swarmed to their volleyball court and took the Lucky Charms aside.

"We're trying to find out what Brooke's got under her shirt," Sophie whispered.

Nathan's face went straight to red.

"No, silly." Willoughby poked him. "She's got something stuffed into the waistband of her track pants."

"Something she's not supposed to have," Maggie said.

"At least that's what we think," Darbie put in.

Fiona rolled her eyes. "If she got it from the Corn Pops, it's definitely contraband."

"What's that?" Kitty said, eyes wide.

"Something she's not supposed to have," Fiona said.

"Here she comes," Jimmy whispered. "What do you want us to do?"

"I'm not pulling something out of her shirt," Nathan said.

"Get her to jump up and down a lot," Sophie said. "Until it falls out."

"Done," Jimmy said.

It wasn't hard. Although Brooke was unnaturally quiet at first and volunteered to stand out and rotate in, they weren't two volleys into a game with the Wheaties' team before she was bouncing like the ball itself and yelling, "That was out! That was *so* out!"

"How about getting it for us?" Vincent said. "It went over there."

Brooke bounded after the ball, and Sophie watched the lumpy-looking bulge under her T-shirt shift to the side.

"I hope it doesn't go down into her pants instead of out." Willoughby gave the expected shriek.

"Hey!" Brooke yelled. "Somebody, catch!"

She heaved the ball so hard she fell after it, right on her tummy.

"My candy!" she cried. "Aw, man!"

Brooke rolled over and yanked a plastic bag from under her shirt. Five different kinds of mini candy bars scattered over the gym floor.

"Dude!" Colton Messik shouted from the next court over. "It's rainin' chocolate!"

Fifty pairs of tennis shoes squealed as Coach Yates blew her whistle.

"Singletary! What are you doing with food in class?"

Sophie only had to look at Julia, Cassie, and Anne-Stuart to know. All three of their glossy upper lips were curled like Fruit Roll-Ups.

"I wonder how much of that she already ate," Maggie said.

If the theory that sugar might make ADHD behavior worse was true, Sophie figured Brooke had downed about a pound. She was crawling around on the floor like a crab, snatching up miniature Snickers and Three Musketeers and shoving them back into the bag.

"I'll relieve you of those, Red," Coach Nanini said as he stood over her.

Darbie looked at Sophie. "I'm sorry, but I wish he would relieve *me* of *her*."

Dr. Devon Downing sighed. It was difficult to make progress when other factors were constantly entering in. But she went on, because the work of a gifted medical researcher could not be abandoned. She had to find a cure, before Raggedy Ann-D-H-D was lost to the—

"Corn Pop Alert," Fiona said.

Sophie looked up in time to see Brooke dallying at the edge of the court where the Pops and Loops were playing. Anne-Stuart whispered something in her ear, which kept Brooke from seeing the ball flying at her until it smacked her in the head.

"Hey!" Brooke yelled at Tod, who was innocently whistling into the air. "I'll kick your—"

"Brooke!" the Corn Flakes shouted in unison.

"It's your serve," Jimmy said.

Brooke gave Tod one last killing look before she bounded back to them.

"Cheated death again," Vincent muttered.

Brooke didn't show up at the Corn Flakes' table at the beginning of lunch, and Darbie gave a happy sigh. "I like having a moment of peace," she said as Sophie handed her the camera bag.

"The moment's over," Willoughby said. "Here she comes. You have those Cheerios ready, Kitty?"

But Brooke stopped at the end of the table and didn't put her tray down.

"I'm sitting with Julia and them," she said.

Everybody looked at Sophie.

"How come?" Sophie said.

"Because Julia's gonna finish doing my nails."

"You hardly have any nails," Maggie said.

"Ma-ags," Willoughby said out the corner of her mouth.

"She's gonna give me fake ones," Brooke said. "She has this really cool file thing—her mom bought it for her at the nail shop—"

"The one with the cat on it?" Kitty said. "That *is* cool."

Nice work, Kitty, Sophie thought.

Brooke nodded, sending her pizza slice dangerously close to the edge of the tray. "She said it cost fifty bucks."

"That's a bit of a horse's hoof, I think," Darbie said.

"Huh?" Brooke said.

"That means Julia's exaggerating," Fiona said. "No nail file costs—"

Fiona was cut off when Brooke's body suddenly lurched forward and her plate crashed to the table. The pizza slice landed pepperoni-down in Sophie's lap, and the contents of a glass of chocolate milk splashed up in Brooke's face. Brooke whirled around to find Tod Ravelli standing behind her, smirking.

"Sorry." His mouth was as unrepentant as anything Sophie had ever seen. "My bad. But you shouldn't be blockin' the aisle like that."

"You did it on purpose!" Brooke said.

Before Sophie could even agree, Brooke grabbed the now-empty tray and brought it down on top of Tod's head.

The cafeteria came to life with shouts of "Fight! Fight!"

Maggie and Darbie pulled Brooke by both arms, and Willoughby jumped on her back. Jimmy stood behind them, hands out like a baseball catcher. Vincent fumbled with the camera.

"Let me at 'im!" Brooke screamed.

"Don't do it!" Sophie tried to shout. But her pip-squeak of a voice was lost in Kitty's panicked cries, Fiona's attempt to talk

Brooke down, and the roar of the entire lunch room urging Brooke and Tod to go at it.

Only Coach Nanini could break up something like that, and he did. Then Mr. Bentley, the principal, hauled the kicking, screaming Brooke out. Mr. DiLoretto, the art teacher, dragged Tod in the direction of the nurse's office. Coach Nanini stood there, shaking his big head.

"Tod ran into her on purpose, Coach," Willoughby said. "We saw him."

"I didn't get it on film, though," Vincent said. "I was too late."

"That's okay." Sophie didn't like the weary sag of Coach Virile's eyebrows. "Red chose to take the matter into her own hands."

"Literally," Fiona said.

Coach gave a grim nod. "There are consequences for that."

"She's gonna get suspended," Maggie said when he was gone.

Darbie looked straight at Sophie. "I told you I didn't think our little project was working."

"What do we do now, Sophie?" Kitty said. She pointed to the cereal box on the table. "I have all these Cheerios."

Sophie felt irritated prickles go up her neck. "I don't know," she said as the bell rang.

"Maybe you'll figure something out by after school." Willoughby nodded until her curls bounced.

Sophie thought she might go "mental" instead from the nonstop itching inside her.

They had barely gathered at their lockers at the end of sixth period when Kitty said, "She's coming!" and ducked behind Maggie.

Brooke marched down the row of lockers, French braid half undone, waving a yellow slip of paper.

"I told you," Maggie said. "She got—"

"I'm suspended for three days!"

Brooke stomped up to Sophie and brought her foot down hard on Sophie's toe. Sophie choked back a yelp.

"Three days!" Brooke said. "And it's *your* fault!" She stormed off, still waving the suspension slip.

"That was just—violent!" Willoughby said.

Sophie sank to the floor and hugged her foot. "It's just because she's frustrated. I read that—"

"I don't care what she is." Fiona squatted beside Sophie. "I personally don't want to be around when she decides to break a tray over one of *our* heads."

"We have enough film to make our movie for class, don't we?" Darbie said.

Maggie consulted the Treasure Book and nodded. Willoughby and Kitty looked down at Sophie.

"Is it settled then?" Fiona put her hand on Sophie's arm. "Is Project Brooke over?"

No! Sophie wanted to shout at them. *I can't give up!*

But she didn't say anything at all.

Seven

The next day, Sophie was sure the rest of the Corn Flakes had taken her silence as a yes. And a yes, she quickly figured out, made everybody happier.

Kitty didn't nervous-giggle as much. Willoughby gave fewer poodle-yips. Darbie declared that she hadn't wanted to call anybody an eejit for a whole day.

So why, Sophie asked herself, didn't she feel all happy and free the way everybody else did now that Project Brooke was over?

One answer she knew right away. Without Brooke there, taking all of Sophie's attention, she couldn't keep her mind off baby Hope. What if nobody could help Hope when she got to be Brooke's age? What if people gave up on her and were glad when she wasn't around? The questions itched like poison ivy that was spreading.

Sophie only knew that if she gave up on Brooke, it would be like giving up on her own little sister. No matter what the other Corn Flakes decided, she had to be ready the minute Brooke came back.

Which was why, after school on Tuesday, Sophie went to the library and logged on to a computer back in the corner. The schedule of every student at GMMS was on a list anybody could pull up. She didn't even need Dr. Devon Downing for that.

Sophie scrolled through the R's and the S's until she came to *Singletary, Brooke.* She poised her gel pen over her notebook, ready to write down room numbers, but she couldn't take her eyes from the screen.

Period 1—Special Education/Language Arts	Room 202
Period 2—Special Education/Study Skills	Room 202
Period 3—Physical Education	Gym

The rest of the classes were Special Ed too. There was even tutoring scheduled after school on Mondays and Wednesdays.

Sophie thought she had to be dreaming. She leaned closer to peer through her glasses, but the words were really there.

I don't remember the Internet saying kids with ADHD were Special Ed, she thought. In fact, she knew they weren't. One article had even said ADHD kids were just as bright as other kids, only they couldn't concentrate enough to get their work done. So what was going on?

Dr. Devon Downing pushed herself back from her microscope and used extreme willpower not to hurl it across the room. Once again, she was confronted with a medical mystery that perhaps she couldn't solve. Something else was wrong with Ann-D-H-D's brain, perhaps something that, like Down syndrome, couldn't be cured. No wonder the subject broke trays over people's heads and stomped on their feet—

"She's not a subject," Sophie said out loud. "She's a person—and I can't help her either."

She left the library before she started throwing books off the shelves.

The urge to throw things didn't go away. That night Sophie couldn't see Jesus' eyes again. She wanted to ask him her questions and belt out her doubts, but it all stuck in her throat.

Maybe he just didn't want to listen to her.

During the break between first and second periods the next morning, when Fiona, Darbie, and Sophie hung outside the classroom talking in frosty breaths, Fiona said, "Don't forget, we have Bible study this afternoon."

"My aunt's bringing snacks," Darbie said.

Sophie didn't say anything. Fiona nudged her.

"You're coming, right, Soph? Boppa's picking us up."

"I guess." Sophie shrugged.

Fiona and Darbie looked at her blankly.

"You guess?" Fiona said. "What's up with that?"

"I don't know," Sophie said. "Maybe I'm just tired of Bible study."

Darbie thrust her head forward. "Now *that's* a bit of the horse's hoof."

"Nobody loves Dr. Peter's class more than you do," Fiona said. "What's going on?"

"The bell's gonna ring." Sophie retreated into the classroom because she didn't want to tell her best friends that she was afraid to go to Bible study. They might all find out she was so mad at God, she wanted to grab an angel's harp and break it over her knee. Or whatever a person did when God didn't send any messages through Jesus that everything would be okay.

I must not allow these personal feelings to interfere with my research, Dr. Devon Downing scolded herself. What should I work on next?

"What do you mean?" Anne-Stuart said. "The assignment is right there on the board."

Sophie blinked and propped her social studies book in front of her, trying to focus on the page. All she saw was Dr. Devon Downing disappearing.

By the time they arrived at the church that afternoon, Sophie felt like a plastic bag full of air. One small punch would be all it took ...

And Dr. Peter landed it the minute they were all situated in their different-colored beanbag chairs, Bibles in matching covers in their laps.

"So what's God been doing in your lives this week?" he said.

"Nothing," Sophie said. "I think he lost my address."

Everyone seemed to stop breathing at the same time. Sophie couldn't move, not even to say, *I'm sorry! I didn't mean that!* Well, she hadn't meant to *say* it, anyway.

Finally, Kitty giggled nervously, and Willoughby's poodle-yip came out as a whimper. Harley, one of the Wheaties, gave a soft snort. Everyone was looking at Dr. Peter, and even Sophie could see why. Nobody in the class had ever said anything like that about God before.

Dr. Peter sat forward in his beanbag chair and let his arms fall across his knees. "Is this something we need to talk about privately, Loodle?"

"Can I say something?" Fiona said.

Dr. Peter nodded at her. Sophie wished miserably that he hadn't.

"If Sophie's thinking that, then we all need to hear what you say."

"She's our friend," Kitty said in a tiny voice.

"Not only that," Darbie said, pushing her hair behind her ears. "If Sophie can go there, then the rest of us are bound to go there too, sometime or other. She knows God better than any of us."

"I thought I did," Sophie said. "Now I'm not so sure."

"Okay," Dr. Peter said. "If it's all right with you, Sophie, we'll all take a look at this doubt issue."

"Whatever," Sophie said. It was useless to keep pretending anyway, she thought. She'd already blurted out the worst thing she could possibly say.

"All right then." Dr. Peter rubbed his hands together the way he always did when they were ready to dig into the scriptures. "Let's open those Bibles to John 20, verse 26."

The air itself felt uneasy as the group thumbed its way to the New Testament. Usually Sophie loved this part and couldn't wait to hear who Dr. Peter wanted them to pretend to be in the story he read. But if it involved Jesus, she was afraid to even step into the scene.

"Imagine that you're the disciple Thomas." Dr. Peter pushed his glasses up with a nose-wrinkle. "Now, you remember that when Jesus rose from the dead, he appeared to the disciples in a locked house."

"John 20:19," Maggie said.

"Wow, Mags," Willoughby said.

"Thomas wasn't with them," Dr. Peter went on. "And when the other disciples told him they'd seen Jesus, he wasn't having any of it. He said unless he saw the nail holes in Jesus' hands and put his finger in them, he wouldn't believe it."

"Gross," Gill the Wheatie said.

"Now it's eight days later, and the disciples are all hanging out again. Thomas is there too, so pretend you're him."

Sophie automatically closed her eyes. Okay. She could be Thomas. All bristly and annoyed because he didn't see any evidence of Jesus anywhere. Sophie felt the fingers of fear. It wasn't really that hard to imagine right now, and that in itself was scary.

"'Though the doors were locked,'" Dr. Peter read, "'Jesus came and stood among them, and said, "Peace be with you!"'"

Sophie/Thomas looked up sharply. How did this intruder get in? The door was locked. Fear clutched his heart.

"'Then he said to Thomas—'"

Sophie/Thomas gasped. He's speaking to me! he thought. He clutched at the front of his robe. This couldn't be—Jesus was dead. He'd left them—abandoned them.

"'Put your finger here; see my hands.'"

Sophie/Thomas shuddered from head to foot. But he couldn't deny this man with the kind eyes who looked so much like his Jesus. Slowly he pressed his finger into the palm of the man's hand. It sank into a hollow, jagged hole. Thomas jerked back.

"'Reach out your hand and put it into my side.'"

Sophie/Thomas didn't want to, but something invisible seemed to push his fingers forward, until he could feel the gash where the Roman soldier had pierced Jesus with his sword—

"It's you!" Sophie/Thomas cried. "My Lord and my God!"

Sophie's eyes flew open. She'd almost forgotten Dr. Peter was reading. He looked at her over the top of his Bible. "'Then Jesus told him, "Because you have seen me, you have believed; blessed are those who have not seen and yet have believed."'"

Maggie raised her hand. "I get it."

"Then tell me," Gill said.

"That guy should've believed it when his friends told him Jesus was alive again," Maggie said. "He shouldn't have made Jesus prove it to him."

"What's that got to do with Sophie being mad at God, though?" Fiona said.

Sophie squirmed. It had felt so good for a moment there, to feel like she was Thomas really seeing Jesus. If only Jesus had stayed in her mind long enough for her to ask him why he seemed so far away lately, why he was giving her so many things to deal with that couldn't be fixed.

"Good question," Dr. Peter said. "If what Maggie just said is true, then Sophie shouldn't have so many doubts."

Sophie felt her eyes start in alarm, but Dr. Peter put his hand up. "It is true that we need the kind of faith that believes without seeing. But most of us don't have that right away and all the time, and it's okay."

Maggie looked up from the paper where, as usual, she was taking notes. "It is?"

"Sure. Faith is alive—it's something that grows stronger over time. We grow at different rates too. Don't we all need to see and hear God for *ourselves*?"

As Dr. Peter looked around the room, Sophie stayed very still.

Dr. Peter went on in his it's-going-to-be-all-right voice. "Jesus knew that poor Thomas didn't have a whole lot of imagination. Back at the Last Supper, when Jesus said the disciples knew where he was going and someday they'd join him, Thomas disagreed. He said he personally had no idea where Jesus was going, and he sure didn't know the way to get there."

"He was a bit thick, that one," Darbie said.

Sophie sat up straighter in her beanbag.

"He just took everything very literally," Dr. Peter said.

"Like Maggie," Fiona said. "No offense, Mags."

"No need to be offended." Dr. Peter grinned at Maggie. "Thomas gave Jesus the opportunity to say that *he* was the way. All they had to do was follow Jesus, even if they didn't know where. That's the whole reason we're here studying him, right? So we can follow?"

"But I don't know where he is right now," Sophie said. "Everything is so—wrong."

"I felt that way when I first got leukemia," Kitty said.

Dr. Peter nodded. "But even before you went into remission, God gave you what you needed to get you through."

"But God won't cure my baby sister," Sophie said. "Once you have Down syndrome, you always have it. There's no remission, either."

All eyes were once again on Dr. Peter.

"All I can say, from my own experience," he said in a thick voice, "is that when God isn't giving you what you're asking him for, he usually has something else—something better—in mind."

Something better? Sophie felt like arguing. But she pinched her lips tight. What could be better than Hope being cured of Down syndrome?

Fiona raised one eyebrow. "Didn't Jesus basically tell Thomas he needed to believe without seeing? And we have to too, right?"

"Yes, but there's something else." Dr. Peter scooted to the edge of his beanbag so he could look right into Sophie's eyes. "It's fine—even *good*—to have doubts about what God's doing at certain times. One Christian writer I really like—a man named Frederick Buechner—said, 'Doubts are the ants in the pants of faith.'"

"Ewww!" Willoughby said. The poodle was back.

Dr. Peter grinned. "Just like ants get you moving, doubts keep your faith stirred up and moving."

"I don't like ants," Sophie said. She could almost feel them on her, making her itch, like she'd been doing for days.

"And you don't like doubts, either, do you?" Dr. Peter's voice was soft. "Nobody ever said having faith was always going to be a picnic."

Fiona grinned. "My Boppa always says, 'What's a picnic without ants?'"

Dr. Peter smiled an almost-sad smile at Sophie. "It's okay to ask questions, Loodle. As long as you don't stop trying to find the answers."

Eight

When class was over and Darbie's aunt Emily brought in cheese, crackers, and juice boxes, everyone leaped for them as if big weights had been removed from their shoulders.

Everyone except Sophie. It was true—she didn't feel quite so itchy now. She was just sad. Squeezy cheese from a can wasn't going to cheer her up.

Dr. Peter leaned on the wall next to her. "This is very hard stuff, isn't it, Loodle?"

"I don't know what to do." Sophie shifted her shoulders. "I keep praying and asking ..."

"Why don't you do what you always do? Make a movie."

Sophie pulled her chin in. "We tried to make a movie with Brooke, but it didn't help her. Besides, everybody hated doing it."

"I was thinking of a video record of your baby sister's first weeks. Not a Film Club production—just a Sophie movie."

"How would I do that?" Sophie said. Hope couldn't exactly follow a script.

"Just film her doing her baby-thing." Dr. Peter grinned down at her. "You're not really Thomas—you *do* have an imagination. That makes it easier for you to accept things on faith. I know you will eventually, once you get your questions answered."

The fear fingers took another grab at Sophie's heart. Making a movie was supposed to take her mind *off* things she didn't want to think about.

She shook her head. "I don't really think a movie about Hope will help."

"Aw, Loodle," Dr. Peter said. "I think she's the perfect place to find God's answers."

Sophie wasn't sure about that. But Dr. Peter had never sent her in the wrong direction before. With those icy fingers still trying to get a hold on her, she took out her camera that night after supper and went in search of her baby sister.

Hope was asleep in her crib. Sophie focused on the little face, which was turned to the side as she lay on her back. Sophie thought her eyes looked normal when they were closed. But the little tongue was, as always, poking out from between her lips. She made funny little squeaky sounds as she breathed.

After about a minute, Sophie turned the camera off.

"You need to do something," she whispered to the baby.

"Don't you dare wake her up." Lacie padded across the thick carpet and leaned over the crib to straighten Hope's blanket. "What are you doing, anyway?"

"Making a movie," Sophie said.

"About Hope?" Lacie said.

"Yeah. I think it's gonna be kinda boring."

"You should tell Mama and Daddy you're doing it. They'll be super relieved."

"Why?"

Lacie gave the baby a soft pat before she turned to Sophie, arms folded. "They're worried that you aren't bonding with her. With you making a movie about her, at least they'll stop thinking you're jealous of her or something."

"Jealous?" That was one of the few bad feelings she *didn't* have about Hope.

"You have to admit it's pretty weird," Lacie said. "You were all over Zeke when he was born, but you don't even want to hold Hope."

"I've held her," Sophie said.

Lacie just looked at her.

"I'll take some footage of you covering her up with the blanket and stuff," Sophie said.

As Sophie focused in, Lacie lifted the blanket and let it float back down over baby Hope's little pink self.

"What's that red thing in there?" Sophie said, still filming.

Lacie pulled a plastic figure out from under the blanket. "What else?" she said. "Spider-Man."

Friday, Brooke was back in PE class, and Sophie felt a wave of sadness when she saw her in the locker room. But when the Flakes reported to the gym for roll check, Brooke herself looked pretty happy. The Pops appeared to be teaching her a cheer.

"I haven't seen them do a routine since they got kicked off the squad," Fiona said.

Brooke stood between Cassie and Anne-Stuart. Julia was in front of them, demonstrating a hip swivel. Sophie had definitely never seen Willoughby or any of the other GMMS cheerleaders do that, and Brooke wasn't quite getting the hang of it. She looked like she was stirring a giant pot of sand.

"You have to move your rear end," Cassie said.

"You're doing fine, Brookie," Julia said. "It's the words that are important."

"Brookie?" Fiona said under her breath. "This is definitely suspicious."

Sophie had to agree. Julia was having far too much fun for a jilted ex-cheerleader passing her skills on to a girl with no rhythm and even less coordination. Brooke's hips actually appeared to go in two different directions.

At the blast of Coach Yates's whistle, everyone but Brooke fell into line. She remained with her back to Coach, still swirling her hips.

"If you're not where you're supposed to be when I get there, Singletary," Coach Yates yelled, "I'm counting you absent."

"I'm here!" Brooke yelled back. When she turned to run toward her place, Sophie saw her face for the first time. She had on so much eye shadow, Sophie wasn't sure how she kept her eyelids open.

"Why's she wearing all that makeup?" Maggie said.

"Because we gave her a makeover." Julia flipped her hair over her shoulder. "We're trying to help her fit in."

"You *are?*" Willoughby said. Sophie could see her stifling a shriek.

"*We* aren't a clique," Anne-Stuart said. "*We* try to include new people."

Cassie narrowed her eyes at Sophie. "Not like *some* people we know."

Sophie put her hand on Fiona's shoulder. She could almost hear her best friend's teeth grinding.

When they got to their volleyball court, Coach Yates came over. "Another team is short a person, and they requested you, Brooke." She nodded her too-tight ponytail toward the Pops/Loops court.

Brooke let out a whoop and attempted a cartwheel in that direction. Although it looked more like somebody falling out of bed, the Corn Pops clapped.

"Okay—now I'm not just suspicious," Fiona said to Sophie. "I've moved on to dead certain. Something's going on."

Whatever it was, Sophie watched it continue through the PE period. The Corn Pops adjusted Brooke's braid and redid her lipstick every time the ball went out of bounds. When Tod told her she stunk at volleyball, Julia said it didn't matter because she looked "too cute" on the court. Tod sent a lot of death stares Brooke's way, but Julia shot him down with a few of her own.

"They're setting somebody up for something," Willoughby said. "So everybody watch your back."

Sophie nodded. That was definitely something they didn't have to see to believe.

In the locker room, Brooke dragged her clothes to the Corn Pops' corner, but they dressed her in an outfit they appeared to have brought from home, complete with a skimpy orange shrug that tied in the front and a matching purse with giant sequins on it. To Sophie she looked like a sparkly pumpkin. As Brooke strutted out of the locker room, several sequins fell off and left a trail behind her.

Sophie had a fidgety feeling inside. She really should go after Brooke and tell her the Corn Pops didn't invite girls like her into their group without an evil reason.

But Brooke was surrounded by Pops, smiling like Queen Julia herself. Was Project Brooke over for the Flakes? Sophie wondered. Could anybody ever really save her?

Sophie couldn't answer that question. Not yet, anyway. But Dr. Peter had said not to stop looking for the answers.

At lunch, Darbie had an answer of her own. "Coach Nanini pulled me out of Miss Imes' class to talk to me," she said.

"I saw that," Fiona said. "What'd he say?"

Sophie could see Darbie trying not to smile. "He said he and some of the other teachers talked about it, and they decided Brooke had too many problems for Round Table to handle. He tried to get her some special help, but he said she won't take it. It's like she won't admit she has ADHD or anything else. Anyway, I'm off the hook."

Fiona looked at Sophie. "So that means we're *all* off the hook."

"Seriously, Sophie," Darbie said. "If Brooke doesn't want help, what are we supposed to do?"

"I guess you're right," Sophie said.

But she was squirmy inside again. As she tore her sandwich into tiny pieces, Dr. Peter's words came back to her: *Doubts are the ants in the pants of faith.* Just like annoying little ants got you moving, itchy doubts kept your faith stirred up and moving.

After school, Sophie picked up her camera from Mr. Stires' storage room. If she intended to keep asking questions, then she'd better keep looking for answers—and be ready to record them.

Saturday morning, she took more footage of Hope sleeping, sometimes on her side, sometimes on her back. Sophie decided babies must sleep a lot because they couldn't do much of anything else. Especially this baby.

It surprised her then, when she was filming Mama feeding her a bottle Saturday afternoon, that Hope found Mama's finger with her tiny ones and wrapped them around it.

"I didn't know she could do that!" Sophie said.

"Isn't it the cutest?" Mama leaned down and kissed the miniature fingers. Baby Hope still held on.

Sophie zoomed in. It was like Hope knew that was Mama and she wasn't letting go for anything. Could that be?

"Come here, Soph," Mama said.

Sophie put the camera in one hand and sat next to her. Mama pulled her finger away from the baby.

"Just put your pinky right in her palm," she said. "Watch what happens."

Moving in slow motion, Sophie placed her little finger against Hope's soft, warm hand. In an instant, Hope was clinging to Sophie. Almost as if she trusted her.

"This is your big sister," Mama cooed to her.

Hope stopped sucking on the bottle and moved her eyes. They stopped as if she was looking right at Mama.

"Hello," Mama said in her softest wisp of a voice. "Is that my Baby Doll?"

"Does she know you?" Sophie said.

"She does." Mama laughed, a little tinkle bell of a laugh. "Of course, we've been together a long time. You keep talking to her, and she'll know your voice too."

"Are you sure?" Sophie said.

"Very sure." Mama looked straight at her. "Sophie, she's a person, just like the rest of us."

Sophie knew her face was turning as red as Nathan's. Mama went back to cooing at Hope, and Sophie went back to filming. Inside, though, she felt something go soft.

While she took movies all weekend, Sophie discovered that Hope turned her head toward Lacie's voice too, and that Zeke's seemed to be her favorite finger to latch onto. He got her to curl her hand around a Spider-Man figure's leg, but Daddy took it away from her.

"You don't know where this thing has been, Little Rookie," he said to her. "I'm afraid to find that out myself."

The filming also showed Sophie that nobody had more fun with baby Hope than Daddy. The best shots she took were of the two of them. He walked around with her tucked into the crook of his arm, kind of like a football, and talked to her as if she could understand everything he said.

Sophie was in Hope's nursery Sunday afternoon, filming Daddy changing her diaper, when something crashed in the direction of Zeke's room.

"Want me to check that out?" Sophie said.

"I'll do it," Daddy said. "If he's halfway up the wall, you won't be able to get him down anyway."

"What about Hope?" Sophie nodded toward the half-dressed baby on the changing table.

"Don't let her fall off. I'll be right back."

"But how do I ..." Her question faded as Daddy made a hasty exit. Sophie looked down at Hope. She lay very still, with only the occasional hand or foot popping up. It was so quiet in the nursery that Sophie could hear her tiny breaths.

This was the first time she'd been alone with her when she was awake. The fear fingers curled around Sophie's heart the way Hope's fingers curled around somebody's pinky. Only these squeezed hard. *What do I do if she starts crying?*

Baby Hope jerked as if she'd read Sophie's mind. Her eyes searched the ceiling, and her arms flailed at her sides. The telltale crumple wrinkled her brow.

"Don't cry," Sophie said. "Come on, don't cry. I don't know what to do if you cry."

Hope let out a frightened squawk and turned her head to the side.

"Don't fall off," Sophie said, leaning her stomach against the changing table.

A mind-flash of her baby sister tumbling to the floor almost blinded her. Sophie scooped the tiny body up in her arms and held her against her chest.

"Don't cry," Sophie whispered to her. "I would never let you fall."

Hope stopped wiggling. The next squawk settled into a sigh, and she breathed tiny whisper breaths against Sophie's neck. Sophie closed her eyes, but she couldn't imagine anything. She could only be right there, holding her baby sister.

"Looks like you two are getting along pretty well," Daddy said from the doorway.

"You should take her." Sophie pressed against her father until he took the baby from her.

Then she fled to her room on the edge of tears. The thing she'd feared all along had happened. She'd started to love a sister who would never be okay.

Nine

The ants-in-the-pants feeling kept Sophie's mind itching until Monday morning. No answers yet, but Dr. Peter had said to keep asking.

So she took the camera to school, just in case, and went to Mr. Stires' room to put it away before first period. The storage room wasn't open yet. He was still in his puffy down jacket, pulling at his mustache as he listened to Julia Cummings, who had her back to the door. Sophie didn't have to see her face to know it was her so-sweet-it's-disgusting voice.

"I'm not trying to get her in trouble," Julia said. "I just wish you'd talk to her before we have our next lab. I don't want to end up with some other animal's insides on me—"

Julia stopped as Mr. Stires' eyes flickered toward Sophie. When Julia glanced over her shoulder, Sophie had the strange sensation that Julia had already known Sophie was there.

"Just leave the camera on the desk, Sophie," Mr. Stires said. "I'll put it away."

Sophie did. As she turned to leave, she caught a satisfied smirk on Julia's face.

"Why is she just now tattling to Mr. Stires about the lizard brain?" Fiona said when Sophie told the Corn Flakes in the gym. "If she wanted to get you in trouble, she would have said something to him right away."

Darbie gave an elaborate sigh. "We always have to have drama. We just get done with Brooke, and now we have the Pops again."

"Oh—my—gosh," Kitty said.

Sophie turned in time to see Brooke bound into the gym wearing Pepto-Bismol-pink tennis shoes and neon-purple track pants with matching jacket.

"Those are Cassie's shoes," Willoughby whispered.

Kitty nodded. "And I've seen Anne-Stuart wear that work-out suit."

Fiona pushed the stubborn strip of hair away from her eye. "But Anne-Stuart didn't accessorize with a boa."

Sophie stared as Brooke pulled a lime green string of feathers out of the jacket.

"Just what do you intend to do with that?" Coach Yates, of course, yelled. Her face looked double-pinched.

"It's for my ch—"

"It's mine." Julia flashed Coach Yates a plastic smile. "I'm letting her use it." She turned oh-so-sweetly to Brooke. "I didn't mean for you to bring it to class. That's for later." And then she winked.

"A wink is not good," Willoughby told the Corn Flakes when they were gathered on their court. "In Corn Pop world, that means something is their little secret."

"An evil secret," Kitty put in.

"Don't let's be doddering on about that now," Darbie said. "She's not our responsibility anymore."

Sophie felt a pang as she caught the ball Jimmy tossed to her and headed for the serving position.

"Sophie," Fiona whispered from outside the court where she was waiting to rotate in.

"What?" Sophie said.

"You're not going to leave it alone, are you?"

"Leave what alone?"

"Brooke—and the Corn Pops."

"You're supposed to serve now," Maggie called from the net.

Sophie held the ball in one hand and swung the other arm back.

"Okay." Fiona sighed. "Find out what you can. I'll cover for you."

Sophie popped the ball up with her fist. She didn't care if it went over the net. Fiona had given her the first reason to smile in a long time. Maybe this was a little bit of an answer.

After class, Fiona walked backward in front of the rest of the Corn Flakes, chattering away about some complicated vocabulary word they just *had* to know. Sophie dawdled by the ball basket until Cassie and Brooke passed through the doorway and headed for the locker room, heads bent together. Cassie was whispering, but Sophie knew Brooke's version of a whisper could be heard from a hundred paces. Sophie gave them about ten and followed, ears perked up.

Cassie sounded like she was saying, *Mutter mutter mutter mutter.*

Brooke said, "I haven't had a chance yet."

"Mutter mutter mutter," said Cassie.

She put her arm around Brooke and pulled her closer, so that Sophie couldn't even hear her muttering.

"Wicked!" Brooke said.

They turned into the locker room with Sophie behind them. She hurried so she wouldn't lose them at the next turn past the showers. When she rounded the corner, only Cassie was standing there with her back to Sophie, blocking her way.

"Um, excuse me," Sophie said.

Cassie didn't answer or budge.

Sophie tried to get past her, but Cassie moved with her. When Sophie jockeyed the other way, Cassie was right there.

"Could I please get by?" Sophie said.

Cassie looked over her shoulder. "Oh, sorry." Her voice had as much expression as the recorded lady on voice mail. "I didn't see you there."

"So—could I get by?" Sophie said.

"Sure."

Cassie stepped aside so Sophie could pass between her and the row of shower stalls. But Sophie didn't get a foot farther before someone grabbed her arm and yanked her behind the first curtain.

"Hope you like cold water!" Brooke said.

The faucet squeaked on, Brooke leaped out of the stall, and Sophie was soaked by liquid ice cubes. Gasping and groping, she finally threw herself out through the shower curtain. Cassie and Brooke were nowhere to be seen.

Shivering right down to her bones, Sophie sloshed down the hall, clothes dripping near-icicles on the floor. Ahead of her, damp footprints led not to the locker area, but in the other direction, straight to a door marked SUPPLIES.

"You always leave a trail, Brooke," Sophie said out loud. She pushed the door open and slipped inside.

It was dark, but Sophie found a switch on the wall and lit up the storage room. Brooke was hidden from the knees up behind an open shelf unit full of paper towels and toilet tissue. At the bottom, though, were a pair of Pepto-Bismol-pink tennis shoes and two legs clad in neon purple.

"I see you, Brooke," Sophie said. "You might as well come out."

"I don't got nothing to say to you."

Sophie rolled her eyes. When did Brooke *not* have anything to say?

"All I want to know is why you pushed me into the shower," Sophie said. "I'm freezing."

"Serves you right. You're just a troublemaker."

"Me?" Sophie's voice squeaked upward.

"Don't play innocent." Brooke's pink shoes shuffled. "I know about you."

"Know what?"

"You're the one who made all of Julia's and Anne-Stuart's friends hate them."

"What are you—"

"You're the one who made Tod Ravelli hate *me*."

Sophie stopped interrupting. The girl who didn't have anything to say was on a roll.

"You're the one who got me suspended too," Brooke said. "Since you're all buddy-buddy with Coach Ninooni—or whatever his name is."

Sophie wrapped her arms around her shivering self, but she was hot on the inside. The Corn Pops had been at work on Brooke, but there was no way to prove it. If she let Brooke talk long enough, she'd probably spill it, but what good would that do? It would be Brooke's word against the Pops', and Brooke hadn't exactly built a reputation for being trustworthy.

But something tripped up that thought. Getting the Pops in trouble wasn't what mattered. It was keeping Brooke *out* of trouble.

"I don't know why you had to do all that stuff to me." There was a quiver in Brooke's voice. "I thought you were my friend—putting me in that movie and everything."

"I was *trying* to be your friend," Sophie said.

"No, you weren't!" The metal shelf unit shook, and a roll of toilet paper tumbled to the floor.

"Would you come out of there before everything falls off?" Sophie said.

"No." Brooke's voice twisted, as if that was the only way she could keep back tears. "I hate you. All I was to you was Project Brooke. My *friends* showed me."

Sophie felt as if she'd just been slapped—and that she deserved it.

In the silence, Coach Yates could be heard down the hall, yelling, "Who left this shower on?"

Brooke stumbled out from behind the shelves, face blotchy. The ends of the green feather boa hung forlornly from the bottom of the purple jacket, and one sleeve was wet. "Are you gonna tell on me?" she said.

Sophie closed her eyes. *Brooke didn't even think about that before she dragged me into the shower.*

"All right," Coach Yates yelled, "you have two minutes before the bell rings."

Brooke looked wildly around the supply room like she was searching for an escape hatch. Sophie's heart pounded. This might as well be happening to her.

After all, she thought, it's my fault. I have to at least try to fix it.

But her "helping" had messed things up before, and Sophie knew it. She'd wanted to fix Brooke and she'd just made her hate the Flakes instead.

Just keep asking the questions. Wasn't that what Dr. Peter had said?

Which way do I go? she prayed to eyes she couldn't see.

"One minute!" Coach Yates yelled.

Her voice was getting farther away. Brooke wedged herself between Sophie and the door.

"They said you'd tell on me, but they'll swear I never came near you—"

"I won't tell, Brooke," Sophie said, "if you'll give me one more chance to help you."

"Help me with what? I'm just fine the way I am—my friends say so."

Sophie pulled her chin in. "Julia and them?"

"Yes—*they* really like me—*they* don't try to change me!"

Before Sophie could point out that the Corn Pops had all but done plastic surgery on her, Brooke shoved her aside and flew out of the room.

Sophie felt like a soggy, shivering lump of failure as she dragged herself out too. When she turned the corner toward the now-empty locker area, she ran into Coach Yates (as Fiona would say) "literally."

Coach Yates looked from Sophie's drenched clothes to the front of her own sweatshirt, now bearing a wet Sophie-print.

"What in the world happened to you, LaCroix?"

"Um, I was in the shower," Sophie said.

"With your clothes on?"

Sophie could only nod.

Coach Yates put up her hand. "I don't even want to know. You have fifteen seconds to get dressed."

Sophie was cold and deflated when she got to Miss Imes' classroom. Julia and Anne-Stuart were just inside the door, and they both spattered laughter into their hands at the same moment. From the glow in their eyes, Sophie figured Brooke had completed her assigned task even more successfully than they could have imagined.

But, then, they never did have much imagination, Sophie thought. Fiona and Darbie, on the other hand, were gaping at her like they were dreaming up the worst.

Before she could get to them, Miss Imes said, "Bad time of year to be walking around with wet hair, Sophie."

"Sorry," Sophie said.

Miss Imes' eyebrows pointed up. "Sorry for what?"

For everything, Sophie thought. She slunk to her desk, slid into her seat, and closed her eyes. She even put her hands over her glasses. But she could still hear the twist of hurt in Brooke's voice when she said, *I hate you. All I was to you was Project Brooke.* There was definitely no room in Sophie's mind-picture for Jesus.

But somehow she had to believe he was there. *I'm trying really hard to follow you*, she prayed silently, *but would you please show me where we're going?*

When Sophie looked up, Fiona was giving her a bug-eyed stare and pointing to her hair as if to say, *What's with the wet head?*

There was no way to communicate back—not with Miss Imes gazing pointedly in every direction. But seeing Fiona made Sophie think of something. As she scribbled down the problems from the board, her mind raced.

How did Brooke find out the Flakes referred to her as Project Brooke?

Sophie glanced at Julia and Anne-Stuart, who were calculating away with their sharpened pencils as if math were their sole purpose in life. Brooke said her "friends" had told her—people who "really liked her" and "didn't try to change her." Sophie gnawed on her stubby pencil. It was crystal clear to her that the Corn Pops *didn't* like Brooke, and that they *were* trying to change her—and using her in the process.

And then Sophie took in a huge breath that threatened to drag her eraser down her windpipe.

The Corn Flakes don't like Brooke, either. And Brooke was right. All we did was try to change her.

"Miss Imes?" Julia said, in a voice as sweet as pancake syrup. "Would you show me how to do number five? I know you explained it, but I need you to show me."

Sophie eyes sprang open.

Show me. I need you to show me.

Brooke hadn't said, "My friends *told* me." Sophie could almost hear her quivery voice again in her mind. She'd said, "My friends *showed* me."

But what did they show her that actually said the words *Project Brooke*? Where was it ever written down? At the risk of being pierced by Miss Imes' pointy look, Sophie scanned the room.

Vincent? No, he and Darbie were always behind the camera.

Fiona? She never wrote anything down. She just dictated to Maggie, who recorded *everything*—even stuff that didn't have anything to do with the movie.

Sophie's pencil fell out of her hand, and she didn't bother to pick it up. She closed her eyes and heard Darbie say, *Brooke's always going through everybody's belongings.*

Sophie watched the clock, fear fingers squeezing the breath out of her. Five long minutes until the bell rang for lunch. An eternity before she'd be able to get to Maggie.

Ten

When the bell finally ended math class, Sophie told Fiona and Darbie everything as they sailed to their lockers.

"So you think Brooke saw the words *Project Brooke* written in our Treasure Book?" Fiona said.

"How could she?" Darbie said. "Maggie would never let her near it."

Sophie talked over her shoulder as she took the last turn into the locker hall. Fiona and Darbie practically ran to keep up. "Brooke said Julia and them *showed* her."

"So you think one of the *Pops* saw it in the Treasure Book?" Fiona said.

Darbie scowled. "How? You know Maggie wouldn't let one of them get a *sniff* of it."

"I don't have the answers." Sophie shook her head. "We don't even know if Maggie wrote it down in there. We just have to ask her."

Maggie, Willoughby, and Kitty were already at their lockers when Sophie squealed her tennis shoes around the end of the row. She took the last few steps in one leap.

"You're not supposed to run in the halls," Maggie said. "You could get in trouble—"

"Maggie!" Sophie said. "Did you ever write the words *Project Brooke* in the Treasure Book?"

Maggie blinked. "I wrote everything down."

Fiona stuck her head between them. "But did you write down those exact words: *Project Brooke*?"

"Yikes, Fiona," Willoughby said. "Why are you all up in Maggie's dentalwork?"

Fiona pointed to Maggie's backpack. "Could you just look?"

Maggie squatted and unzipped her pack, which was on the floor. She grew as still as a stump.

"Isn't it in there?" Fiona said.

"It's in here. Just not in the place I always keep it."

Sophie's heart nearly stopped as Maggie held up the Treasure Book. Or, at least, what was left of it. Its former shiny purple cover was all jagged strips that hung from the binding like a tattered flag. Some of the cuts dug deep into the pages.

"How long has it been like *that*, Mags?" Fiona asked.

"I didn't know it *was* like that!"

Sophie knelt beside Maggie. "How did somebody get in your backpack?"

"Or did you leave the book out someplace?" Kitty said.

"I never do that!" Willoughby said, "Well, then *somebody* got into your backpack *somehow* — "

Sophie put her hands over her ears. "Stop!"

The Corn Flakes froze as one.

"Sorry, Mags," Fiona said. "It's not your fault."

The bell rang, and Darbie shooed them all toward the cafeteria, explaining to Kitty, Willoughby, and Maggie what Brooke had said to Sophie in the supply closet.

Maggie trudged next to Sophie, hugging her bag to her chest. She didn't utter so much as a grunt even when they were all settled at the table. Nobody opened a lunch. Sophie thought she might be sick.

"Fiona is right, Mags," Sophie said. "It's not your fault. It's mine for ever thinking of doing that stupid movie in the first place."

"No, it's mine," Fiona said. "I named it Project Brooke. That was *so* un-Corn Flake."

"It's mine for even writing it down," Maggie muttered.

"Maybe you didn't." Kitty looked doubtfully at what used to be the Treasure Book. "'Course, there's no way to tell now."

Fiona nodded. "I looked. When you push the strips together, you can see it: 'Project Brooke.'"

"I'd like to say something." Darbie jammed her hair behind her ears. "It isn't any of *our* faults that somebody got into our private property and cut it all in flitters."

"*Somebody?*" Willoughby said. "We know it was Brooke."

Fiona nodded. "We just don't know how and when."

"But we know why." Sophie's voice squeaked like a clarinet some beginner student couldn't play.

"Who cares why?" Maggie said. "She broke a rule, and she has to take the consequences."

"That's right." Darbie looked right at Sophie. "I hope you don't think we should let this go just because we feel bad that we hurt Brooke's feelings."

Sophie looked miserably at the Treasure Book. Maggie was smoothing down its hopeless cover, as if she could make it whole again.

"The Corn Pops told her a bunch of lies," Sophie said. "And I bet when she saw this she just got mad like she does." Sophie looked again at the book that had held so many of their dreams. "I want to try to help her one more time. Let's just give it another day."

"Why?" Darbie said. "I'm about to eat the head off somebody, but you don't see me looking for Brooke so I can reef her."

"You don't have to," Willoughby whispered. "'Cause here she comes."

Kitty whimpered and hid her face behind Maggie's shoulder. Sophie slid the Treasure Book into her lap under the table, just as Brooke arrived.

"Oh, my—what's this show?" Darbie muttered.

Brooke was still in Anne-Stuart's purple track outfit, but she'd had some other changes made since Sophie last saw her.

Her red hair was in a folded ponytail on top of her head, held in place by a blue-sequined scrunchie. Sophie was sure someone had applied makeup to her face with a spatula, especially the lipstick. There appeared to be an entire tube of Shimmering Cherry on her lips. The effect of clown-at-a-fashion-show was completed with the green feather boa Brooke had draped over her shoulders and wrapped around each arm like stripes on barber poles.

"Hi, Brooke." Willoughby wore her automatic cheerleader smile. "You look—"

"Interesting!" Sophie said. "Don't you guys think she looks interesting?"

"Fascinating," Fiona said.

Kitty pulled out the cereal box. "Want some Cheerios?"

Brooke only looked over her shoulder. Then she straightened up and closed her eyes for a second, as if she were concentrating.

"Are you okay?" Sophie said.

Brooke slapped her hands together and threw her arms over her head, green feathers and all. She looked like a parrot trying out for cheerleading.

"Ready?" she shouted. "Okay! Give me an F !"

Nobody answered so she answered herself and went on with, "Give me an L!"

"This is embarrassing," Kitty whispered to Sophie.

But Sophie said, "*L.*"

Brooke flung her arms into a point over her head. "Now give me an *A!*"

"Come on, you guys," Sophie said through gritted teeth. "*A!*"

The arms took a flying turn to the side. "Give me a *K* !"

"*K!*" Sophie said. Kitty and Willoughby joined in feebly.

Face now as red as Nathan's had ever gotten, Brooke screamed, "Give me an—" She paused, made-up brow furrowing like a wad of clay. "Oh—give me an *E!*"

"*E!*" cried half the cafeteria.

"Sophie, stop!" Fiona hissed at her. "Don't you hear what she's spelling?"

"Give—me—an—*S!*"

Sophie saw the word in her head, where she'd pictured it hundreds of special times. She went cold.

"What do we have?" Brooke yelled.

There was a slight pause.

"What *do* we have?" Gill the Wheatie said at the other end of the table.

"Flakes?" said Vincent across the aisle.

Willoughby plastered her hands over her mouth. The other Corn Flakes looked too stunned to move.

"Flakes!" Brooke swiveled her hips in a clumsy circle. "Coooorn Flakes! That's what they call themselves!" Plunging toward the table end, she straightened her arms, grabbed on, and stuck out both legs to the sides.

"Don't, Brooke!" Willoughby cried. "You won't make it!"

Brooke didn't. What looked like an attempt to land a pike on top of the table ended in Brooke halfway *under* the table on her hind end. But she wasn't finished. She scrambled up, amid screaming middle-school laughter, and hoisted herself onto her knees on the table. With her hands cupped around her mouth, she shouted, "These are the Corn Flakes!"

"The what?" somebody shouted back.

The noise died down a level. Brooke pointed at Sophie's head, and then Fiona's. Sophie was sure she was going to throw up, right there. Beside her, Fiona was as stiff as a pole.

"They call themselves the Corn Flakes," Brooke cried. "That's because they *are* flakes. A clique full of flakes. Don't ever be their friend because you can't trust them."

Gill and Harley both stood up, and some of the other Wheaties too. "That's not true!" one of them said.

"I trust them," Jimmy said. Nathan nodded, face the color of a match head.

Vincent got to his feet. "Where did you get this information? Sounds like you made it up to me."

"No." Brooke pulled the back of her hand, still clad in green feathers, across her lips. Titters erupted from the crowd as she wiped lipstick from mouth to ear. "I'm not making it up. I got the 411 from my friends, who are *not* flakes, even though *these* flakes have wrecked everything for them."

She flung a hand toward Sophie's Corn Flakes, whose faces were frozen into portraits of shock.

"Name your source," Vincent said to Brooke.

"Huh?" Brooke said.

"Who told you?"

"They're right over—" Brooke jabbed a finger toward the Pops' table. It was empty. Not even Tod and Colton were there. The feather boa slid off one arm. "They *were* over there," Brooke said. "It's Jul—"

"Brooke, get down," Sophie said.

As the cafeteria buzzed around them, Darbie thawed from her frozen state and grabbed one of Brooke's arms. Fiona took the other. Brooke stared at them and then at herself, as if she'd just noticed she was on top of the table.

Darbie and Fiona hauled her into a chair. With lipstick smeared across her face and sweat making streams through the makeup, Brooke looked like a little girl who'd just been caught in her mother's cosmetics.

She really is a little girl, Sophie thought. It took away some of her urge to stuff the feather boa down Brooke's throat. While Darbie muttered and Fiona gritted her teeth and Kitty whined into Maggie's unmoving shoulder, Sophie watched Brooke crane her neck toward the cafeteria door. She looked desperate, as if that same little girl had completely *lost* her mother.

"Who are you looking for?" Sophie said.

"My friends."

Darbie snorted. "You mean the *friends* that took off and left you making an eejit of yourself?"

Brooke came halfway off the seat, but Sophie grabbed her arm.

"Did your, um, friends tell you we called ourselves the Corn Flakes?" Sophie said.

"No. I read it." Brooke looked as if she wanted to bite her tongue off when Maggie pulled the mangled Treasure Book from Sophie's lap and laid it on the table.

"Did you read it in here?" Maggie said.

Sophie could almost see the possible lies flipping through Brooke's mind. Again she half rose from the seat and threw glances at every corner of the room.

"Okay," Fiona said, "let me just tell you what probably happened, and you can tell me if I'm right."

Darbie and Maggie wore matching scowls, but Sophie said, "Good idea."

Brooke lowered herself back into the seat and stared down at the Treasure Book.

Fiona folded her hands on the table. "When we were making the movie, the Po—uh, Julia and your other *friends* asked you if you'd ever seen inside our book. You said no, and they said if you looked in it, you'd find out what we were *really* like." Fiona brushed her hair aside. "How am I doing so far?"

"That's *maybe* what happened." Brooke wrapped the end of the boa around her finger, so that it too was coated with lipstick.

"So," Fiona went on, "you got into Maggie's backpack, sometime when she wasn't looking, and you found the book. When you saw that we called the movie Project Brooke, you were incensed, and you stabbed it multiple times with—something."

"I didn't use incense," Brooke said.

"No," Sophie said. "She means you got mad."

"And then you went back and told your *friends*." Fiona made quotation marks with her fingers. "And you also told them that the book said we were the Corn Flakes."

Willoughby's curls bounced. "So they taught you a cheer about Corn Flakes. They dressed you up like Ronald McDonald and told you to do the cheer in front of everybody."

Brooke looked at Sophie. "You all make it sound like they were trying to make me look stupid."

"No," Sophie said. "They were using you to make *us* look stupid."

"Because if they'd done it themselves," Maggie said, "they'd get in trouble."

"But they're nice! They let me wear their clothes—they wanted me on their team."

Fiona leaned toward her. "And where are they now?"

"They'll be back."

"No, they won't." Kitty looked at Brooke from over Maggie's shoulder. "I used to be in their group, and all they did was use me too."

"Me, three," Willoughby said.

"Personally, I think they even use each other." Fiona sat back, arms folded. "You can believe them if you want to, but it's only going to get worse if you do."

"*Don't* believe Julia and the rest of them, Brooke," Sophie said. "I mean it. We were wrong before when we made you our project, but we honestly wanted to help you because—"

"Because I mess everything up." Brooke wound the boa around her neck. "Everybody tells me that all the time."

"We were trying to help you *not* mess things up, only we did it the wrong way. We're sorry." Sophie glanced around the table at the friends who suddenly wouldn't look at her. "Well, *I'm* sorry, anyway."

The rest of the Corn Flakes were quiet for the longest minute Sophie had ever lived. Questions in her own mind tortured her.

What if nobody had learned anything? What if the Corn Flakes really were nothing but a clique? If they abandoned Brooke now, were they really any better than the Corn Pops?

Sophie was so afraid of the answers, she almost ran from them, right out the door.

Brooke pointed at the Treasure Book. "What about that?"

"You mean, are we gonna turn you in?" Willoughby said.

Maggie cradled the book in her hands. "You can't just go around tearing people's stuff up because you get your feelings hurt."

"I don't know how come I did it." Brooke tightened the boa. "I just do stuff, and I don't even know why."

"That's why we were trying to help you," Sophie said. "And we—well, I—still will."

The Corn Flakes still wouldn't look at Sophie, but Brooke did. For a second, she reminded Sophie of baby Hope turning her head toward a voice, like maybe—just *maybe*—she could trust it.

So—*is this the Jesus-way?* Sophie wondered. It sure looked like it.

But Brooke's eyes sprang open as if some sudden thought terrified her.

"You won't help me!" Brooke cried. "You won't help me when you find out!"

She bolted from the seat, and feet pounded toward the door. The feather boa trailed behind her.

Eleven

The bell rang, and the cafeteria erupted in one big push toward the door. Sophie sank back into her chair.

"What's wrong, Corn Flake?" some kid said to her as he pointed to her still-wet hair. "Too soggy to move?"

For a moment, Sophie had forgotten that Brooke had just told the middle-school world their secret name. She sagged—sogged—further into the seat.

"Like he even knows what a Corn Flake really is," Fiona said. She nudged Sophie to a standing position.

"Do *we*?" Sophie said.

"Do we what?"

"Know what a Corn Flake is?"

Willoughby looped her arm through Sophie's on the other side and tugged her along behind the crowd going out the door.

"We know what it isn't," Darbie said.

Sophie knew she was talking about Brooke and the Pops, but she didn't feel much different from any of them as she trudged toward Mr. Stires' classroom. She tried to ignore the stares of people who stopped whispering as she, Fiona, and Darbie went by.

Mr. Stires stopped them in the doorway. For a minute, Sophie thought he was going to confront her about the lizard brain in Julia's hair. But his face was as cheerful as always.

"How's that film coming along?" he said.

You mean that heinous piece of trash that ruined everything? Sophie wanted to say.

"Uh, we still have a lot of editing to do," Fiona said.

Mr. Stires bobbed his head. "Why don't I take a look at what you have while you're in groups today?"

Sophie felt numb as she nodded. "I'll get it. It's in my camera bag."

She didn't even look at Julia and Anne-Stuart as she headed for the storage room, but she could feel their victory smiles. She was just too tired to care.

The bag was on a shelf above its usual place, and Sophie had to stand on tiptoe to pull it down. Maybe they wouldn't even do any more films, she thought as she grabbed the strap. Maybe everything was just going to be different from now on—

Her thoughts tripped themselves to a stop as the bag fell into her hands. It rattled. It had never rattled before. It wasn't *supposed* to rattle.

The old fear fingers gripped Sophie's heart as she set the bag on a low shelf and squatted to open it. Something was wrong. Way wrong.

Hands sweaty, Sophie unzipped the cover and peered inside. All she saw were broken pieces of what used to be her video camera.

"Hey, Soph," Fiona said from the doorway. "What's taking so long? Mr. Stires is putting us in groups."

"It's ruined," Sophie said. Her voice sounded as wooden as Maggie's.

"No, it's not," Fiona said. "He'll probably put us in the same group."

Sophie didn't answer. She just pointed into the bag as Fiona crossed the storage room. When she looked in, her magic-gray eyes went wide, as if she were staring into headlights.

"It's been pulverized," she said.

If that meant the keeper of their many dreams was now reduced to shards of glass and pieces of bashed-in metal, Fiona was right. Sophie was sure her heart had stopped beating.

"Mr. Stires said to hurry up," said another voice from the doorway. "Why are you foostering—" Darbie took a sharp intake of breath. "What's wrong?" She too gasped into the camera bag. Then she said, "Brooke again."

Sophie couldn't argue with her. Who else was angry enough to smash up the thing that was most important to the girls who made her feel like a project?

Who else indeed? Because as Sophie gazed down into the bag in disbelief, she saw something shiny that wasn't a hunk of camera lens. It looked like the sparkly head of a cat.

"Julia's nail file," she said out loud.

"Where?" Fiona said.

"Right there." Sophie pushed aside some of what was now junk with her finger. The cat on Julia's fancy file seemed to give her an evil smile.

"I don't get it," Fiona said.

"Last call for groups," Mr. Stires called from the classroom.

Sophie slapped the top closed and zipped the zipper.

"What are you doing, Sophie?" Darbie said. "We can't let this go. We have to tell!"

"No," Sophie said. "Brooke has to tell. And first she has to tell me."

"What are you talking about?" Darbie said.

Sophie pulled the memory stick out of the front pocket and slung the rattling camera bag over her shoulder by the strap. "I don't care if everybody thinks the Corn Flakes are a stupid clique. I'm still going to be one, even if I have to do it by myself."

"Who said anything about us not being Corn Flakes anymore?" Fiona's face was the color of Cream of Wheat.

"Nobody said *anything*," Sophie said. "That's just it. At lunch just now, nobody said a word about helping her take back her power from the Corn Pops. Everybody just stood there until she ran off."

"All right, ladies," Mr. Stires said from the doorway. "Darbie, you and Fiona are a group. Sophie, I put you with Jimmy. You have the memory stick so I can look at your film?"

Sophie handed it to him and brushed past Darbie and Fiona to a seat next to Jimmy.

"You okay?" Jimmy's blue eyes were so kind Sophie almost cried—except there was no time for tears.

"No," Sophie said.

"I'm sorry about what Brooke did. I think Corn Flakes is a cool name."

Sophie winced.

"I get it if you don't feel like working right now," Jimmy said. "I'll just do part of the assignment, and you can do the rest for homework."

She nodded. She even wanted to tell him about the camera and ask him to help her make some kind of plan for Brooke. But she just couldn't. This was a Corn Flake problem. Even if she was the only Flake who knew it.

While Jimmy worked, Sophie tried to write down what to do next. She didn't get much further than, *Go to Brooke's tutoring room after school.*

But Fiona and Darbie obviously made more progress. They were waiting for her outside when she left fifth period, and they flanked her as they pulled her down the hall. Sophie could almost see idea light bulbs popping over their heads.

"We didn't get any work done," Fiona said.

"But we weren't foostering about," Darbie said. "We might have a plan."

Sophie stopped just short of their sixth-period classroom. "You changed your minds about helping Brooke?"

"Here's the deal," Fiona said. "Now that everybody on the entire planet knows we call ourselves the Corn Flakes, we can really show them what that means."

"That we aren't some clique," Darbie said. "That we help people take back their power to be who they really are—just like we do for ourselves."

Sophie looked from one of them to the other. They weren't watching her like they were waiting for her to tell them what to do. They looked like they already knew.

"Don't you want to know how we came up with that?" Fiona said.

Without waiting for Sophie to answer, Darbie said, "We did just what you always do. We imagined Jesus."

When Maggie, Willoughby, and Kitty arrived, they gathered in the back of the art room while a substitute teacher wrote her name and THIS IS A STUDY PERIOD on the chalkboard.

"Yikes," Fiona said, "that Jesus-thing works faster than I thought."

They spent the period with their heads bent together, bringing Maggie and the others up to date and wrestling a plan into place. A Jesus-way, they named it.

A few times they all looked at Sophie, as if waiting for her to tell them the right thing to do. But it didn't make her itchy anymore. She knew without seeing that inside each of them there was a little doubt, a little fear, a little being smart about things, a little love. No, a *lot* of love. The things that made them all Corn Flakes.

"Okay," Maggie said when the bell rang. "We have until the late bus to make this happen, right?"

"If we don't, we go to Coach Nanini with the camera first thing tomorrow," Darbie said.

"Whatever happens," Sophie said, "we'll know we did it the Jesus-way."

After a big Corn Flake hug, they split up to go to their stations.

Sophie looked at her watch every five feet as she headed for the Special Ed hall. Like that would make time slow down, she thought. She wished she'd pushed Maggie a little on the deadline. But they had to do it the Jesus-way.

Still, every "What if ...?" from *What if Brooke didn't go to her tutoring session today?* to *What if she tied herself up with that stupid boa?* went through Sophie's head until she reached Brooke's classroom door.

. She stood on tiptoe to see through the little window. Before she could even get her nose to the glass, the door opened. Sophie stumbled in, straight into Brooke.

They stared at each other long enough for Sophie to see that Brooke had attempted to undo the makeup job. The lipstick and eye shadow had been pushed to the sides of her face along with raised rows of foundation makeup. It looked to Sophie as if a mask had been partly peeled back to reveal the real Brooke.

And the real Brooke looked as if she were staring straight into the face of Godzilla. Sophie took advantage of the frozen moment to pull the camera bag from behind her back and hold it in front of her.

"We need to talk," Sophie said.

Brooke shook her head. "I knew you wouldn't help me when you found out." Then she looked as if she wanted to chomp her tongue off.

Sophie just nodded. "We already figured out you did it. But we don't think you did it alone."

Sophie slipped her hand into the outside pocket of the camera bag and pulled out Julia's nail file. Brooke went so pale that every freckle stood out from her face. She grabbed for the file, but Sophie slid it back into the pocket and pulled her out into the hall.

"Let's talk right here," she said. That had been Darbie's idea. She said if Sophie tried to take Brooke too far, she would make a getaway. If she did try, Sophie knew the next step in the plan. She just hoped Willoughby remembered.

Brooke stood against the wall, kicking at it with her heel while she stared at the camera bag. "I have to give that nail file back to Julia," she said. "I thought I lost it, and she said I was gonna have to pay for it."

"Did you sort of *borrow* it from her?" Sophie said.

"I didn't swipe it! She told me to use it to open your camera and mess with stuff so it wouldn't work. Only first I read that thing about me being a project and how dumb you thought I was." She switched heels. "I was still so mad when Julia got me the camera, and then I couldn't get it open. So I just jumped up and down on it until I heard that teacher with the mustache coming. I guess I left the nail file in there on accident."

Sophie sucked in a huge breath. With a picture in her mind of Brooke stomping on her camera like it was a soda can, it was mega hard to go on with the Jesus-way. But another picture—of Julia tucking the nail file into Brooke's hand and purring instructions—was even clearer.

"We still want to help you," Sophie said.

Brooke shook her head. "Nobody wants to help me. Nobody even likes me."

Sophie felt as if her chest were caving in.

"See?" Brooke said. "You can't say, 'Sure, I like you.'"

No, Sophie thought. *I can't*. Not if she was being her real, honest self.

She swallowed hard. "It's hard to like you because of some of the stuff you do. Only, some of that stuff you sorta can't help because nobody ever helped you with your ADHD—"

Brooke let out a scream that ripped through Sophie. "I don't have that! And I'm not a retard, either!"

She pushed herself away from the wall and, eyes wild, stormed down the hall. Bounding after her, Sophie threw herself onto Brooke's back, and wrapped her arms around her shoulders. She got a face full of red hair.

"Get off me!" Brooke screamed.

"No!" Sophie screamed back—although hers went up into the atmosphere someplace. "Not until you let us help you."

Brooke whipped herself around in the other direction, so that Sophie had to squeeze tight to stay on. There in front of them was Willoughby, standing with her hands on her hips and a cheerleader grin on her face.

"Ready!" she said.

If Sophie hadn't known the plan, she would have thought she was about to do a cheer. She could feel Brooke tighten under her.

"Come on, Brooke," Sophie said into her ear. "Just give us a chance. We'll help you turn yourself in so you won't get into as much trouble, and you can get real help."

"We'll stand by you." Willoughby raised her arms as if she were holding a pair of pom-poms. "We'll be your cheerleaders."

"I hate cheerleaders," Brooke said.

But Sophie felt some of the tightness go out of Brooke's shoulders.

"You don't have to like us," Sophie said. "Just let us help you. That's what Corn Flakes do."

It actually felt good to say it out loud to somebody who wasn't a Corn Flake. And at least Brooke let go a tiny bit more.

"We'll bring Julia and Cassie and Anne-Stuart to you, and you can ask them to tell you the truth about whether they're really your friends," Sophie said.

"And we'll be right there, in hiding," Willoughby said.

"Then you can make your own decision." Sophie hugged Brooke's shoulders. "You're smart enough to do that."

Brooke went so limp, Sophie slid to the floor. Slowly she studied Brooke, and deep inside a question was answered.

After all the Internet research, the Dr. Devon Downing pretending, and the good-girl-Brooke rewards they'd gotten on film, the way to help Brooke was looking right back at her.

Brooke was suddenly a girl that somebody believed in.

Twelve

✿ ⌂ ✹

O kay," Brooke said. "But you can't leave me."

"No way we'll leave you," Willoughby said.

So Brooke trudged behind Willoughby toward the locker hall with Sophie at her side. When they reached the corner, Willoughby pointed to a row of four big garbage cans.

"We'll be right back here, cheering you on," she said.

Brooke sucked at her lip and rounded the corner.

Sophie felt a tap on her shoulder. Kitty motioned for her and Willoughby to duck with her behind the row of trash containers where Maggie was already crouched, notepad and pen in hand. Sophie didn't ask how they'd managed to come up with four honkin' huge garbage cans and drag them there. It was their part of the plan, and they'd done it.

"Did Darbie and Fiona find the Corn Pops?" Sophie whispered to Kitty.

"Some of them," she whispered back. "Fiona's still looking, and Darbie went to get—"

Maggie cut them off by pushing Sophie's head down. Sophie had just hidden behind the middle can when she heard Julia say, "*There* you are. So, do you have my nail file, or what?"

There was silence. Sophie peeked through an opening between garbage cans. She could barely see Brooke nodding.

"She's saying yes," Sophie whispered.

Maggie wrote it down.

"So give it back," Julia said. "And it better not be messed up, or you still have to pay for it."

"And we *know* you can't afford it," Cassie said.

Sophie frowned as her gaze grew focused and very narrow.

"I can't give it back to you right now," Brooke said.

Sophie hoped she wasn't looking back toward the trash cans for cheers. The Pops needed to think this was Brooke's idea.

"I thought you said you had it," Julia said.

"I do—well, I don't ..."

Sophie closed her eyes. *Please, God, let her believe we want to help her. Please let her believe it.*

"She doesn't have it, Julia," Cassie said. "Let's just report that she stole it. Your mom'll buy you another one."

"I didn't steal it!" Brooke said. "You gave it to me, and you told me to use it to mess up Sophie's camera!"

"And you did," Julia said. "And now I want it back."

Sophie didn't have to see her to know that she was holding her hand out like a queen waiting for somebody to kiss it, and that Cassie was ready to do the Corn Pop beheading if Brooke didn't. It had been the crossroads for so many girls before her: Kitty, Willoughby, B.J.

"I'm gonna turn it in with the camera," Brooke said.

"Turn it in to who?" Julia's voice was shrill.

"Whoever Sophie and them tell me to. That way, I won't get in so much trouble."

"Get ready," Willoughby whispered. She grabbed one of Sophie's hands and Kitty grabbed the other. Maggie just kept writing. Sophie wondered if, when Julia attacked Brooke, Maggie would stay there and get down every last word while the rest of them went into the next phase of the plan.

But there was a sudden quiet down the locker row. Then Julia said, in a voice Sophie had to strain to hear, "Before you turn into a little Corn Flake and go confessing, let's make sure you have your facts straight."

"I do."

"Except the part about the nail file. Do you know whose idea that was?"

"Yours."

"Uh, hel-*lo-o*. No-o-o. *I* didn't want you taking any kind of risks. It was all Anne-Stuart."

"It was?" Cassie said.

"Shut up, Cassie. You don't know everything Anne-Stuart and I talk about."

During Cassie's stung silence, Julia's voice went even lower. "I hated the idea so much, Brookie, that I will even tell whoever you plan to tell that Anne-Stuart was the one who messed up Sophie's camera, not you. Then you don't even have to mention the nail file, and neither one of *us* will get in trouble."

Sophie heard a loud sniff that couldn't belong to anyone else but Anne-Stuart herself.

"Good job, Fiona," Willoughby whispered.

Sophie saw Maggie make a large check mark on the plan.

"You are *so* not serious, Julia," Anne-Stuart said. "You would actually lie and say I did it, when it was all *your* idea?"

"It was yours, Anne-Stuart," Cassie said.

"Like you so know everything Julia and I talk about, Cassie." Another sniff. "Brooke, Julia's making that up about me so you won't get her in trouble."

"Shut up, Anne-Stuart." It sounded like Julia's teeth were in a vicious clench.

"Don't tell me to shut up."

"Since when do you tell me what to say, Anne-Stuart? I tell *you*—"

"And you know what? I'm sick of it." Anne-Stuart's voice clogged from *not* sniffing. "I've gone along with everything you ever wanted to do to bring down the goody girls—"

"Corn Flakes!" Julia cried. "They're the Corn Flake clique—and if it wasn't for *me*, we never would have found that out. If it wasn't for *me*, they could just go on making everybody think they're all perfect while they take everything away from me that I deserve!"

"Oh, and I didn't help at all," Anne-Stuart said.

"You did what I told you."

"And now you plan to let me take all the blame?" Anne-Stuart's words screeched like a bad microphone. "How could you take *Brooke's* side?"

"Because I need her to keep the Corn Flakes down. So either trust me to get you out of it, or go back to being the loser you were before I found you."

There was a loud smack. Only when Julia gasped did Sophie realize Anne-Stuart had just slapped her. Sophie peered between the trash cans in time to see Anne-Stuart nearly mow Darbie down as she bolted from the scene. Or what Sophie could see of Darbie. She was half hidden by the hulking form of Coach Virile.

"Catfight?" he said.

Sophie couldn't see Julia, Cassie, or Brooke now, but she clearly heard Julia say, "You should go after her, Coach. She destroyed Sophie LaCroix's camera and tried to blame it on poor Brooke."

Sophie could feel her Corn Flakes holding their breath. But she had to believe—

"No, she didn't," Brooke said. "I did it."

"With the nail file she stole from Julia!" Cassie said.

241

"Shut up, Cassie!" Julia said. "Would you just get out of my life!"

It appeared that Cassie did, as fast as she could. Her retreating footsteps echoed down the locker hall.

"I came late to this party," Coach Nanini said, "so excuse me if I'm a little confused."

"Those guys'll tell you," Brooke said. "I did it."

"What guys?"

"Back there."

Sophie rose slowly from behind the trash cans, pulling Willoughby and Kitty with her. Fiona emerged from the opposite bank of lockers. Julia's hair seemed to stop in mid-toss, as if the Corn Pop life had just been sucked out of it.

"Anybody want to clear this up for me?" Coach Nanini said. "Little Bit?"

Sophie opened her mouth, but Brooke dodged around Darbie, tripping on her shoelaces in the process. She landed with her face close to Coach's chest. When she looked up at him, Sophie saw tears making trails through the stale makeup, as if they were washing away the last of Project Brooke.

"I did it, and I know it was horrible. I know I'm gonna get in trouble, but I want—" Her mouth snapped shut, and she turned to the Corn Flakes.

"You can do it, Brooke," Willoughby said.

Heads bobbed. Darbie even said, "You won't make a bags of it. Go on then."

Brooke squeezed her eyes tight. "I want help," she said.

"All right," Coach Nanini said. "Let's see if we can't get you some." He looked up at Julia. "Expect to hear from Mr. Bentley first thing tomorrow. This isn't over for you."

Then he walked away with Brooke, head bent toward her like an understanding bear.

"I wouldn't believe that just happened if I hadn't seen it with my own eyes," Darbie said.

"We *didn't* see it," Willoughby said. She nudged Kitty. "Nice hiding place."

But Kitty just slipped her hand into Sophie's. "We didn't have to see it to believe it, did we?"

Fiona coughed and nodded down the locker row. Julia was still standing there, staring toward where Anne-Stuart had left, as if she knew she'd reappear any moment to pay the queen her rightful homage. It was either wait there or face the unbelievable truth: Julia'd been abandoned, and without the Pops, she was powerless.

"I wrote down everything they said," Maggie murmured to Sophie.

Sophie shrugged. "We may not actually need it now. I think the Corn Pops are no more."

"What about the Corn *Flakes*?" Kitty said. "Do we still call ourselves that, now that everybody knows?"

They all looked at Sophie.

"I don't think it matters what we're called," she said. "It's all about who we are. That's what counts."

Sophie didn't miss her camera as much as she thought she would. In fact, it was a whole two weeks before she wished she had it. It wasn't to film Brooke telling about her new counselor—Dr. Peter Topping—or Julia becoming so almost-invisible at school that Sophie started praying for her. It definitely wasn't to make a movie about a dream character. None showed up in her mind to try to solve some problem.

No, she decided on a Saturday afternoon when she walked into the family room where Daddy was watching a basketball game with a sleepy baby Hope in his arms. Her tiny sister was the one she wanted to film.

Daddy looked up at Sophie. "I don't think our little rookie cares about the Boston Celtics," he said. "You want to put her in her crib?"

Sophie smiled and put out her arms.

"Way to be a team player, Soph," Daddy said.

Sophie took the steps one by one and placed Hope in her baby bed. She stood looking down at the eyes lightly closed in fairylike sleep. Eyes that were uniquely Hope Celeste LaCroix.

"Maybe my daydreaming days are over," Sophie whispered to her. "I'll always have an imagination—you need one, you know. All Corn Flakes and other authentic people have imaginations—and they're themselves—and they never put anybody down. In fact, they even help people they don't like because they follow the Jesus-way."

Sophie heard her own voice get husky with tears. "I wish you could be a Corn Flake," she whispered. "Maybe I just have to believe God will let you, no matter how different you are."

And then it occurred to her, the truth that—at some level—she'd always known. It made her lean down and kiss her sister's soft forehead.

"I don't have to try to fix you. You are your own unique self. Just like me, and Fiona, and Darbie—"

Hope's eyes fluttered open. She searched Sophie's face as if she were waiting for something.

"Do you want to be a baby Corn Flake?" Sophie whispered.

The little tongue popped out. And then Hope's face brightened into a smile. A wonderful, toothless, knowing smile.

An I-want-to-be-a-Corn-Flake smile.

Sophie smiled back.

And she believed without seeing that Hope would most certainly be one.

Glossary

Attention Deficit Hyperactivity Disorder (uh-TEN-shun DEF-uh-set hy-pur-ak-TIV-eh-tee dis-or-dur) also known as ADHD, it is a brain disorder (or problem with the brain) that makes it hard to pay attention to the right things

the bejeebers (beh-JEE-burs) no one quite knows what bejeebers are, but when someone scares them out of you, it means you feel like your stomach almost jumped out of your body in fright

chromosomes (KROH-muh-zohms) these are super long pieces of DNA that have everything a baby needs to become a human. They decide things like your hair color, or if you're going to be a boy or a girl.

clique (clik) a bunch of friends who don't let anyone else join their group

contraband (KAHN-tra-band) something that is against the rules, and you have to sneak in

defect (DEE-fekt) something that isn't the way it should be

dire (DY-er) horrible, disastrous, and can only lead to bad things

eejit (EE-jit) the way someone from Ireland might say "idiot"

flitters (fli-turs) 1) a feeling you get when you're really excited, like when your body gets all shaky; 2) description of something that's all in pieces

foostering about (foo-stur-ing a-bout) an Irish way of saying "wasting time"

the full shilling (the full SHILL-ing) not all there in the head; acting like your brain cells are missing

genes (jeans) stuff in DNA that your parents pass on to you, which make you who you are. So if you and your mom both giggle the same way, it's because you have her genes.

heinous (HEY-nus) unbelievably mean and cruel

hysteria (hiss-TAYR-ee-uh) crazy and out of control

impulsivity (im-puhl-SIV-eh-tee) always doing things right away instead of thinking about it first; doing things you don't plan on

incense (IN-sents) being really angry

jilted (JILL-ted) describes someone who was suddenly ditched

literally (LIH-ter-uhl-ee) actual fact. So if your homework was eaten by an iguana, it literally happened. Or if you believe something that's meant to be a joke, then you took it too literally or as fact.

make a bags of (mayk a bags of) do a poor job or screw things up

microscope (my-cro-skohp) science equipment that makes very tiny things bigger so that you can see them

mondo (MAHN-doh) another word for "extremely"; describes something that's much bigger or louder than it needs to be

obnoxious (ob-NAWK-shus) really, really annoying

reef (reef) an Irish word that means to beat someone up

remission (re-MIH-shun) when a disease, like cancer, disappears with treatment. If the disease doesn't come back for many years, the person may be cured.

shenanigans (sheh-NAN-eh-gans) playing around and possibly being a little naughty

somber (SAHM-bur) super serious, and not smiling or finding things funny

unrepentant (un-rhee-PEN-tent) not feeling bad about something you did and refusing to apologize

Sophie and Friends

Nancy Rue

Meet Sophie LaCroix, a creative soul with a desire to become a great film director someday, and she definitely has a flair for drama! Her overactive imagination frequently lands her in trouble, but her faith and friends always save the day. This bindup includes two-books-in-one.

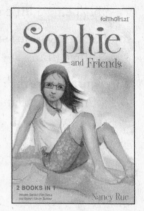

Sophie's First Dance: Sophie and her friends, the Corn Flakes, are in a tizzy over the end-of-school dance – especially when invitations start coming – from boys! Will the Flakes break up, or can Sophie direct a happy ending?

Sophie's Stormy Summer: One of the Flakes is struck with cancer, and Sophie severely struggles with the shocking news, until she finds that friends – and faith – show the way to a new adventure called growing up.

Sophie Flakes Out

Nancy Rue

Meet Sophie LaCroix, a creative soul with a desire to become a great film director someday, and she definitely has a flair for drama! Her overactive imagination frequently lands her in trouble, but her faith and friends always save the day. From best-selling author, Nancy Rue, comes two-in-one bindups of the popular Sophie series.

Sophie Flakes Out: Sophie wants more privacy like her friend Willoughby, who has plenty, until Willoughby's father finds out about her fast, new friends. His harsh punishment makes Sophie wonder what rules they need to follow.

Sophie Loves Jimmy: Sophie doesn't get why a rumor should stop her from being Jimmy's friend – until the Corn Flakes start believing the whispers. Now Sophie wonders how she and the Flakes can ever be friends again!

Available in stores and online!

Sophie Steps Up

Nancy Rue

Sophie LaCroix is a creative soul with a desire to become a great film director someday, and she definitely has a flair for drama! Her overactive imagination frequently lands her in trouble, but her faith and friends always save the day. This bindup includes two-books-in-one, Sophie Under Pressure and Sophie Steps Up.

Sophie's Friendship Fiasco

Nancy Rue

Meet Sophie LaCroix, a creative soul with a desire to become a great film director someday, and she definitely has a flair for drama! Her overactive imagination frequently lands her in trouble, but her faith and friends always save the day. From best-selling author, Nancy Rue, comes two-in-one bindups of the popular Sophie series.

Sophie's Friendship Fiasco: Sophie tries living up to other's expectations, but lately she's letting everyone down. When she misrepresents the Flakes – with good intentions – she loses their friendship. Will they ever forgive her?

Sophie and the New Girl: Sophie likes the new girl who joins the film club. She's witty and unique, even if she is a bit bizarre. When the camera goes missing, the other Flakes are quick to accuse. Will Sophie be able to identify the real thief?

Available in stores and online!

Faithgirlz Journal

My Doodles, Dreams and Devotion

Looking for a place to dream, doodle, and record your innermost questions and secrets? You will find what you seek within the pages of the Faithgirlz Journal, which has plenty of space for you to discover who you are, explore who God is shaping you to be, or write down whatever inspires you. Each journal page has awesome quotes and powerful Bible verses to encourage you on  your walk with God! So grab a pen, colored pencils, or even a handful of markers. Whatever you write is just between you and God.

NIV Faithgirlz! Backpack Bible, Revised Edition

Small enough to fit into a backpack or bag, this Bible can go anywhere a girl does.

Features include:

- Fun Italian Duo-Tone™ design
- Twelve full-color pages of Faithgirlz fun that helps girls learn the "Beauty of Believing!"
- Words of Christ in red
- Ribbon marker
- Complete text of the bestselling NIV translation

Available in stores and online!

NIV Faithgirlz! Bible, Revised Edition

Nancy Rue

Every girl wants to know she's totally unique and special. This Bible says that with Faithgirlz! sparkle. Through the many in-text features found only in the Faithgirlz! Bible, girls will grow closer to God as they discover the journey of a lifetime.

Features include:

- Book introductions—Read about the who, when, where, and what of each book.

- Dream Girl—Use your imagination to put yourself in the story.

- Bring It On!—Take quizzes to really get to know yourself.

- Is There a Little (Eve, Ruth, Isaiah) in You?—See for yourself what you have in common.

- Words to Live By—Check out these Bible verses that are great for memorizing.

- What Happens Next?—Create a list of events to tell a Bible story in your own words.

- Oh, I Get It!—Find answers to Bible questions you've wondered about.

- The complete NIV translation

- Features written by bestselling author Nancy Rue

Available in stores and online!

ZONDERVAN®
.com

Talk It Up!

Want free books?
First looks at the best new fiction?
Awesome exclusive merchandise?

We want to hear from you!

Give us your opinions on titles, covers, and stories.
Join the Z Street Team.

Email us at zstreetteam@zondervan.com
to sign up today!

Also—Friend us on Facebook!

www.facebook.com/goodteenreads

- Video Trailers
- Connect with your favorite authors
- Sneak peeks at new releases
- Giveaways
- Fun discussions
- And much more!